SCRAPPING PLANS

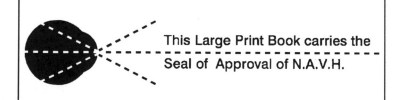

This Large Print Book carries the
Seal of Approval of N.A.V.H.

SISTERS, INK, BOOK 3

SCRAPPING PLANS

A SISTERS, INK NOVEL

REBECA SEITZ

THORNDIKE PRESS
A part of Gale, Cengage Learning

GALE
CENGAGE Learning™

Detroit • New York • San Francisco • New Haven, Conn • Waterville, Maine • London

GALE
CENGAGE Learning™

LIBRARY OF CONGRESS CATALOGING-IN-PUBLICATION DATA

Seitz, Rebeca, 1977–
    Scrapping plans : a sisters, ink novel / by Rebeca Seitz.
        p. cm.
    ISBN-13: 978-1-4104-1629-2 (hardcover : alk. paper)
    ISBN-10: 1-4104-1629-1 (hardcover : alk. paper)
    1. Sisters—Fiction. 2. Adoptees—Fiction. 3.
Scrapbooks—Fiction. 4. Scrapbook journaling—Fiction. 5. Large
type books. I. Title.
PS3619.E427S37 2009
813'.6—dc22   2009012446

Published in 2009 by arrangement with Riggins International Rights Services Inc.

Printed in the United States of America
1 2 3 4 5 6 7 13 12 11 10 09

To my wonderful husband, Charlie,
who makes my life a
true fairy tale. I love raising a
family with you.

ACKNOWLEDGMENTS

As with every endeavor I undertake, this book would not have been possible without the support and patience of my precious husband, Charlie. His ability to overlook my craziness in talking to the characters rattling around my head — even arguing with them out loud! — is invaluable. He treats my writing as a serious activity that must be supported and encouraged. For that I am incredibly grateful.

Joy's story would have been nearly impossible for me to write without the help of Charlie's sister, Sara Fawcett. Sara, you are one of the most gracious, elegant women I've had the pleasure of knowing in this lifetime. I admire your dedication to both family and career and am thrilled that you and Louis have realized your dream of parenthood through the adoption of Maddie. Thank you for sharing your story of traveling to China to get Maddie and for letting me share a portion of it with my readers.

When Charlie and I moved to Kentucky to be closer to my family, I didn't know how helpful that would be to my writing. My parents, Herman and Linda DeBoard, have astounded me with their support and praise (and probably sold more books than any bookstore in the country!). I know I wasn't the easiest child in the world to raise, guys, but thanks for teaching me God's ways and turning me to Him. I love being your daughter. I also have to thank my sister, Christie Ricketts, and her family — Randall, Alex, and Katie. I have no idea how many hours y'all have spent watching Andy so that I could write and Charlie could get things done outside. Thanks for making my life work!

As always, I'm blessed to work with some truly outstanding people in the publishing industry. My fabulous editor, Karen Ball, kept me going when I wrote my way into a corner. Thank you, my friend, for the ideas and encouragement throughout the writing of this story. My "guru" agent, Steve Laube, steers me with unfailing wisdom and wit. Thanks, Steve, for representing my writing and for walking me through the sticky situations that inevitably arise in the process.

Since releasing the first Sisters, Ink book, I've been so honored to receive tons of e-mail from you, the readers. I love hearing your feedback and I keep all of your e-mails! Thank you for taking the time to let me know what you think of these characters and stories as well as for sharing your personal struggles and triumphs with me. Keep those e-mails coming: Rebeca@sistersink.net.

Finally, thank You, Lord, for giving me stories to write and for creating a path of publication for me. I love how You use this unworthy but willing woman and am so astounded to be a part of Your story. I know I don't deserve any of the treasures of this life you've written and I thank You for granting me worth and value as Your daughter. As long as You give me breath and purpose it for me, I'll praise You and write the stories You let me see. I love You.

ONE

I've tried to be happy. I try so very hard. Yet the frigid granite beneath my fingertips is a blazing desert compared to the barren iceberg of my womb. What woman could be happy with a monolith of ice blocking her very female essence?

This kitchen is perfectly planned. If Martha Stewart visited, she'd be envious of my exquisite arrangement of pears and apricots, dusted with the slightest coating of glaze and balanced artfully in Momma's old bowl. She would gasp at the coordination of stripe to check, plaid to French country print, that draws the eye around the room. Her Tod-slippered feet could sweep across my stone floor and arrive unspecked at their destination.

And if the Great Martha were to stop there, I would measure up. My life would hold a semblance of value, of worthiness.

Most stop there.

Thank God.

I don't mean that irreverently. How can I be irreverent? I'm the grateful adoptee of an upright preacher man and his loving wife. I'm the epitome of "grateful recipient." All of Stars Hill would tell you that.

They don't look past my kitchen.

Thank God.

But I don't have much time to stand here, staring at a *House Beautiful* workspace. Scott will be home in two hours. And duck a l'orange is not an easy dish for even one so seasoned as I.

Is it odd that I love French food yet Chinese blood runs through my veins? Hmm. Perhaps if I'd been raised on the soil my mother trod, I would know and appreciate more of the cuisine of the Asian world. I might even be privy to which province most suits me.

I should visit China.

Did I just think that?

I can't visit China. Daddy, that blessed preacher man, would be hurt if I went in search of a mother who was never Momma. Of a woman who took one look at me, then left me bawling on a doorstep in the dead of night.

Then again, Daddy has Zelda these days.

Now Zelda, there's a woman who follows

every fancy. What a strange little bird she is. Those fiery red spikes in her hair make me think of a surprised woodpecker — or the recipient of an errant lightning bolt. When she smiles, her whole face turns upward. I hear we have that in common. I wish I could remember seeing a smile on my face. But when I'm alone, with a mirror reflecting the mystery of me, it isn't a smile that comes to bear. Besides, what kind of lady wears spurs on her cowboy boots? Honestly, spurs! Why, one of these days she's going to rip a gash in Daddy's ankle while they do do-si-dos around the Heartland dance floor.

I assume that's what happens inside that wretched place. How Kendra and Tandy can spend their Friday nights there is beyond me. To each her own, I suppose. Though my own will never involve cowboy boots and a twanging fiddle.

Do fiddles twang?

Maybe I meant guitar.

No matter. I have a duck to prepare.

"Did you see her?"

Kendra tripped over the uneven sidewalk and grabbed Tandy's arm. Cold gusts of wind beat at them, pelting them with snatches of icy rain.

"Hey, watch it, sister!"

"Sorry." Kendra kept walking, shooting a murderous look back at the beguiling concrete. "We need to bring up sidewalk maintenance at the next town meeting."

Tandy patted the coffee-colored hand still crooked in her elbow. "Now, Kendra, don't be getting all drastic on me. Can you imagine what poor Tanner would do if we dared question the maintenance of our fair Stars Hill?"

"Huh." Kendra huffed and let go of Tandy to stuff her hands in her pockets. "Probably remind us of all he's done to keep this town in antique replica streetlights and ten o'clock curfews."

"At least the curfews are gone."

They pulled their hoods up and stepped down from the sidewalk to cross College Street.

"I wonder how many times Daddy would have had to bail us out if they had that curfew when we were in high school?"

Tandy tucked a curl behind her ear and took long strides toward Clay's Diner. "I seem to recall a certain sister needing to be bailed out anyway."

"There was no bail involved. Just a minor misunderstanding."

"That the whole town talked about for months." Tandy grinned and pulled open

14

the door of the diner. Heated air billowed out a welcome. "After you, con woman."

"Yeah, keep it up, sis. I can always bring up improper car racing at the next town meeting." Kendra sailed through the entry, ignoring Tandy's rejoinder of "You wouldn't!" and hung her dripping coat on one of the hooks by the door.

Tandy sloughed off her own navy pea coat and stamped her yellow rain boots. "Would you?"

Kendra spun on a heel and walked off toward "their" booth in the back corner. "Wouldn't you like to know?"

"There's my darling wife!" Clay Kelner came around the counter toward them.

Kendra rolled her eyes and snatched up a menu. "Oh, spare me. Shouldn't the newlywed bliss have worn off by now?"

"What are you upset about?" Clay allowed a quick glance for his sister-in-law, then bent and dropped a peck on Tandy's upturned lips. "Are you and Darin fighting?"

"No."

"Yes." Tandy leveled a gaze at her sister. "Because Kendra is too busy spying on Joy to pay attention to her man and get their wedding planned."

"Joy? The perfect one? Mrs. Plan-Everything-to-Death?" Clay's eyebrows

15

rose. "Why are you spying on Joy?"

"Because something's wrong and I'm the only one in this family paying attention, that's why." Kendra slapped the menu on the table top. "And wedding plans are coming along just fine, thank you very much."

"Sure you're not just being your usual dramatic self?" Clay fast-stepped back before Kendra could swat him. "*Lovable* dramatic self, I mean!"

"Ha ha. Very funny." Kendra pointed the menu at Clay, then Tandy. "You laugh now, but something's up and we need to find out what before it gets so bad we can't fix it."

"Well, can we at least get some food first?" Tandy snatched the menu and put it back in its holder. "I can't think on an empty stomach."

"The usual?"

Both girls nodded, and Clay turned back toward the kitchen.

When he'd gone, Kendra studied her sister. "Tandy, I know you think I'm nuts. But didn't you see her at Darnell's? I mean, she stood over that display of oranges for at least a full minute, just staring into space!"

"Yeah, I saw her, Ken." Tandy sighed. "But you know Joy. She's not going to appreciate us marching into her house and demanding to know what's wrong."

"She wouldn't care if Meg did it." Kendra sniffed.

"Yes, she would. And she's closer to Meg because this is exactly the kind of thing Meg *wouldn't* do."

Kendra huffed and turned away. Rain sluiced down the windows, making the streetlights outside sparkle. Inside every table was filled with Stars Hill town folk happily spooning up chili and vegetable soup. *If we don't figure this out soon, they will. And then Joy will be the talk of the town.* She pulled out her cell phone and punched buttons.

"Who are you calling?"

"Meg." Her faux ruby ring glinted in the light when she held up a finger to stop Tandy's objection. "Hey, Meg, it's Kendra. Tandy and I are at the diner and wondered if you could drop by. Call me as soon as you get this." She snapped the phone closed and dropped it back in her giant suede bag, now splashed with raindrops.

"And what will that accomplish?"

"We're going to have Meg talk to Joy about this."

"Since when can we get Meg to do *anything*? Did you discover a magic wand I don't know about?"

Kendra pushed her mahogany-colored

spirals back into the burgundy head wrap from which they had escaped. "She's been wanting me to paint a mural on Hannah's wall for a month. I think she'll do just about anything to see it finished."

Tandy leaned back in the seat and whistled low. "Remind me never to underestimate you, sister."

Kendra stopped fixing her hair and leveled a stare at Tandy. "You better believe it."

Two

Vivaldi. I love the lyrical playfulness of Vivaldi. Kendra can have her Otis Redding, and Tandy can listen to Martina McBride all day long. But give me a season set to Vivaldi and I am a happy woman.

At least as happy as is possible these days. Scott is late getting home. That's under-standable. Why rush home when the only thing there to greet you is a frozen shrew of a woman? That's what I'm becoming. I'll bet anything that's what he sees when he looks at me.

Which isn't often.

I remember how his gaze landed on me in the early years of our marriage. Like I was a prize, a beautifully kept prize, just for him. I would catch him staring over the flickering candlelight on the dinner table and he'd smile, and I would know just what he wanted for dessert.

He wanted me then.

Before the wanting was replaced by the function of me.

I wish I could remember exactly when that happened. When I decided to be a birthing vessel rather than his wife. If I had realized the two could be separated, that being unable to be one would give the other lordship over our marriage, perhaps I —

No. I couldn't. Haven't I proven how unable I am? Despite following every step in every book. Months of testing, minute after minute ticking away as we waited for the extra pink line to appear. That expectant look on his face when I stepped out of the bathroom. The fallen features when I shook my head.

Again.

And again.

And again.

My life's irony cuts deep. My mother did not want to birth me. And all I want is to give birth.

"Hail, hail, the gang's all here." Clay's voice boomed across the counter. "Meg, what can I get you?"

Meg plopped into the booth beside Tandy and glanced at their dishes. "Chili and tea, Clay. Thanks."

Clay nodded and turned toward the

kitchen.

Meg focused a laser-sharp gaze on Kendra. "And *you* can tell me why I just left my house so fast my socks don't match and my scarf is hanging in my hall closet."

Kendra sat up straight. "Who cares about your socks when Joy's in trouble?"

"What trouble? Joy doesn't get into trouble unless there's a six-step system for it."

"That's what I've been saying." Tandy twirled her straw.

Kendra tapped the table with a long purple fingernail. "If Joy wasn't in trouble, then why did she stand stock-still in the middle of Darnell's staring at oranges like they held the secret to Jesus' return?"

"You're kidding me, right?" Meg slumped in the booth. "She was probably checking them out for orange rot or whatever disease oranges get."

Tandy's curls rustled as she shook her head. "No, she wasn't. She stared, but not at the oranges. At, I don't know, something *else.*"

Meg looked back and forth between her sisters. "What are you two talking about?"

"It's like I tried to tell you on the phone. There's something wrong with Joy."

"There's nothing —"

"And we think you should find out what." Kendra dropped her gaze and became seriously interested in the fried green beans on her plate.

"Whoa. What? You think I'm going to jump all up in Joy's private business because you two saw her look at an orange funny? Maybe the orange rot is in your brains."

Kendra leaned across the table. "I'm serious, Meg. Something's up and either you find out what, or I start shadowing her everywhere until I figure it out."

Meg sighed and crossed her arms over her chest. "Please tell me you have more to go on besides Joy investigating oranges."

"Oh yeah, lots more." Kendra shifted in her seat. "She was working on my hair last Tuesday, and right there in the middle of cutting, she froze. Had my hair in between her fingers and scissors ready to go. I thought she must have seen something out the window, so I tried to turn and look. That pulled my hair out of her hand, which woke her up."

"Did you ask her what she saw?"

"Of course I did. She acted like nothing had happened."

"What?" Meg looked to Tandy, who nodded confirmation.

"And did you see her at church on Sunday? She didn't take the first note of Daddy's sermon."

"Are you sure?" Meg scrunched her nose. "Joy has been taking sermon notes since we were in junior high."

"Not one drop of ink touched the page. I watched the whole time."

"Maybe she was just distracted."

"Meg." Tandy's low voice hummed a warning. "This isn't all in Kendra's head. I'll admit, Joy hasn't done anything that anyone who doesn't know her would think is odd. But we know her. You best of all. Does it sound like everything's all right?"

Meg chewed on her lip. Joy hadn't returned her last phone call and it had been . . . an entire week. Oh no. Here she was running around like four firemen with a ten-alarm blaze and no water hose just keeping up with her kids, and Joy was over at her house with a monster problem.

And Kendra had been the one to notice.

She dropped her arms. *I've got to get my house on a better schedule. Spend more time with the sisters.* "Okay."

"Okay?" Kendra's eyebrows rose. "Okay you'll help us figure out what's going on?"

"Okay, I'll talk to Joy. I can't believe I missed this." Meg rubbed her forehead. "Between the kids and these stupid headaches —"

"You're still getting the headaches?" Tandy turned in her seat, her forehead wrinkling. "I thought they went away."

"They did. They had." Meg saw Clay approaching with food and smiled. "I'm fine. I probably just need to eat."

"And I'll do my best to help with that." Clay slid a bowl of chili in front of Meg and winked at Tandy. "You ladies get Joy all figured out?"

"Not yet, but Meg's going to work on it." Kendra swiped a fry through some ketchup and chomped down.

Clay shook his head. "Careful what you let these two rope you into, Meg."

"Hey, you're supposed to be on my side." Tandy flicked a straw wrapper his direction.

"Which is why I didn't tell her to get out of here before she got in too deep." Clay winked and walked back to the kitchen, whistling all the way.

Meg dipped her spoon into the steaming bowl. "That husband of yours has a streak of wisdom."

"Yeah, combine it with his streak of wit and you've got one smart-aleck comedian who occasionally gets it right."

"Somebody should warn Robin Williams."

"Oh, I think he's safe." Kendra ducked as

Tandy threw the rest of the straw paper her way.

"You know, we need to address this tendency of yours to throw things at people."

Tandy rolled her eyes and Meg swallowed her chili. It did nothing to dispel the iceberg of worry in her throat.

THREE

"Before I incur Joy's wrath, do we have any idea what could be wrong?"

Kendra shrugged. "I've thought and thought. All I can come up with is husband troubles."

"Or baby troubles. They've been trying to get pregnant." Tandy sipped her drink.

"Or both." Meg thought for a second and nodded. "I'm betting on both. Joy can't get pregnant, which means she'd find a doctor who could help. And that would tick off Scott because he can't stand to be incapable of something."

"What is it with men and their inability to ask for help?" Kendra huffed.

Meg scooped more chili. She held it aloft and watched the steam. "I think it's wired into their genetic makeup."

"Then Scott better get his wires fixed, or he's going to have three ticked-off sisters to deal with."

"Remind me again why it's our business whether or not Scott wants to see a doctor?" Meg popped her spoon in her mouth.

"Because, nutcase," Tandy's voice sounded like a schoolmarm patiently instructing a six-year-old, "his not seeing the doctor is making Joy crazy."

"And when Joy's crazy . . ."

"We're all crazy. I get it, I get it."

Kendra nodded. "You know, if the whole world would just do as we say, things would run a lot more smooth."

"Speaking of doing what we say, have either of you talked to Daddy lately?" Meg said.

"Why would we talk to Daddy? He's not doing anything but preaching and taking Zelda dancing every Friday."

"I know." Meg tilted her chin down and raised her eyebrows. "Think about it."

Tandy looked across the table at Kendra while all around them conversations buzzed along. She shook her head. "I give."

"Me too. What's there to talk to Daddy about?"

"You don't think it's odd how much time he's spending with Zelda these days?"

"What time? He goes dancing with her on Fridays." Kendra shrugged.

"And grocery shopping with her on

Mondays."

"What?"

Meg smiled. "Yep. Every Monday, like clockwork, you can find him and her over at Darnell's. *Like clockwork.*"

"No big deal. So they're sharing grocery shopping." Tandy held up her empty glass and nodded when she caught Clay's eye. "I don't think I'd put that in the 'to be concerned about' column. Who likes to shop alone?"

"Daddy, until he met Zelda." Meg held up her hands to stop their protests. "I'm just saying, they're sharing a lot. Grocery shopping. Dancing. Church."

"Okay, now stop." Kendra pushed her plate aside. "She goes to our church. Daddy's the preacher. I don't think that counts as a date."

"Are you so deep into wedding plans that you haven't noticed where Zelda now sits?" Meg watched both sisters think through the past Sunday. Understanding dawned on Kendra's face first.

"In the second pew on the left." Her hushed voice barely carried across the table. "Right by the aisle."

"Bingo." Meg went back to her chili.

"Are you sure?" Tandy squinted as if trying to see into the past. "I don't remember seeing her there."

"You have *got* to be the least observant person on the planet."

"Says the sister who didn't even notice Joy's messed up right now."

Meg winced. "You're right, you're right. I'm off my game."

"How long has she been sitting there?"

"Joy?" Meg looked around the diner, trying to spot her baby sister.

"No, nutcase. Zelda."

"Oh, this last Sunday was her fourth Sunday there."

"What?" Tandy sat up straight. "Tell me you're kidding. How did I not notice this?"

"Got me. All the blue hairs noticed it. They've been asking Daddy if he's got a question up his sleeve."

"A question? What kind of question?"

"*The* question. As in, 'pop the question.' "

Tandy nearly fell out of the booth. "Absolutely not. No way. Daddy is not asking Zelda to marry him. That's the most absurd thing I have ever heard come out of your mouth."

"Hey, don't shoot the messenger, sister, dear. It's the blue hairs saying it, not me. And you can't really blame them, since Zelda is now sitting in Momma's spot every Sunday."

"Well, the blue hairs can go find themselves another rumor to float, because this one doesn't hold water. Nobody in their right mind would believe Daddy could possibly think of asking another woman to marry him. Not after what he and Momma shared."

"Amen to that, sister." Kendra crossed her arms over her chest. "Don't tell me you're okay with this, Meg."

Meg grimaced. "Of course not. Why do you think I brought it up with you two? Daddy listens to y'all. So get to talking."

"What do you propose we say? 'Hey, Daddy, Meg heard some of the old women at church talking and, seeing as how everybody thinks you're about to propose to Zelda, we thought we should let you know we're not okay with it.' Does that work?" Tandy shook her head.

"Works for me."

"Meg, stop it. Much as it pains me to admit it, Tandy's got a point. This isn't something we can be proactive about."

"Aren't you the one who was just telling me to march into Joy's house and ask her what's going on?"

"That's different." Kendra looked out across the patrons still merrily chomping away on their burgers. "We *know* something's wrong there. With Daddy, it's just the blue hairs talking."

"Yeah, it could be nothing." Tandy's voice held the hope of Christmas morning.

Meg shook her head. "Happy with your heads in the sand there, ladies?"

"You better believe it."

But Kendra's voice held a note of worry.

Four

The candlelight flickers. Its warm light doesn't feel right for this room. Candlelight is for conversation, for whispered promises, for easy laughter. Those things aren't a part of our dinners. Not anymore.

Scott looks exhausted. Lines crease his forehead, and my heart hurts with the knowledge that my inability has caused such a physical change in my husband.

We must go see a doctor. I know a doctor could help us figure out why we cannot seem to conceive. Yet broaching the subject will only cause that line to deepen. Scott does not like asking for help.

In high school I thought that was heroic.

Now I think it is idiotic and selfish.

He may not need help, but I certainly do. And what man cannot ask for help on behalf of his wife? Why can't he see that his stubbornness only makes this situation worse?

He likes the duck I've made. I know he

does, even though he doesn't tell me. He rarely says anything positive to me anymore.

"How was work today?"

His eyes stay low, looking at the dish rather than me. "Fine."

"Did you manage to close that sale over on Ralston Road?"

He nods.

I wait. I'm not certain why. I know he will not contribute to this conversation unless I force him to do so. A part of me hopes, though, that today he will decide to be the Scott I married. The happy man with a positive outlook on life.

The man I forced away with my barren womb.

The notes of a toccata fall from speakers hidden in the walls. They should create an atmosphere of frivolity, but even music has limits. Music is too honest to ignore reality or overwhelm it.

I push orange glaze around my plate, watching it swirl against the white bone china. The candlelight dances on the plate's platinum rim, and, for a moment, I am lost in the simple beauty of that dance.

Scott clears his throat, and reality blots out beauty.

"Joy, I think it's time we accept that perhaps we aren't meant to be parents."

It's a conversation we have had too many times these past weeks.

"Scott, we're nowhere near that yet. We haven't even been to see a doctor to find out what might be blocking us from conceiving."

"And we're not going to see a doctor, Joy. You know my heart on that. Must you continue on a subject we've closed repeatedly?"

"It's closed only to you."

"Since I'm half of this marriage, then I should have a say in how we handle this situation."

"More of a say than me?"

"Than I."

"Do *not* correct my grammar, Scott Lasky. You are *not* the end-all, be-all of marriage. You do *not* have all the answers. And, right now, you do *not* get to tell me I cannot go visit a doctor and find out if the problem is me." My voice doesn't sound like my own, but this reckless feeling of finally doing something about our situation instead of treading water feels right. I stand up, needing to end the conversation before Scott talks me out of it. "I'll call Dr. Goodman in the morning for an appointment. Good night, Scott."

My ears feel closed, like I've stepped off

the edge and plunged into the deep recesses of a lake. I know my feet are carrying me away from more than just a cold dinner.

I don't think I care.

"Come on, Kendra! Get in here before my rear end gets frostbite!" Tandy held open the front door of the house that had been home since her adoption nearly three decades ago.

"I'm coming, I'm coming." Kendra's mittens prevented her from getting a good grip on the stair rail and her feet slid on the stairs.

"Watch out!" Tandy jumped out the door, and Kendra caught her extended hand just in time.

"Whew. That was close."

"We'll just call you Grace from now on." Tandy pulled Kendra through the door and shut out the cold winter air.

The sisters walked through the house and into the kitchen. Tandy picked up a red-checkered towel and opened the oven. The door's old hinges creaked as she knelt down to check out the batch of double-chocolate-chip cookies inside. "I think these are about done. It's hard to tell since they're already brown."

"Are the chips melted on top?"

"Yeah, I think so."

"Then pull those babies out. We've got scrapping and planning to do."

Tandy retrieved the cookie tray and set it on a cooling rack. She turned to Kendra and tossed the towel back on the counter. "Shouldn't we call this what it is? We're not planning. We're conniving."

Kendra shrugged off her coat and hung it on the back of a nearby Windsor chair. "That sounds too evil. We're not doing anything bad here, are we? We're just making sure Daddy doesn't do something stupid."

"I don't know, Ken. Part of me thinks his dating life should be his business."

"Forgetting the fact that 'dating life' and 'Daddy' in the same sentence still gives me the creeps, we need to focus on the greater good here."

"You're right." Tandy heaved a sigh. "I wish Momma were here."

"Me too."

Silence fell between them, and Tandy's thoughts filled with memories. Momma's sure presence, her unwavering love of the whole Sinclair family. Momma always had the right word to say or hug to give when life threw a curveball. She hadn't been perfect, but she'd sure been the best momma Tandy could imagine. Why couldn't Momma be the one pulling cookies from the oven now, just like she'd done for years and years?

Because cancer is no determiner of people.

Tandy cleared her throat and opened the cabinet to the right of the old porcelain sink. "Grab the milk, Ken. We've got to get this situation under control."

Kendra moved toward the refrigerator, her lavender boots squeaking on the linoleum floor. "So are we going to talk to Daddy? I should warn you, I haven't come up with anything better than that little speech you gave Meg at the diner."

"Me either." Tandy held out the glasses while Kendra poured. "But maybe there's a way to put the brakes on this without talking to Daddy or Zelda."

Kendra put the cap back on the milk jug and placed it back in the refrigerator. "Okay, sounds good. How?"

Tandy chomped down on a cookie and chewed. "I haven't figured that part out yet. That's what you're here for."

"Oh, good to know your expectations aren't too high." Kendra picked up the plate of cookies and turned to leave the kitchen. "Before we get too deep into this, we're sure we don't want them getting married, right?"

"Kendra Sinclair! What do you mean?" Tandy snatched up their milk glasses and followed Kendra up the stairs toward Momma's scrapping studio. "You *want* Daddy bringing another woman in here, letting her put her clothes in Momma's drawers, her makeup in Momma's bathroom? Spraying her perfume so all traces of Momma's smell are gone? Washing her clothes in Momma's washing machine? Pushing her mop across Momma's kitchen floor?"

"Ugh. I hadn't thought through that part of it."

"Well, think it through then. Marriage is huge. She'd be to Daddy what Momma was. And then she'd try to be to us what Momma was, and I don't think I'm a good enough actress to put up with that the rest of my life."

They made it to the top of the second flight of stairs and crossed the worn hardwood planks to a giant square table. Kendra pulled out a stool and plopped down, cookie in hand. "Okay, genius. I'm all in. How do we stop this? Is there anything in Zelda's past that would make Daddy break up with her?"

"I don't think so. I tried that angle back when I first came home. Clay backed her up, remember, because he knew her as a marine wife back in his enlisted days. Her personal life isn't going to quash Daddy's feelings. Besides, they've probably talked through their pasts by now if Meg's right about the amount of time they've been spending together."

"True." Kendra nodded. "What about letting Zelda know we don't want her around?"

"Do you think Zelda would care?"

"Maybe."

"Ken, if she cared, she'd have left Daddy long ago. None of us has been exactly silent on our feelings about her being in Daddy's life."

"No, but we haven't been overly vocal either. We've been mannered and kind and put up with her."

"Yeah. See where that got us?"

"Exactly." Kendra brushed the crumbs off her hands, her diamond engagement ring glinting in the light, and walked over to the shelf holding the layouts she was currently working on. "We've been nice, and she's taken that for approval. So we stop being nice. She'll get the hint and, at the very least, cut back on all the time she's spending with Daddy. Daddy's not dumb. He'll get the message that she's losing interest, and the whole thing will run its course in a few weeks."

Tandy stared as Kendra began setting out papers and embellishments as if she hadn't a care in the world. The clock ticked while she waited for Kendra to laugh.

"You're serious," Tandy finally said.

Kendra looked up. "Yeah. It's a good plan, don't you think?"

"No! It's not a plan at all. 'Stop being nice'? That's your grand plan?" Tandy stomped over to the same shelf and jerked her materials off so hard some of them fell to the floor. She knelt and began picking them up. "Kendra, come on. That's not going to work. Zelda's just going to tell Daddy that we aren't being nice, and then Daddy will talk to us in that voice — you know, the one that guilts us into being angels again — and then the whole thing will just bring them closer together. They will have *parented* us together."

"How can we be parented when we're in our twenties and thirties already?"

Tandy finished retrieving her embellishments and dumped the whole mess across the table from Kendra's spot. Narrowing her eyes, she looked at Kendra. "You don't want to stop this, do you?"

Kendra's shoulders slumped. "It's not that I don't *want* to, T. It's that I don't know *how.* Short of telling Zelda we don't want her to get serious with Daddy — which we know won't work — or telling Daddy none of us are ready for this — which isn't really fair to him — I don't know of a way to make sure they don't fall in love."

Tandy's heart stopped. "You think he loves her?"

"If he's been letting her sit in Momma's seat for a month, yeah, I'd say he loves her."

Tandy dropped onto a stool, defeat falling on her like a storm cloud. "How did we miss that?"

"You just got married." Kendra shrugged. "You're busy starting your own home. And my whole world is bridesmaids' dresses and boutonnieres right now."

"But I shouldn't be losing touch with my old home just because I'm starting my new one."

"Isn't that the 'leave and cleave' part of marriage?"

Tandy bit her tongue and turned her gaze to the layout now spilled out all over her side of the table. A sharp retort would help, but Kendra had a point there. Her marriage to Clay *should* be her priority, and it had been ever since their wedding. But letting herself focus on Clay to the detriment of Daddy? Was that really what marriage was supposed to be?

Clay would tell her Zelda wasn't a detriment to anything good in the world. And he might be right. Keeping Momma's memory alive, though, meant a lot. And how could they do that with Zelda in Momma's kitchen cooking breakfast and in her laundry room doing the wash and in her living room rocking in Momma's rocker? They wouldn't even be able to talk about Momma in the house, probably, because it would make Zelda uncomfortable!

Tandy picked up a photo and began organizing the mess before her. "Look, Ken, if you don't want to help me, that's fine. But I'm not going to stand by silently while Daddy gets rid of all trace of Momma from this house and our lives because he's found someone new to love."

"You think he'd do that?"

"I don't think he'd mean to, but I can't see anything else being fair to Zelda. She's not going to live forever in a house that reminds her of her husband's first wife. I wouldn't expect her to. Would you?"

"I guess not." Kendra slid a blade across a photo, cutting off the extra part of it. "But, T, are we absolutely certain that the blue hairs are right? That Daddy's thinking of popping the question?"

"No, I'm never sure of anything those

women say."

"Well, I think we need to know if there's a situation to deal with before we take steps to address it, don't you?"

"I do." Tandy stood up. "Let's go see."

Kendra hurried to follow Tandy down the stairs. "See what?"

"See if Daddy's thinking about marrying Zelda."

"What are we going to do? Ask him?"

"No." Tandy turned and marched into her parents' bedroom. "We're going to ask his stuff."

"Oh, Tandy, you can't be serious. We're going through Daddy's things? That's a huge invasion of his privacy!"

Tandy spun on her heel and stared Kendra down. "Remember when we came home from school and Daddy and Momma were sitting on your bed with your journal in their hands?"

Kendra nodded. "Yeah, they found out I'd been sneaking out with Tyrel Parks, and I got grounded for three months from everything but church."

"And what did they say when you yelled at them for invading your privacy by reading your journal?"

"They said they were doing what had to be done to make sure I was taken care of,

43

safe, and making wise judgments."

"Yep." Tandy walked over and yanked open the top drawer of an old mahogany chest that had sat in this same spot for thirty years. "And that's precisely what we're doing. If we're right and Daddy's in love with Zelda," she riffled through the folded white undershirts, "then he's not in the right frame of mind to be making wise judgments. We're just making sure he's taken care of."

Kendra hesitated for a second longer. With a shake of her spiral curls, she huffed and strode over to the chest's matching dresser. "I'm not sure I buy your logic, sister, but I've never deserted you before and I'm not about to now."

"Thanks, Ken." Tandy slammed the drawer shut and moved quickly to the one below it.

"Thank me when we're done and out of here without Daddy being any the wiser."

Tandy shut her mouth and searched as fast as her fingers could fly.

FIVE

The rose bushes in my back garden look dead. Every plant out there does. Leafless trees and brown grass. No color at all. I should have put evergreens or pansies within view of this window. Instead I'm left with death staring toward my bedroom. A death created by my own hands.

I've never loved anyone as deeply as I love Scott Lasky. Is it possible to hate someone even while you love them? Because I hate him now. I love him, of course. I'll always love him. But I hate him too. I hate how stubborn he is. I hate how sure he is. I hate how unsure he is. I hate how silent he is. I hate how scared he is.

I hate that most.

I know he's scared. Does he think I don't know? That I could have lived with him for years, made his meals, ordered his house, shared his bed, and not know when he's scared?

I just can't decide if he is more scared that the problem is me or that it's him. If I'm the one keeping us from getting pregnant, then he might not be able to love me. I can be honest about that. Scott's accustomed to getting what he wants. He's always believed that if he works hard enough and follows the appropriate steps, he can attain the goal he has set.

We share that vision.

Pregnancy isn't falling into line, though. It relies on body parts outside of our control. And even a certain amount of magic, I think. Or miracle.

Yes, miracle.

Miracles don't come from hard work. They come from prayer and from the will of a God with whom we're not allowed to reason. A God whose character or motivation I cannot fully grasp. I thought God wanted us all to be happy. But if that's the case, we would be pregnant by now.

Meg said our life's purpose isn't to be happy; it's to bring glory to God.

Didn't God tell us to be fruitful and multiply? How can I be faithful to His command, glorify Him in my obedience, if He's given me a womb that doesn't work?

Then again, the problem could be Scott. I don't know if he'd survive that knowledge.

If he could comprehend being *unable* to do what he wants. If he's the problem, I'll bet he finds a solution. Scott wouldn't rest until he'd found a way to overcome whatever issue life presented.

I love that about him.

"I can't believe this, Tandy." Kendra unwound her purple, red, yellow, and orange striped scarf, tossing it atop the desk on which she sat. She clicked the switch on a leopard print lamp at her side. The feathered finish around the edges left no question as to whose desk this was, sitting proudly in all its eclectic glory in the Sisters, Ink office.

"Me, either." Tandy wore a shell-shocked expression — eyes glazed over, fixed on nothing in particular, but fixed nonetheless. Her own brass lamp with green hood and short gold pull cord testified to previous days spent slaving over briefs in an Orlando law office.

Kendra leaned forward and snapped her fingers. "Hey, Earth to sister. Come in, sister."

Tandy blinked and turned her head. "I just can't believe this."

Kendra wrinkled her forehead. "Weren't you the one telling me 'Daddy's in love with her' and all that jazz? Why are you so surprised?"

"I guess I hoped I was wrong." Tandy leaned back in her desk chair and steepled her fingers, looking for all the world like the attorney she had once been. "You know? Saying it out loud sounded so ridiculous that it just had to be wrong."

"Well, news flash. That box means he's not only planning to pop the question, he's not scrimping on the diamond. And he went to Lindell Jewelers. They're in Brentwood. That's where Darin designed my ring. And their diamonds don't come with a small price tag or an everyday setting."

"So he's been planning this for a while."

"If he went to Lindell, I'm betting he's done what Darin did and designed the ring himself. So yeah, he's been planning this a while."

"How did we miss this?"

Kendra slapped her hands on her jean-clad thighs. "Beats me. Who cares? What's done is done. He's in love. He's bought a ring, and he may even have plans to give it soon. If we're stopping this train, it's time to throw ourselves on the tracks."

Tandy stood and headed toward the back.

"Where are you going?" Kendra hopped down from the desk and trailed after her sister. "We're having a conversation here!"

"I know, but my hands need to move so I can think. I did my best strategizing in Orlando in the files room."

"Bet the paralegals loved you."

Tandy gave a wry smile and entered their storage room. Boxes of products bearing the Sisters, Ink logo nearly filled the room. T-shirts, pens, scrapbooking tools and embellishments, club identification cards, and the usual office supplies of stationery and envelopes crammed every shelf. Tandy attacked the jumble in front of her, pulling rubber bands from pens and staples. Kendra chewed a fingernail while Tandy quickly created a rubber-band ball.

"This can't happen, Ken. Daddy can't get married."

"Agreed. Now what do we do to keep that ring off Zelda's finger?"

Tandy snapped a rubber band. "We've got to get ruthless."

"Okay."

"Really?"

"Really."

"I thought you were only in this to support me."

"Let's just say the sight of a jeweler's receipt in Daddy's nightstand drawer was enough to bring home the reality."

Tandy nodded. "Okay then. If we can't

find something in Zelda's past to make Daddy break up with her, then we'll just have to find something in Daddy's to make Zelda break up with him."

"What in the world does Daddy have in his past that anybody would care about?"

"Nothing that we know of. But we also didn't know he'd bought a ring. Maybe there are other things we don't know."

Kendra shook her head. "No, I don't think that's going to work. Daddy's been a straight arrow ever since we've known him. Short of killing somebody in his teenage years, we're not going to find anything bad enough to make Zelda walk away. Besides, like you said before, they've probably already talked through their pasts."

"So we go with your plan."

"What plan?"

"We'll stop being nice."

"You mean the plan you hated?"

"I hated it in its *first* stage. We're going to escalate to a stage that works."

"Based on your reaction the first time we talked about this, I'm betting that's about stage twenty."

"Exactly. Not only will we stop being nice, we're going to be downright rude."

"Meg will never go for this."

"She doesn't have to. Two of us being rude

to Zelda will probably be enough."

"Maybe, but it'd be more effective if all four of us sent the message."

"Then we'll do whatever it takes to convince Meg and Joy that the *right* thing here is to be rude."

"Good luck with that. I'm pretty sure Joy equates rude with the seven deadly sins."

"And we wouldn't want Joy to go against her principles."

Tandy and Kendra spun around at the new voice.

"Zelda!" Tandy dropped her rubber-band ball. It bounced lightly, then rolled across the commercial carpet to stop at Zelda's boots.

"Hello, girls." Zelda retrieved the ball, then straightened.

"H–how are you? We didn't hear you come in." Kendra pushed her hair behind her ears.

"I guess not. Though I'll say your rude campaign is off to a great start."

"Oh, we didn't —"

"Yeah, I guess so." Tandy put her hands on her hips. "Was there something you needed or do you always go around butting into people's private conversations?"

Zelda smiled while the feeble storage room light glinted off her red spiky hair. "Yes, I'd say you would have done well at

51

this campaign."

Tandy raised an eyebrow. "Would have?"

Zelda shook her head and her big silver jewelry clanked. "You can call it off."

"I don't think so." Tandy took a step toward Zelda and pointed. "So long as you're around, you should know there's no more nice daughter for you. Daddy's having a friend to hang out with is fine. Shoot, even grocery shopping together is fine. But we have a mother, and we certainly don't need some red-haired marine widow walking in here and trying to take Momma's place just because she's gone home to heaven."

Zelda's face hardened, and Kendra saw the strength of a military wife shine through. "The very fact that you'd think I'd try," her voice could have cut glass, "is enough for me to know this won't work. I told Jack we should keep things casual. That you girls weren't ready for anything else. But from the sound of things, he didn't listen."

Tandy sneered. "Oh, sure. Getting married is all Daddy's idea. You haven't thought a bit about living in our house or enjoying your status as the preacher's wife, right? Don't try to sell me that line. You've been sitting in Momma's seat for a month now. And that's another thing that's about to change. Don't even think about trying it this Sunday. We're on to you. We'll put up with your presence in Daddy's life. But your little plan for marriage is over right now. Got it?"

Zelda stared at Tandy, tension tightening the distance between them. Kendra's gaze darted back and forth. A brawl at the Sisters, Ink office wouldn't go unnoticed by townsfolk.

"Look, ladies —"

"No, Kendra." Zelda held up a small hand, exhaustion lowering her tone. "Don't bother. I care a lot about your daddy. Enough to know that being with me isn't worth hurting his relationship with his daughters." She moved to go, then turned back and tossed the rubber-band ball. Tandy caught it in reflex. "I'll be gone by tomorrow, Tandy. Tell your daddy whatever you want about why."

"Wait, Zelda." Kendra stepped forward. "Where are you going?"

Her smile held sadness and the remembrance of familiar heartache. "Somewhere quiet, Kendra. Somewhere my presence doesn't cause so much pain."

The thud of her boots receded, punctuating Kendra's racing thoughts. Had they done the right thing? Would Daddy be mad? Well, of course he'd be mad. But how long would it take for him to see they'd done this because they were looking out for him?

Kendra thought back to Tyrel Parks. She didn't get over that for a month. And that had been a high school crush two weeks in the making. Daddy and Zelda had been together for almost a year now. She'd been at Tandy's wedding.

Shoot, she's on the guest list for my wedding.

Kendra turned to find that same shell-shocked expression on Tandy's face.

"Should we go after her?" Kendra's whisper barely covered the space between them.

Tandy shook her head. "I don't think so. Just be grateful she's gone and things can get back to normal."

Normal? What did that mean?

One look at her sister's face convinced Kendra it was better not to ask.

Six

Meg popped an aspirin and washed it down with a swig from the bottled water in her cupholder. *If I spent more time drinking water, I wouldn't get dehydration headaches.* She checked her face in the rearview mirror, decided there wasn't much to be done about it, and stepped out of the van.

Joy's cobblestone driveway looked as it always had — immaculate and historical. Meg's loafers slid a bit on the moss lightly coating the bricks.

Moss? When had that been allowed to take root?

No matter. Whatever had invaded Joy's life to cause these lapses in memory or character, Meg would talk to Joy about them and, together, they'd fix whatever was wrong. Nothing on earth couldn't be defeated by the power of Sinclair sisterhood. Through all kinds of craziness, the sisterhood hung together. They held each other up when life's waves pounded mercilessly. They threw punches when one went down. They spoke when one lost her words. They prayed when one lost her faith. Hadn't they held true to that promise for nearly three decades now?

Meg reached the top of the stairway and squared her shoulders to Joy's massive wooden door. No matter what lay on the other side, they'd face it. Together.

The wind kicked up, and Meg shivered as dead leaves rustled.

Dead leaves?

She turned to see brown leaves bunched up in the corners of the flower beds on either side of the stairs. *Moss and dead leaves.* Meg took a deep breath and pushed the doorbell like a warrior sounding a battle cry.

A light rain began falling, and Meg huddled closer to the door. Why didn't someone answer? She pushed the doorbell again, hearing its muffled signal on the other side of the wood. Joy had to be home. When Meg dropped by the salon, the receptionist informed her that Joy had taken a sick day.

A sick day. Moss. Dead leaves. Meg rubbed her temple and prayed for relief from the incessant throbbing. She needed to think.

What could have rocked Joy's world so hard that she'd skip work and let the grounds go?

Finally the door opened a crack. Meg tried not to gasp at the sight of Joy but failed.

"Hi, Meg." Joy's beautiful blue eyes were glued to the floor. Faint purple moons hung below her black lashes.

"Hey, Joy." Meg stepped into the house, pushing fear to the back of her mind. A pall hung in the air, as if someone were sick or dying. "I stopped by Styles, and they said you'd called in sick. Everything okay?"

Joy lifted a tiny shoulder and looked at the corner of the room. "Sure."

"Really? Because you don't look okay. Can I help?"

If the chandelier's light hadn't moved on her ebony hair, Meg would have missed Joy's slight shake of the head. "No, we're fine."

"Hey, Joy?" Meg waited an eternity for Joy to meet her eyes. "I think we both know everything's not fine. If you don't want to tell me whatever it is, you don't have to. But you're going to have to do a better job of covering it up because Tandy and Kendra know something's up. And I'm guessing you'd rather they not apply their fix-it principles to whatever's going on."

The bands around Meg's heart eased a bit with Joy's slight smile.

"How about you and I drink about a gallon of sweet tea each and pretend the sugar won't go right to our hips?" She gingerly placed an arm around Joy's shoulders and steered her down the wide gallery hallway. Each painting hung perfectly parallel to the next and Meg could find no knickknack out of place.

Still, something in this house gave her a chill that the rain outside couldn't have produced in its wildest dreams. The oriental carpet muffled their steps, and Meg cast about for a safe topic of conversation.

The words died on her lips when they entered the kitchen. Dishes littered the granite countertops. Some sort of orange glaze had dried and cracked on several of the plates and a large baking dish. Wine glasses stood sentinel by the sink, their glass cloudy and dull. Black-striped towels that Meg remembered buying with Joy at Crate & Barrel were bunched up on the stove, which sported drops of a dark-brown liquid on the surface. Meg looked closely and saw spatters of something — dried milk? — on the floor by the far counter. A bowl in the sink half full of milk — from cereal — confirmed the milk spots.

"I've been a little preoccupied." The small voice came from beneath her arm.

"No problem. Everybody gets tired of cleaning sometimes." She led Joy over to one of the tall chairs scooted under the outcropping of granite that formed the bar. "How about you take a load off and let me clean up for you?"

Joy nodded and looked off toward the corner again. Meg swallowed. In all her years of living here, Joy had never let any of them clean the kitchen. "It's an insult to the guest," she'd declared every time they offered. Didn't matter that family wasn't a guest. Not to Martha Stewart, so not to Joy.

Meg searched around and found some dishwashing liquid. Of course, it couldn't be something as familiar as Palmolive. Meg hoped designer dishwashing liquid performed as well as the stuff she bought at Target.

In a few minutes warm suds built in the giant sink and Meg scraped dishes in its other side.

"So do you want to tell me what's going on, sis?"

"Nothing's going on."

"Yeah, I can see that." Meg gestured with the red-and-white scrubber, encompassing the room. "This is normal for your house."

"You said it yourself. I grew weary of cleaning."

"Who are you and what have you done with my sister?" Maybe humor would help.

Joy half-laughed, but the sound held no mirth. "She died after the ninth pregnancy test."

Meg turned, then thought better of facing her. If Joy could talk more easily without their looking at each other, she'd grant that. "Ninth? Wow, that's a lot. I didn't realize you'd been trying for so long."

Again came the dry laugh. "You asked when Joy left. There have been tests without her."

"Oh." Meg scrubbed. "How many tests, exactly?"

"I lost count."

"Have you seen a doctor?"

"I will this afternoon. People do that on their sick days, don't they?"

"That they do. Who are you seeing?"

"Dr. Goodman."

"Are you meeting Scott there?"

The laugh that Meg had already begun hating came again. "I'm not meeting Scott anywhere."

"What does that mean?"

"Nothing."

"I think it may mean something, sis."

"Not really. It just means I'm not meeting him anywhere. Not in our home. Not in our marriage. And certainly not in Dr. Goodman's office."

Meg sank her hands into the warmth of the dishwater and cleaned away what mess she could. A redbird landed on the block of birdseed hanging from a dogwood outside the kitchen window. Meg noticed the birdseed had nearly all been eaten. So did the bird, who pecked a bit and flew off, still hungry.

"Did you have a fight?"

"Hmm. I think a fight implies communication. No, we didn't have a fight."

"How about a silent argument?"

"No, that implies a commitment to caring. We definitely didn't have an argument."

Meg held in her frustration. If Joy wanted to play word games for a while, then she'd play.

"How about a disagreement? Neither party has to talk to the other past the airing of the disagreement. And it doesn't mean either of them cares, just that they disagree."

Silence answered her and Meg let it go. She finished scrubbing away the orange glaze from the platinum rim of a plate and moved on to the next.

"Yes, we had a disagreement." Joy's voice

had softened another notch.

"About what?"

"Oh, about a lot of whats. Actually, about a lot of abouts. It's hard to know which ones caused the others."

"Name them and we'll figure it out."

"About going to the doctor. About whether we should be parents. About whether it's his fault. About whether it's mine. About whether it matters whose fault it is. About why I can't let it go. About why he can't care enough to not let it go. About what this means for our marriage."

"That *is* a lot of abouts."

"You were warned."

"Which about do you care about the most?"

No hesitation. "About whose fault it is."

"Thus the visit to Dr. Goodman?"

"Yes."

Meg waited again, cleaning the dishes and letting the words swirl in her pounding brain. When had pregnancy become so important to Joy?

"Why does it matter whose fault it is?"

"Because when you have a problem, you find out what's causing it. If you know the cause, you might be able to fix the problem." Meg nodded. That made sense. "And Scott doesn't want to find out the cause of the problem?"

"Scott doesn't acknowledge there *is* a problem." Anger filled Joy's voice with a passion she hadn't shown since Meg walked in the door. "He thinks we should just keep trying and praying and somehow all the stars will fall into alignment and we'll get pregnant."

"That's annoying."

"Precisely!" Joy slapped the counter.

Meg cheered inside at this sign of life.

"I show him the research that advises any couple who's tried for six months with no success to see a fertility specialist. He shows me one that says to wait until twelve months. So I wait twelve months. We get to twelve months and he says we should give it another twelve, just to be sure. Meanwhile, neither I nor my ovaries are getting any younger. At this rate, I'll be in a nursing home by the time my husband decides, perhaps, just perhaps, something isn't working correctly in our systems."

"So you decided to see Dr. Goodman without him."

"At least then I'll know if I'm the problem."

"And what if you are? Any treatments are going to be expensive and probably painful."

"So? I've never shied away from pain."

"No, and I didn't mean you would now. I meant it will be helpful to have Scott's support while you go through that."

"I doubt he'll support me. He might leave me when he finds out I've gone to see Dr. Goodman."

"You can't be serious."

"I don't know if I'm serious or not. I know he's serious about believing there is no problem. Going to Dr. Goodman is a pretty clear indication that I think there's a problem, wouldn't you agree?"

"Yes."

"That's not a small matter over which to disagree with your husband."

"Well, no. But it's not big enough to end your marriage over."

"Oh, I don't know if he'd end our marriage. He may just interrupt it for a while."

Meg reached for one of the black-and-white towels and dried the suds from her hands. She joined Joy at the countertop and reached for one of her sister's small, cold hands. "Is finding out the cause worth 'interrupting' your marriage?"

Joy turned her breathtaking blue eyes toward Meg, and Meg's heart broke at the tears held captive there.

"I don't have a choice. It's been interrupted since the ninth test." Joy closed her eyes and fat tears rolled beneath the thick black lashes, down her delicate cheeks.

Meg pulled Joy's head to hers and ached over a pain she didn't know if they could fight.

"Kendra Diane Sinclair!" Daddy's voice boomed across the house and up the stairway. "Tandy Ann Sinclair Kelner! I know you're here, and I better see your sorry faces in front of mine in three seconds or I'm coming up there!"

Tandy dropped her glue runner and raised dread-filled eyes to Kendra. "What do we do?"

"I think we face the music."

"Are you kidding? He's going to tan our hides!"

Kendra rolled her eyes. "Oh, Tandy, we're adults. He can't spank us or ground us. We'll just tell him there was a misunderstanding, and he'll get over it."

"What misunderstanding? Zelda heard us scheming how to break her and Daddy up, and we broke her and Daddy up. What, exactly, was misunderstood in that exchange?"

"I don't know, but we better figure it out fast because our three seconds are up, and judging from his voice, he's talked to Zelda."

Daddy's footfalls pounded up the stairs, and both sisters braced for his appearance.

"I want to know what in tarnation you two thought you were doing." The words came before his head had cleared the landing. Tandy gulped as he got to the top and crossed the room, one finger pointing. "I've done nothing but love you girls as long as I've known you. Your mother and I raised you better than this, and I'll have you know you've shamed the both of us with your behavior toward Zelda. And to know you would have kept this from me if I hadn't run into her at Darnell's! Now tell me exactly what you thought authorized you to go meddling in my relationship like this."

"She told you we were meddling?"

"She didn't have to, and don't you take that tone, Tandy Ann. Zelda's been worried about the two of you since the first time I said 'I love you.' I told her she shouldn't worry. I told her my girls were mature enough to let their daddy love again. I was wrong about that, but don't prove I was wrong about your respect."

"Daddy, we only wanted what was best for you."

"And who told you I couldn't make that

decision, Kendra?"

"Daddy, you know you wouldn't see anything negative about Zelda." Tandy searched for reason. "You said yourself you love her. We see her without the rose-colored glasses you wear."

"And what do you see with that perfect vision, missy?"

"A woman who wants the status of being the preacher's wife, who sees this nice, big house and all that farmland outside and sees a good life she could have."

"You think she's a gold digger?" Daddy's eyes widened.

"I think she may be."

"So I'm just a dumb farmer and preacher who can't tell he's being swindled. Is that it?"

"Daddy! I would never think that of you!"

"Then I must be so desperate for companionship I'll take the first woman that comes along, right?"

"No!"

"Then tell me, Tandy. What does your opinion of Zelda say about your opinion of me?"

"I don't think that's what Tandy means, Daddy."

"What does she mean, then, Kendra? I'm all ears. Tell me what the two of you were thinking when you ran off the woman I love?"

"You really love her, Daddy?" Tandy's voice sounded twenty years younger than the body from which it came.

Daddy paused. His words, when they came, were soft. "Yes, sweet girl. I love her."

Tandy squeezed her eyes shut. Kendra walked around to Tandy's side and held up her hand to stop Daddy from joining them. "We figured this would come sometime, T," she whispered into Tandy's ear. "She's who he's picked." Tandy took a deep breath and Kendra pulled her into a hug. "If she makes Daddy happy, then we might need to let her in."

"But —"

"Not into Momma's space. Into a new space. A Zelda space."

Tandy let out her breath, and Kendra met Daddy's eyes over her sister's head. Daddy smiled his gratitude. Kendra patted Tandy's back. Tandy stepped back and looked up to Kendra's face. "A Zelda space? Aren't we too old to make space for new folks?"

"I sure hope not. Or Darin's in a world of hurt."

Tandy chuckled. "You're right." She swiped at a tear and turned to Daddy. "You really do love her?"

Daddy nodded. "Yes. Not like your momma. And Zelda doesn't love me like her first husband. It's different. But it's still love. Neither of us will replace that first love for the other."

Tandy put one balled-up fist on a hip. "Okay, then. We'll just have to get her back here."

"I don't think it will be that easy. She was pretty hurt by you two, and she's not going to do anything she thinks will hurt my relationship with you girls."

"We'll see about that, Daddy. Don't worry. I can fix this."

Daddy threw his hands up. "You're going to try whether I agree or not, so okay. Just keep me in the loop, please."

"You've got it."

"And Tandy?"

"Yeah, Daddy?"

"The next time you think I'm walking down the wrong path or making wrong decisions, how about you come to me directly?"

Tandy ducked her head and smiled.

SEVEN

Meg turned another page in the worn *Real Simple* magazine and glanced at her watch.

"I told you this might take a while." Joy picked a piece of lint from her black corduroy pants.

"I know." Meg put the magazine down. "I'm not in a hurry, I'm just wondering if they forgot about us."

"We've only been back here half an hour, Meg." Joy turned back to the book she'd brought from home. "That's a normal wait time for him, and we know the nurse worked me into the schedule. I'd say we might wait another half hour before he gets back here."

"Are you kidding me?"

"No."

"You wait half an hour every time you come to the doctor?"

"You don't?"

Meg tried to think of the last time she'd been to the doctor other than rushing the kids to the ER for various emergencies. "I can't remember."

Joy smiled. "Be grateful for your health."

Meg nodded and picked up another magazine. Convincing Joy to let her come to this appointment had taken some doing, so there was no way on earth she'd walk out before the doctor told them the results of Joy's exam. Whether Scott had figured out that Joy had been to that first visit yet, neither of them knew. According to Joy, Scott continued to practically live at the office, and when he was home, he stuck his nose in a book or hid behind the newspaper. Joy even gave up cooking dinner a few nights ago. What was the point if Scott didn't appreciate it? What if their marriage couldn't recover from the hurts each of them dealt every day?

"Hi, Joy. Sorry to keep you waiting." Dr. Goodman entered the office and held out a hand in greeting.

"No problem, Dr. Goodman. Thanks for working me in." Joy shook his hand and settled back into her seat. "This is my sister, Megan."

"Nice to meet you, Megan."

"Likewise." Meg shook his hand and focused back on the room. "I'm hoping you have good news for my sister."

Dr. Goodman took his seat and smoothed his tie. "Well, yes and no. The good news is, we could find no abnormalities in any of your tests, Joy. Your fallopian tubes have no blockages, your uterus has no cysts, and your reproductive processes seem to be functioning properly. As far as we can tell, all within you is normal."

Joy grinned. "That's great news!"

"What's the bad news?"

The doctor grimaced and leaned forward onto his desk. "If you're checking out fine, and you haven't been able to get pregnant in over a year, then I have a strong suspicion that Scott should be tested immediately."

Joy's lips tightened into a thin line. "You're saying the problem is Scott."

"No. I'm saying there's a strong likelihood the problem is in Scott's reproductive system, not yours. Be sure to keep the blame where it belongs, Joy. Not on the person but on the system. He doesn't control his system anymore than you control yours. You do what you can — eat right, exercise, get enough sleep — but genetics are what they are."

"He'll never agree to testing."

Dr. Goodman leaned back in his chair. "Has he said that?"

"Pretty much."

"He might change his mind now that we know everything is working properly in your system."

Joy sat still for a moment, then picked up her purse. Standing, she held out her hand. "Thank you, Dr. Goodman."

The doctor shook Joy's hand and nodded. "You're more than welcome. Let me know if I can help."

Joy let go of the doctor's hand and walked out the door.

Meg scrambled to follow, shooting a smile of gratitude over her shoulder for Dr. Goodman.

Joy didn't speak until they'd gone down five floors in the elevator, walked the long hallway to the parking garage, traipsed across the garage to their car, and buckled in.

"Either he gets tested, or he gets a new wife."

Meg opened her mouth to warn about ultimatums, but the look on Joy's face stopped her cold.

Joy pushed a button and the quiet purr of the Lexus's motor began. The minor notes of a Mozart piece filled the car's cabin. Joy ejected the disc and inserted another, then turned the volume knob and hummed along.

"What are we listening to?" Meg nearly shouted over the music.

"It's from *Hansel and Gretel* by Engelbert Humperdinck. This is the aria the witch sings as she tries to put Hansel and Gretel into her oven. It played at the Met this month, so the music is popular again."

"How do you know what played at the Met this month?"

"Oh, didn't I tell you? They're streaming the performances live into movie theaters across the country. I drive up to Nashville and watch an opera every single month."

"You go to the movie theater to watch an opera?"

"I do. Isn't it wonderful?"

"Fantastic." Where did Joy get this love of classical music, and how did no other Sinclair sister get it?

"I couldn't believe our good fortune when the series started. Imagine! No more flying up to New York to see good opera. And experiencing it in the theater is even better. I don't have to be in a ball gown, and I can even eat popcorn while I watch! Though I wouldn't admit that last part in public."

"Never."

Joy grinned and Meg thanked God for the presence of a real smile on her sister's face. "Congrats, by the way, on being normal."

Joy flashed a happy face her way before turning back to the driving. "Thanks. You have no idea what a relief it is to know I haven't been the one holding us up all this time."

"I'd advise you not to tell Scott's he's been 'holding you up.' That might not sit very well."

"Oh, I'll try to be a bit more tactful." Joy turned the radio volume down. "Though not much. Tact gives him the opportunity to decline my request for him to see a doctor. He has to understand this isn't a request, that it's a necessity for our marriage."

"You really want to hang your marriage on whether he'll take a medical test?"

"It's more than that." Joy stopped at a red light and faced Meg. "Taking the test means he wants a baby as much as I do. That he wants to do what it takes for us to make a family. To have children. All this time he's been saying that having children is as important to him as it is to me. The time has come for him to, as Kendra would say, put up or shut up."

"I cannot believe you just said that." Meg giggled.

"Me either. And it goes in the same category as popcorn at the opera."

Meg made an *X* sign over her chest. "Cross my heart."

"It's more than just a bra."

"Amen, sister."

Meg laid her head on the headrest and closed her eyes. The stress of the day pounded in her temples, and she tried to think of what she'd eaten all day. Not much. And not much water either.

Another dehydration headache. I have got to remember to drink more water!

The whir of the tires lulled her, and Meg allowed the sound to wash away the last vestiges of consciousness, slipping blissfully into a Lexus-induced nap.

"We're going to need Meg and Joy on this." Kendra's face reflected the blue glow of her computer screen.

"Tell me again why we had to come down here and work at —" Tandy checked her watch — "seven o'clock at night?"

Kendra entered another new member name and hit the print button to create a club identification card. "Because breaking up our dad's relationship took time away from the business. And Sisters, Ink won't continue on a successful track if we don't pay attention to what needs doing."

Tandy sighed and plopped back into her

desk chair. "Fine. I'll help you with the ID cards and do the ones that came in over the past three days, okay?"

"Thank you." Kendra started entering information for a new card. "But before you get started, call Meg and see if she'll set something up with Joy. We need to find out what's going on there anyway. And if anybody knows how to properly handle a reconciliation, it's Joy."

"Okay." Tandy flipped open her cell and punched the speed dial for Meg's phone.

"Hey, Meg, it's Tandy. Are you with Joy by any chance?"

"Hey, Tandy. Yeah, she's right here. What's up?"

"Kendra and I kind of made a mess, and we need you guys to tell us the best way to clean it up."

Meg's laughter flowed across the phone lines. "Why am I not surprised? Hang on, let me talk to Joy."

Muffled voices sounded, and Tandy busied herself pulling up the new member applications.

"Tandy?"

"Still here."

"She says to come to her house in about an hour. And you might be repaying her for clean-up knowledge by disposing of her husband's body."

"Uh oh. What did Scott do?"

"It's more what he won't do. I'll let Joy tell you all about it when you get here. Be prepared though for a very different Joy."

"So she's finished staring holes into oranges?"

"Oh, yeah. We're way past produce here."

"Okay, see you guys in a little bit."

Tandy flipped her phone closed and typed information into the form on the screen. "Joy wants us over in about an hour."

Kendra nodded. "Did I hear you say Scott did something?"

"Meg says it's more what he won't do and that Joy will explain when we get there."

Kendra stopped typing and took a drink from her Diet Dr. Pepper. "Scott won't do something Joy wants? That doesn't sound right. The man practically worships the ground she walks on."

"That's all the detail she gave me. We'll find out everything when we get there. So could you stop swigging DP and get these new folks entered into the system?"

Kendra set the bottle back down and went back to typing. "Slave driver."

"That's me."

An hour later Tandy and Kendra stood outside Joy's door shivering and holding down the doorbell.

Meg opened the door wide for both sisters to rush in. "You are *so* not funny. Do you have any idea how annoying that doorbell is in the first place? What possessed you to hold it down all that time?"

"We needed to make sure you understood our imminent conversion to blocks of ice if you didn't get a move on."

"Message received. Get your frozen fannies in here."

The trio trouped down the hallway to find Joy in the kitchen stirring a large steaming pot on the stove.

"What's cookin', Toots?" Kendra pulled off her scarf and draped it over a chair on her way to the stove. "Ooh! Hot chocolate!"

"Is there anything else more appropriate for a frozen Stars Hill night?"

"Not that I can think of." Kendra popped a marshmallow into her mouth and snagged another from the bag on the counter before Joy snatched it up.

"Try to leave some for the drinks."

Kendra stuck her marshmallow-covered tongue out and twirled around the room. "I *love* marshmallows!"

Meg laughed. "Are you ever halfway about anything? I mean, do you ever just *like* something?"

"What's the good of halfway? Either go big or go home, baby!"

Joy chuckled as she stirred. "I never thought I'd see the day I would say this, but I'm with you, Kendra. Go big or go home."

Kendra stopped twirling so abruptly she fell against the edge of the countertop. "Excuse me?"

Joy raised her eyebrows. "What?"

"Did you just say 'go big or go home'?" Tandy looked to Meg for explanation, who shook her head.

"I did."

Joy waved a hand at the shocked silence. "Stop acting like I'm a robot who can't ever have any fun."

"We've never acted that way. You have."

"I have? I act like I don't have any fun?"

"Okay, no, not exactly. But you're always proper, always organized, always calm, always methodical. Not really the 'go big' kinda girl, you know?"

"Well, phooey on that from this point on. I'm a healthy, living, breathing twenty-something and it's about time I enjoyed that, right?"

"Um, right." Kendra sat down on a stool. "I trust from this strange conversion you already have ideas for how you're going to enjoy your newfound self?"

"I'm going to have a baby."

"You're pregnant?!" Tandy shot off the stool. "That's fabulous!" She rushed over to hug Joy but stopped at Joy's upheld hand.

"No, I'm not pregnant yet. But I'm going to get that way soon."

Tandy looked back and forth between Meg and Joy. "I think Kendra and I missed a few steps here. What's going on?"

"Dr. Goodman gave her a clean bill of health today," Meg explained.

"That's great!"

"Not all great," Kendra chimed in. "If you're completely healthy, then why do I not have niece or nephew Lasky on the way yet?"

Joy began taking mugs down from the cabinet. "Dr. Goodman thinks we need to test Scott to find out. And I think he's right."

"How did Scott take that news?"

"Not well." Meg slid off her stool and went to help Joy. "I hid in the kitchen when she told him, and I didn't have to strain to hear his voice."

"Scott *yelled?*" Kendra stole another marshmallow. "Seriously?"

"Yelled. Ranted. Raved. Then yelled some more." Joy dipped a ladle into the hot chocolate and transferred it to the mugs whose rims were lined with red cardinals on snow-covered limbs.

"Did you yell back?" Tandy returned to her stool.

"Not only did she yell, she threw things." Meg took a steaming mug from Joy. "That big glass dish that was on display on the sideboard? History."

"But you loved that plate!" Kendra took a mug as well.

"No, I didn't. I acted like I loved that plate because Scott's mother gave it to me. It was hideous, just like his attitude on this topic." Joy finished filling the last cup and brought it, along with her own, to Tandy. She settled on one of the stools.

Tandy and Kendra looked at each other, then at Joy. They blinked.

Joy laughed. "I can't believe it. You two are speechless simultaneously? I wasn't *that* boring of a person before, was I?"

"No, no, of course not." Kendra patted Joy's arm.

Joy gave a wry smile. "Next time you lie to me, at least try to make it believable. I know I'm no Kendra Sinclair, but I've enjoyed my life up until this point. And I'll enjoy it again as soon as my husband realizes what a jerk he's being. If I have to smash a hideous plate here and there or

82

make him fix his own dinner, I'm certain he'll survive in the end. It isn't as if I threw the plate *at* him." She set down her mug and looked out the window. "Although it may come to that if he doesn't call Dr. Goodman soon."

"You're kidding, right?" Kendra looked to Meg and Tandy. "She's kidding."

Tandy shrugged. "I'm still trying to picture her throwing inanimate objects."

"Well, what would you do?" Joy returned her gaze to the sisters. "I've wanted a baby for so long that I've begun to forget what life was like before the longing. My marriage is mired deeper in no-baby muck than Tandy's tires were the last time she went mudding." Joy shivered. "I still don't understand the attraction of that, by the way."

"It's fun!" Tandy defended. "So long as you're trying out new experiences, you ought to come with me. We got enough rain the other night that we could find some great places."

"No, thank you. My new experiences are focused on getting Scott to that doctor's office."

"Has he told you why he won't go?"

"Not explicitly. Knowing him, I'd bet it's that he can't admit he might have a problem he is unable to fix himself."

"But that's dumb."

"Ha!" Meg shook her head. "You try telling an otherwise healthy, always capable, built-his-business-from-the-ground-up man that there's a hill he can't climb."

"Are you talking about Scott or Jamison?" Tandy tucked a curl behind her ear.

"Scott, of course." Meg looked into her mug. "Jamison and I are fine."

"You're about as convincing a liar as Kendra, sis," Tandy said. "Something going on we can help with?"

"Oh, no. We'll be fine. Just a little hiccup. Forget about us. Scott's the topic here."

Joy's eyebrows raised. "You're having problems with Jamison? I'm so sorry, Meg. I've been so preoccupied with the difficulties in my own marriage that I haven't asked you in weeks how things are going in your family."

"Hey." Meg took Joy's hand. "If I have anything that I need to talk through or get help on, don't worry. You'll know about it." The sisters shared a look.

Kendra cleared her throat. "Okay, so enough about Meg. Joy, tell us what the plan is for Scott and how we can help."

Joy sighed. "I'm not certain you can help, but thanks for the offer. I suppose I'm hoping that my behavior tonight communicates to him the lengths to which I will go to convince him he needs a doctor."

"Where is he now?"

"He left. I assume he's driven down to the office to work. That's what he does when he needs comfort."

They all heard the garage door begin to rise on the other side of the kitchen wall.

"I guess he got the comfort he needed." Kendra turned her mug up and downed the last of her hot chocolate. "Which is our cue to scram. You going to be okay here?"

Joy nodded. "Yeah, I'll be fine." Her eyes narrowed. "I'm not making any promises for him though."

Tandy picked up Kendra's mug and took them both to the sink. "You want us to stick around?"

"No. It's all right."

"Okay, then. I'll see you at the salon tomorrow for my cut?"

"Unless I'm in jail for homicide."

"Don't even kid about that." Kendra pushed her arms into her coat sleeves. "He might be acting like inconsiderate scum right now, but baby-less with him is better than baby without him."

"You're right. You're exactly right." Joy deflated a bit but then rallied and sat up straighter. "But baby-less by choice isn't an option."

The sisters nodded, said hurried good-byes, and escaped down the gallery hallway and through the front door.

EIGHT

If Scott comes through that door angry, I think I'll sleep somewhere else tonight. Meg, Kendra, and Tandy may not understand or accept that decision at first, but they love me enough to support me anyway. In all the uncertainty of my future, I can rely on their love.

Scott's, on the other hand, isn't such a sure thing right now.

I cannot believe I threw a plate. When it smashed, I felt so strong. So powerful. The mess was enormous. Still is. Every shard still litters the dining room floor and glitters when I turn on the chandelier. Each refraction of light bolsters my courage, embodies my hopes and dreams of a baby. If Scott wants to leave them lying on the floor, then that's his business. For now, I can't bear to sweep them away as if they don't exist.

"Hi, honey." His voice blows hope into my soul. A term of endearment. He wouldn't use that if he still defied my desires, would he?

"Hi." I keep the greeting noncommittal. If he has decided to call the doctor, I'll thaw faster than a block of ice on a Miami sidewalk. But until I know for sure, I can't run the risk.

"How are the sisters?"

"They're fine. We were just sharing some hot chocolate." I nod toward the pot on our stove.

"Did I get as roasted as the marshmallows?" That grin of his has been my undoing in a lot of disagreements. But we've never disagreed on something of this magnitude.

"Perhaps. How was the office?"

He sits his briefcase on the countertop and stands before me. "I didn't go to the office." At my questioning look, he continues. "I left intending to go there, but I couldn't think. The sight of you with a plate in your hand kept playing through my mind, and I decided to drive out Ralston Road instead."

"What's on Ralston Road?"

"Nothing. That's why I went. No street lights. No other cars. Just miles of country road and quiet night."

I stay silent, unsure of the decisions he's

88

made under dark skies and twinkling stars. He takes my hand and I feel the cold of outdoors through his fingertips.

"I love you, Joy Sinclair Lasky. Can't you see that I can't handle finding out my body won't give you your dream — our dream — of a baby? I've spent our entire marriage working to take care of you, to surround you with beauty and love. If all of that means nothing because I can't give you this one thing, then what does that say about how you value me? How you love me? Whether you find worth in any of the time or things I've given you so far?"

I had not thought of that. I'm not certain I can think of that. What is a painting in comparison to a child?

I open my mouth, but he keeps going before I can assure him of my love or question the equitableness of art to life or point out that having a medical difficulty isn't necessarily a failure.

"I understand that giving you a home and the life we share isn't the same as us sharing a child together."

This man has always understood me before I even understand myself. It's why I fell in love with him. Why I married him.

"But it's important to me that I not lose all value to you if I can't get you pregnant.

And that's what you said tonight. You're prepared to walk out of this house, of this life, if I can't get you pregnant."

"That is *not* what I said, Scott." I cannot let him continue. He has missed such an important point. "My anger at you is not because we haven't gotten pregnant; my anger is in your unwillingness to find out *why*. Whether it's my body or your body doesn't matter to me. What matters is that you won't find out if it's you."

"If it doesn't matter which one of us is to blame, then why do you care if I find out?"

"Because knowing the problem means exploring solutions. Do you have any idea of the plethora of obstacles to getting pregnant? I do! I've been reading and researching for months. And the vast majority of those obstacles now have methods to overcome. But we can't find a solution until we know which problem we are facing."

He closes his eyes and I don't know whether we're about to enter a new phase of this argument or if he finally understands my position.

When he opens them, I can see the tiny red lines in the whites of his eyes. He has not slept lately. There are new lines around the edges of his lids and more gray at his temple, now that I take the time to see it.

"So that I'm clear, you have no plans to leave me if we find out the problem is me?"

"Of course not! Why would you think that?"

His sudden embrace nearly knocks me from my seat. Have I been so cold as to make him believe a pregnancy means more than our marriage?

Hadn't I just said as much to the sisters? If I am asking him to get honest with his physical condition, I have an obligation to get honest with my mental one. That's fair. But I never meant to convey that I'd leave if his physical problem — if there even is one — is insurmountable. I wouldn't do that.

I pull back and make him look at me. "Scott, I love you. I hate what we're going through right now, and I'd do anything to take it all away. The fastest method I can see for taking it away is to define exactly what we're up against. And that means you getting tested."

"I agree."

Did he say that? Or is my imagination crafting reality?

"You agree?"

"I do. If you want me to get tested and you promise me that you aren't going to stop loving me no matter what those tests say, then I'll go."

"Oh, Scott." His heart beats hard beneath my ear as I lay my head on his chest. I can feel my own heart beating harder than a hummingbird's as it hovers over a feeder. He *does* love me. Enough to avoid a course of action that might make me leave.

Why is communication so difficult in a marriage? Even when I'm certain I have been nothing but clear, the message received can be so very far from the one I intended.

"I love you." That, at least, cannot be misunderstood.

His arms tighten around me. "I love you too."

The next morning Tandy's tires crunched as she steered her BMW into the driveway of Zelda's house. No sign of life presented itself, but Tandy couldn't be sure if that was due to the dead of winter or Zelda's real absence. Surely she wouldn't have moved away within twenty-four hours?

She shoved the car in park and pulled up on the emergency brake. This wouldn't be easy, but Daddy deserved to love the woman he'd chosen.

Taking a deep breath, Tandy stepped into the frosty wind and bent her head against the cold. Within seconds, it had invaded her coat to chill her skin. She shivered as she approached the doorbell and pushed its button.

Give her a few seconds. Even if they feel like hours with this frigid air swirling all over the place. When no one answered the door, Tandy pushed the doorbell again and followed it up with a knock.

"She ain't there." An older man, his white hair buffeted by the wind, appeared from the far corner of the next house. He pulled a large trash can behind, its wheels grating on the gravel of the shared driveway.

"Excuse me?"

"You looking for Zelda?"

"Yes. I need to talk to her."

"Ain't here. Packed up all her stuff in one of them big U-Haul things and left. Wouldn't have said so much as a good-bye if I hadn't been coming outside anyway."

Tandy struggled to process the information. Zelda packed up her whole house and left in a day?

"Did she say where she was going?"

"Hmmph." The trash can must have felt like dragging boulders, as stooped as his shoulders and back were. Tandy hurried off the porch and to his side.

"Here, how about I help with that while you tell me where I might be able to find Ms. Zelda?" She took the handle from him.

"Much obliged." He stuffed the weathered hand that had been pulling the trash can into the pocket of his army surplus jacket.

Tandy walked toward the end of the driveway, slowing her step so the man could keep up.

"Far as I know, she went down to Florida."

"Florida?" Where Tandy used to live. "Did she say which part?"

"Sure did. Now, let me think here. What was the name of that town? Same as one in Italy. I remember because when she told me, I thought she was up and going to Europe."

"Naples?"

"That's it. Naples. Said it was good and warm there this time of year and she wanted to thaw out her old bones." They reached the end of the drive and Tandy positioned the trash can so the sanitation workers would pick it up. "Thought for a bit about joining up with her, but too much heat in winter ain't good for a body, you know what I'm saying? Body needs seasons to get itself in order, and they ain't no seasons in Florida. Just sunshine and heat all the time. Can't tell whether it's Christmas or the Fourth of July unless you look at a calendar."

Tandy smiled, remembering her struggle

to get into the holiday mood when the thermometer read seventy-two degrees. "I understand. So she's driving the U-Haul to Naples herself?"

They started back up the drive. "Tried to tell her the foolishness of that, too, but she said she drove it here from her last place and she could just as well drive it to her new place. That's one tough woman, you ask me."

"She's definitely that."

"Tough and mad."

"Mad?" Tandy glanced over at the old man, but his face remained turned to the stones on which they walked.

"As a wet hornet. Don't know what got up in her craw, but something sure did. Ain't seen a woman that mad since I came home with my bride, Annalise."

"Your new wife was mad at you?"

"Not her. Lord, no. Anna was sweet as pie every day of her life, God rest her soul. Betty Livingston though didn't take too kindly to her man coming home from war with a French bride."

Tandy chuckled. "No, I guess she wouldn't."

"Them French women, they got a thing or two to teach these Stars Hill girls."

"Anna was French?"

"With enough of her grandmother's Swedish blood to be the sweetest, kindest French girl you'd ever have the good fortune of meeting, I tell you."

"She sounds lovely."

"Lovely as they come."

They reached his porch and Tandy waited while he struggled up the two wooden steps. "Thanks for telling me about Zelda."

"Pleasure's been mine. I'm Homer Tuck, by the way."

Tandy grasped his gnarled hand and shook it. "Tandy Sinclair Kelner."

A grin spread across Homer's face, and Tandy marveled at all those wrinkles forming little smiles. "You're Tandy?"

"Yes, sir. Do you know me?"

Homer released her hand and slapped his thigh. "Zelda talked you up one side and down the other the whole time she was loading up that truck. If I was you, I'd stay as far away from Florida as I could. She's got a couple forms of torture that we didn't even use in the war lined up for your backside."

Tandy smiled. "I'd love to, and I thank you for the warning. But I've got to get her back here."

"Get her back?" He shook his head. "I don't think you've got yourself a good grasp of that woman."

"Unfortunately I do." Tandy sighed. "I just hope she's as quick to forgive as she is to get angry."

Silence stretched while gray clouds built above them and the wind kicked up again. A trip to Florida might not be all bad. At least she could get some sun on her skin. Maybe even take a dip in the ocean in between bouts of begging Zelda to return to Stars Hill.

Fat snowflakes began to fall, calling Tandy back from sun-kissed beaches and warm, wet sand. She looked up and found Homer's wise gaze upon her.

"I ain't sure what you said or did, Tandy Sinclair Kelner, but I do know a thing or two about the power of forgiveness. I'll be putting you in my prayers."

Tandy's throat closed up and she struggled to respond. "Thanks, Mr. Tuck."

"Call me Homer."

She nodded and stuffed her hands in her coat pockets. Backing away from his porch, Tandy moved toward her car. "Thanks, Homer."

"You're mighty welcome." Homer turned and walked into his house while Tandy crunched across the wide gravel driveway. She settled into her car and punched the button to activate the seat warmer.

So Zelda had fled to Florida.

Tandy turned the key in the ignition and put the car in gear. She backed out of the driveway and pointed the car toward the Sisters, Ink office where Kendra should be by now. Shifting gears, she sped along and hatched a plan as fast as the indicator rose on her speedometer.

By the time she parked outside the office and cut the motor, Tandy had a plan.

NINE

"So Scott's agreed to see the doctor."

Kendra's voice reminded Tandy that Zelda wasn't their only problem right now. She stomped her boots on the mat at the back door, leaving little clumps of snow behind.

"It's snowing."

"Yeah, I can see." Kendra looked up from her computer and gestured toward the big front window that overlooked Lindell Street. "It's getting slippery out there. Did you hear what I said? Scott's going to get tested."

"After hearing about Joy's tantrum, I can't say I'm surprised."

"Me either. That woman's wrath would scare me into submission faster than an atheist at the throne of Jesus."

"Mm-hmm." Tandy turned on her laptop and waited for it to boot up.

"You know, I expected a little more re-action from you. Last night Joy's telling us she's smashing plates and today I tell you

Scott gave in and all you can say is 'mm-hmm'?"

"Sorry." Tandy opened up a Web browser and surfed over to Travelocity. "I've got to get us tickets to Florida, so I'm a little pre-occupied."

"What are you talking about?"

"We're going to Naples."

"Italy?"

"Florida."

"Why?"

"Because that's where Zelda's moved to."

"Tandy, hold up. It's barely been two days. No way has she had time to pack up all her stuff and move to Florida."

"According to Homer, that's exactly what she did. Yesterday."

"Who's Homer?"

Tandy filled her in while she clicked through the reservation procedure online. "I don't think a phone call will get her back up here. So we're going to Florida."

"And we're not driving because . . . ?"

"Because Naples is way south. It'll take forever to get down there, and the longer we wait the longer she has to get madder and madder. We can probably get a deal on a last-minute flight and leave tonight or tomorrow morning."

"Have you talked to Clay about this?"

"I'll talk to him as soon as I find flight information." She clicked a couple more times. "There! There's a flight leaving at 6:30 in the morning. It goes through Atlanta and gets us to Fort Myers at 11:00. We can be at her door by lunchtime. Fort Myers is about a forty-five-minute drive from Naples."

"And when are we coming back?"

"I don't know. This is a one-way flight. Hopefully, we'll be driving back with her in a U-Haul with all her stuff."

"What if she says no?"

"Then we book another flight home, but let's not think about that. She's *got* to come back."

"No, she doesn't. She can kick our sorry behinds to the curb and tell us to leave her alone."

"She could. Except that she loves Daddy. She said so herself. If we get out of the way, she'll come back to him. I'm sure of it."

"Then call her and tell her we're getting out of the way. As much as I would love to go soak up some Florida sun, I've got stuff to do here and so do you. Call her and see if she'll let Ma Bell deliver our apology."

"Kendra, think about it for a second. What if she hangs up on us? Then she knows that we know where she is. Besides, I highly doubt she's got a phone hooked up this fast. And even if she does, there's no way to get the number."

"So get her cell phone number from Daddy."

"Then *he'll* know where she is."

"Good. He can go to Florida and get her. Even better."

"Not better. Worse. If he goes to Florida, then she won't know whether we're sorry or he's just ignoring our wishes. And the whole reason she left was to keep from getting between us and Daddy."

Kendra chewed on a fingernail. "I'm still not sure whether I agree with her on that point, by the way."

"Whether you agree with her or not doesn't matter as much as the fact that *she* feels that way. Which means we've got to make sure she knows we're okay with her and Daddy getting married."

"Just so I'm clear — we really *are* okay with that now, right?"

Tandy sighed. "Yeah, we are. She won't take Momma's place, and she's not going to try. And Daddy's waited a long time to love and be loved. He's happy with Zelda, miserable without her."

"And he's got a ring. Might as well have a finger to put it on."

"And that, yeah."

"I still think we should try to call her cell first."

"We messed up big, Kendra. The apology has to be big too."

Kendra leaned back her chair, and Tandy remained silent while she thought. Eventually Kendra would see that going to Florida presented the best option for Zelda to believe they were sorry and wanted her to come back.

"Okay."

Tandy grinned and Kendra shot a rubber band at her.

"You knew I would say that, didn't you?"

Tandy picked up the phone and dialed the number for the diner. "I had a sneaking suspicion you might." She turned her back to the next rubber-band bullet and waited for Clay to answer the phone so she could tell her husband she was heading back to Florida.

"I'm going to miss you tonight." Clay kissed Tandy's forehead the next morning and snuggled up to her back. "This bed isn't made for one person."

Tandy looked across the expanse of white down comforter and leaned into her husband. "I hear ya. But you do understand why I have to go, right?"

Stars Hill citizens walked down the sidewalk below their second-floor bedroom window, their shoulders hunched against the chilly weather. Thank goodness none of them raised their heads since she'd forgotten to close the blinds last night.

"Yeah. You messed up and you've got to make it right."

"Exactly."

"You know, if you had told me how you felt about Zelda, this whole thing probably wouldn't have gotten so out of hand. I could have told you she'd never try to take Marian's place in your heart or your dad's."

"I honestly didn't think it would get this crazy this fast. I mean, one minute I'm talking to Kendra about Zelda, and the next Zelda's packing a U-Haul and headed to Naples."

Clay lay his cheek against the top of her head. "That's what I'm talking about. You found the time to talk to Kendra but not to me."

Tandy turned to face him. "I know, but you've been so busy with the diner and I spend a lot of time with Kendra over at the office."

"And I understand that. Still, I'm not too busy to know what's bugging you, okay?"

She nodded. "Okay. We knew it would be hard for me to *not* tell Kendra everything in the world the way I've always done though."

"I'm not asking you to keep anything from Kendra. Y'all are sisters and I want you to be close like you always have. Just keep me in the loop too. I don't want to be one of those husbands on the evening news saying, 'I don't know how my wife flipped out. We didn't talk too much. If you really want to know about her, go talk to her sister.' "

Tandy laughed. "Okay, I hear you. Tell husband as much as sister. Roger that."

"Good." He rolled away from her and stood up.

Tandy paused to admire his physique. "You know, you are one *hot* man, Mr. Kelner."

Clay grinned. "Then perhaps you'll accept my invitation to a shower, Mrs. Kelner."

Tandy pushed the covers back, shivering at the sudden loss of warmth. "I think it's my civic duty, sir. You know, saving water is good for the environment."

Clay wiggled his eyebrows. "Then let's definitely do our part for conservation."

She giggled and walked toward the bathroom, putting an extra sway in her hips when she saw Clay following behind.

"I can't promise, though, that we won't be in there long enough for the hot water to run out."

"Don't forget I've got a plane to catch."

They reached the bathroom and he slid an arm around her waist. Turning her toward him, he leaned in for a kiss. "Then you'll have to pack a little faster."

As the heat from his lips flooded through her, Tandy resolved to pack the fastest suitcase in the history of womankind.

TEN

"Kendra, wake up." Tandy shoved her sister's shoulder as the plane descended into Fort Myers and the pilot's voice overhead advised they were beginning their descent. "We're about to land."

"Mmph." Kendra turned her head toward the window.

Tandy pulled an ear bud from Kendra's ear. "Hey, Sleeping Beauty, wake up. Time to grovel."

Kendra popped one eye open and cut it toward Tandy. "The next time you tell me we're taking a 6:30 a.m. flight, the answer is no."

The flight attendant's voice replaced the captain's as she advised everyone to return to their seats in preparation for landing. Tandy obediently stuffed her carry-on under the seat in front of her. "It was either this cheap flight or three times the price for a convenient departure time."

Kendra yawned and sat up in her seat. "Yeah, yeah, yeah. So, what's the plan once we land?"

"I told you this on the way to Nashville. We land, pick up our rental car, and go to Naples. Clay said Zelda used to talk about Wyndemere Country Club, so we'll check there first."

"If you think I remember anything about a crack-of-dawn drive, you're out of your mind. I've blocked everything out, including that manhandling security guy who thought the glitter in my hair products was bomb-making material. Gosh, that guy was on a power trip."

Tandy chuckled. "I'm in total agreement, but let's not talk about bombs while we're on a plane, okay?"

Kendra huffed and refastened her seat belt. "Whatever."

A few minutes later they filed out of the plane and followed the signs to the rental car counters.

"Which one is us?"

"That one." Tandy pointed three desks down and wheeled her suitcase over to the rental desk. "Hi, you have a reservation for Tandy Kelner?"

An Asian man with long black hair held in a sleek ponytail, whose nametag identified him as Chuck, tapped on the keyboard in front of him. The diamond in his earlobe sparkled, and Tandy wondered how a rental car salesman could afford such a bauble. "I'm sorry, I do not show a reservation for Klein."

"No, Kelner. K-E-L-N-E-R."

Make that how an *inept* rental car salesman could afford that rock. She shared a look with Kendra while Chuck typed again. "No, no reservation for that name either. Do you have a reservation number?"

"Oh, for the love of Pete. Hang on." Tandy dug through her big black bag. "A-ha!" She pulled out her reservation and slapped it on the counter. "Here it is."

Chuck took the paper, looked at it, then tapped more keys. The confused look on his face gave the sisters a split second of warning. "It says here you reserved the car with a credit card in the name of Tandy Sinclair?"

"Yes. That's my maiden name."

"We cannot allow a reservation made by someone other than the driver."

"But it's not someone other than the driver. It's me. *I'm* Tandy Sinclair."

"I thought you were Tandy Kelner?"

"I am. I *was* Tandy Sinclair. I got married. Now I'm Tandy Kelner. Surely you've heard of women taking their husband's last name?" Tandy winced as Kendra's elbow found her side.

Chuck stiffened. "Yes, ma'am. But you should have made the reservation in your married name."

"Well, I'll be sure to do that next time, when I've gotten the new credit card with my married name on it. Thanks for that advice."

"You're welcome." Chuck handed her back her reservation paper, then walked away.

"Hey, wait a minute!" Tandy pushed the paper back into her bag. "You didn't give me my keys and I haven't signed the paperwork yet."

"You wish to rent a car?"

"Um, yes. That's why I made a reservation."

Chuck walked back over to his computer and tapped keys. "The rate will be $59.95 per day for mid-size."

"No, my rate is $39.95. It's right here on my reservation." She pulled the paper from her bag again and showed it to him. "See?"

"I see a reservation there for Tandy Sinclair. You are Tandy Sinclair?"

"Yes!" Tandy ran a hand through her hair. "That's what I've been trying to tell you."

"I'll need a driver's license and credit card."

Tandy took out her wallet and handed over her license and credit card.

"The names on these cards do not match." He held them out across the counter. "Do you have two forms of ID that are in the same name?"

"You have *got* to be kidding me. Are you a moron?" Tandy's raised voice drew the looks of several bystanders. "I got married. My name changed. I haven't changed all my credit cards over yet."

"I must have two forms of ID to proceed with your rental. That is the policy."

"Listen, you dumb —"

"Chuck," Kendra stepped in front of Tandy, "we completely understand your policy and think it's a great one. We'd love to tell your boss what a good job you've done in enforcing that policy. Could you get your boss for me, please?" She gave him a full-wattage smile, and Tandy swallowed the anger threatening to spew from her mouth.

"Certainly." Chuck walked away again, eager to please the understanding client.

"That man is about forty-nine cards shy of a deck."

"Which is why we're getting his boss

rather than standing here at the counter for an hour arguing with him. What happened to all your lawyerly reconciliation methods?"

"I left them in Orlando when I moved back to Stars Hill." Tandy crossed her arms. "But I bet I could make a case for prejudice against newlyweds if I had to."

A short woman came through the door where Chuck had escaped moments before. A neat bun of dark brown hair sat at her nape, and a small gold cross hung from her neck. Her nametag read *Lucy.* "Hello. Chuck tells me you've been happy with his service today?"

"Hi, Lucy. I'm Kendra Sinclair and this is my sister, Tandy Sinclair Kelner. She got married a few months ago and hasn't managed to get all her credit cards changed over to her married name. She reserved our car in her maiden name, but her license now shows her married name. Chuck was having a little difficulty understanding the situation, and we were hoping you could help us out."

Lucy's smile was so genuine, Tandy found herself smiling back. "Sure, I can help. And I apologize for Chuck. He's very good at following rules and procedures — that's why we employ him. But sometimes his disability gets in the way of bending the rules a bit to accommodate the customers."

"His disability?" A sense of dread filled Tandy's chest.

"Yes." Lucy tapped keys, glancing back and forth between the screen and the sisters. "He's part of our Work for the Willing program where we help developmentally disabled people come into the workforce. I try to stay out here with him in case situations like this arise, but I had to go back there and get the copy machine going again, so he was alone. I'm so sorry if he caused any problem."

"Oh no, no problem at all." Tandy didn't need Kendra's reproving glare to realize what a moron *she'd* been.

"Thank goodness." Lucy smiled. "Okay, will you be needing rental insurance today?"

Tandy went through the usual questions with Lucy, eventually taking the keys to the Sebring that would be theirs for however long they were in Florida.

The sisters walked away from the counter and toward the doors to the parking garage. "I'm a horrible person."

"No, you're not," Kendra assured her. "You didn't do anything any normal person wouldn't have done."

"I called him a moron!"

"Not really. You asked if he was a moron.

Not much of a difference, but still."

"I can't believe how mean I was."

"Did you have your caffeine this morning?"

"No, and I've got a raging headache as a result. But that's no excuse."

Kendra snagged the keys from Tandy's hand. "No more talking about Chuck until you've had your Dew and are thinking clearly again. Which stall did she say our car was in?"

"C-3. And I ought to be able to act like a Christian even when I haven't had my caffeine."

"You're right, you should. But you didn't. And we're not talking about this anymore until you have. Ah, there it is." Kendra came to a stop behind a white Sebring. She pressed a button on the keychain and the trunk popped open. "Toss your bag in and let's go find a burger joint."

Tandy lifted her suitcase in and trudged around the passenger side. "Zelda is going to wipe the floor with my mean self."

Kendra rolled her eyes and opened the driver's door. "No, she's not. She'll see how sorry you are and rush back into Daddy's arms as fast as her U-Haul truck can go." She revved the engine. "Any preferences for lunch?"

"Humble pie?"

Kendra undid the latches on the convertible top, then pushed the button to open their car to the air. "I think you've already had a few helpings of that, sweetie." She turned and draped a long brown arm across the back of Tandy's seat as she glanced behind them before backing up.

Tandy gave a feeble smile. "Whatever you can find on the way to I-75 is fine with me."

Kendra nodded and put the car into reverse. "You've got it."

They circled the garage, finally emerging into daylight. The sun's rays streamed into the car and thawed their chilly skin in seconds. Tandy closed her eyes and remembered the warmth of the Florida sun she'd left behind a year ago. "Man, that feels good."

Kendra slowed and handed their rental agreement to the booth attendant. "How about we stay a couple days and veg out on the beach?"

"Because my husband is warmer than this sun will ever be and he's back home in frigid Stars Hill."

"Oh, come on. He'll still be there in a couple of days, and you'll have a new tan for him to admire."

Tandy shook her head. "Nice try, sister."

Kendra harrumphed and turned on the radio.

Tandy reclined her seat and lay back. Closing her eyes, she smiled as she remembered Clay's good-bye not more than a few hours ago.

No way would she stay in Florida one second longer than it took to get Zelda back in Stars Hill — where they both belonged.

"Scott, telephone," Joy spoke into the intercom on the kitchen wall. "It's Clay."

"Thanks, honey," crackled back through the speaker.

Joy returned to the pot on her stove and stirred the vegetable soup just beginning to simmer. An apron covered the Sunday clothes she still wore. "Did she say when they'd be coming home?"

"Hopefully tomorrow." Meg placed a small square of cheese on a cracker at the kitchen table. "She said they're staying as long as it takes to change Zelda's mind about leaving Stars Hill."

Joy put the ladle back into a red ceramic spoon rest and faced Meg. "I can't believe she and Kendra just flew off to Florida without telling us. More than that, I'm astounded that they could have run Zelda off *and* had a blowup with Daddy without

116

either of us finding out about it."

"I think Tandy wanted to fix things before she told us. She didn't bank on Daddy talking to us at church this morning."

"Mommy!" Savannah's blonde ringlets bounced as the little girl came running into the kitchen. "James is being mean again!"

"Was not!" James appeared a second after his sister, two bright spots of indignant color on his cheeks. "She is!"

Savannah placed her small fists on her equally small hips. "Was not either. You took Laura."

"Only because you took Larry."

"Wait, wait." Meg held up one hand. "One at a time. Savannah, did you take a toy from James?"

"He was playing with Laura, Mommy! Everybody knows Laura is a girl!"

"She's a carrot, dummy. Not a girl."

"James, do not call your sister a dummy."

"But she is."

"James." Meg filled her voice with warning. "I don't care if someone is acting in a certain way. Calling people names is never justified and is certainly not right for a gentleman. Understand?"

James hung his little head. "Yes, ma'am."

"As for you, Savannah. Taking toys from someone isn't right either. If James wants to play with Laura, then he can play with Laura. You play with Larry, don't you?"

"Yes." Savannah's voice had become small, deflated of indignation in the face of Meg's correction.

"If you can play with Larry the boy cucumber, then James can play with Laura the girl carrot. Now, is the VeggieTales video over?"

"No."

"Then get back in there or I'm going to turn it off."

Both children ran back toward the play room. "We're watching! We're watching!" Savannah's tinny voice bounced off the hallway walls.

"If I could bottle half their energy, I'd be a millionaire," Joy said.

"I'd find a million to pay you for it." Meg cut another slice of cheese. "A four-year-old and seven-year-old would be enough, but as soon as I catch up with those two, Hannah comes toddling along and there goes the last of my energy."

"You have been looking a little tired lately. You know I'm happy to watch them anytime, right?"

"Yeah, it's just I feel like I shouldn't need a babysitter when I'm a stay-at-home mom, you know?"

"Even full-time moms need a break every now and then, Meg."

"I don't know. Maybe."

"Definitely. Why don't you leave them here for the afternoon and go get some rest? Read a book or take a nap or something. I'll bring them back sometime tonight."

"I don't think you know what you're offering."

"Of course I do. Besides, I need you rested up enough to deal with me when we get Scott's test results tomorrow, and hearing little feet running through these halls in the meantime will be nice."

"You'll hear running feet, all right. I'm not kidding, Joy. They don't slow down. It's full tilt all day long."

"So I'll take them up to Chuck E. Cheese's for dinner and wear them out. I'll get some fun scrapping pictures, and it should give you an easy bedtime tonight."

Meg shook her head. "I don't want to look a gift horse in the mouth, but —"

"Then don't. Eat your soup and get out of here. Leave those two to me. Jamison's mom has Hannah all day, right?"

Meg nodded. "When they get to be about Savannah's age, she's not so enamored anymore."

Joy's mouth twisted. "That explains a lot

about Jamison."

"Yeah, he's having a hard time figuring out what to do with a seven-year-old son."

"He's smart. He'll find a solution. Meanwhile, here." Joy set a steaming bowl of soup on the table in front of Meg. "Eat up and go home."

"Why, Joy, that's the most inhospitable, sweetest thing you've said to me in a long time."

Joy scooped soup into another bowl and set it on the tray beside the stove. "I'll just run this up to Scott. Be right back."

Meg spooned soup into her mouth and contemplated the few hours of freedom she'd suddenly been given.

The smart thing would be to take a long, hot bath and a nap. Her neck ached with stress and exhaustion. When was the last time her neck didn't hurt? When had her energy stopped coming back in the morning?

The soup warmed her from the inside, and Meg felt her eyelids drooping. She finished within a few minutes and took the bowl over to the sink.

"All done?" Joy reentered the kitchen.

"Yep. Last chance to back out of kid duty."

"I wouldn't dream of it. Get out of here."

"Thanks, Joy."

"You know I'm happy to watch my niece and nephew. What are sisters for?"

Meg scooped up her coat. "I'll run let them know."

Joy nodded and Meg left down the grand hallway. She stopped long enough to give James and Savannah the good news that they were staying at Aunt Joy's for the day, then practically ran to her van.

Hot bath, bubbles, and a good book — here I come!

Eleven

After a hot lunch and half-hour nap between Fort Myers and Naples, Tandy felt much better. Confident she wouldn't take Zelda's head off in the same manner she'd treated poor Chuck, she followed her Google Map directions to Wyndemere with hope in her heart.

Kendra flipped her phone closed. "Meg says to call when we have an update. I don't think she and Joy are happy we didn't tell them what went down with Zelda."

"They'll get over it. We've got other worries right now. Like how to get past that."

They pulled into the country club's entrance and were immediately greeted by archways covered in mounds of purple bougainvillea, locked gates, and a guard shack — if by shack she meant two-story brick structure with French windows. Tandy pulled up to the "shack" and rolled down her window.

"Good afternoon." The guard's warm smile encouraged her.

"Hi. I'm surprising a friend of mine who came in yesterday — Zelda Swearingen."

"You're right. Ms. Swearingen got in just yesterday. I was on duty when she came through. So she's not expecting you?"

There's an understatement. "No, I hope not or the surprise would be ruined!"

"Hmm." The guard scratched his head, then adjusted his square-framed glasses. "I'm sorry, but I can't let you in. Only announced visitors are allowed. How about I call Ms. Swearingen and see if she'll let you through?"

"But then we won't be able to surprise her!"

He shrugged and wore a true expression of regret. "I wish I could help you, but you wouldn't believe the things folks try to get in here when they have no good reason to do it."

"Could you maybe just tell her a friend from Stars Hill is here?"

"Sorry. She'll have to approve you, and I'll need to see your ID."

Tandy bit her lip and thought. No way would she get through those gates without Zelda knowing first. All she could do was take the chance that curiosity would be enough for Zelda to allow them entry.

"All right, then. Could you tell her Tandy Kelner and Kendra Sinclair are here?"

"Sure thing. Can I see your ID, please?"

Tandy handed it over, and the guard stepped back a couple of steps to a telephone. She waited while he spoke, wondering if Zelda would screech through the phone. When he came back, he wore the same smile as before.

"Go right on through. Take the first road to your right and keep bearing to the right at every fork until you get to Edgemere. She's number 254."

"Thanks so much."

"You're welcome." He tipped his hat. "You ladies have a nice day."

Tandy waited until the gates parted, then touched the gas. "She knows we're coming, Ken."

"Yeah, which means she has time to load."

"Not funny."

"Who says I was kidding?"

They fell silent as Tandy wound the car through the streets. Tall trees and exquisitely manicured lawns greeted them at every turn. Hibiscus blossoms the size of dinner plates swayed in the slight breeze, their bases covered in petunias of purple, red, white, and pink.

"They sure don't skimp on the landscaping." Kendra turned this way and that, trying in vain to see every flower.

"Isn't it gorgeous?"

"I forgot this much color was possible in nature."

"Winter in Stars Hill will do that to you."

"I could paint forever in here."

"I bet you could."

"Hey, there's the sign." Kendra pointed off to the right. "Edgemere."

"What number did he say?"

"Um, 254, I think. There's 248, slow down."

Tandy slowed the car to a crawl until they came to 254. Red stone pavers composed the driveway, bordered on one side by a giant palm and bush with white star-shaped flowers and more giant palms on the other. The house itself was a salmon color that should have been awful but instead blended into the lush landscaping perfectly.

"She can afford *this* and she lived in Stars Hill?" Tandy pulled into the driveway too scared of unknown country club rules to park on the street. "I'm confused."

"Didn't Clay tell you she came there because he told so many Stars Hill stories while he served in the Marine Corps?"

"Yeah, but I never guessed she had this

125

kind of financial freedom. Here I've been thinking of her as a gold digger, and instead she's got a second home in a country club in Naples. Clay definitely didn't mention this. He said she just talked about Wyndemere a lot. No way did she buy this in a day and move down here."

"No, you're right. She had to have had this before."

Birds chirped in the palms overhead while Tandy wondered what to do next.

"What now?" Kendra checked her hair in the visor mirror.

"I guess we get out of the car."

"Sounds like a logical first step. Any idea what we're going to say to her?"

"Provided she doesn't shoot us on sight, I think the words 'I'm sorry' are going to come out of my mouth about a hundred times."

"Good plan. Let's go." Kendra pushed open her door, and Tandy followed suit.

They walked down the driveway and turned left onto a sidewalk whose edges were lined with more lush plants. A white metal gate greeted them at the end. It had no lock. To its right they could see the front door. Zelda was nowhere in sight.

With a shaking hand, Tandy lifted the gate's latch and walked through.

■ ■ ■ ■

Meg stepped in to water so hot that steam curled away from the line of it pouring out of the faucet. Mounds of bubbles grew where the water fell, pushing toward the back of the tub.

She closed her eyes in absolute pleasure, then couldn't decide which made her more happy at this moment — the warm water, the thousands of bubbles, or the knowledge that no child would be running through the door with a need for Mommy. Deciding it didn't matter in the long run, she slowly eased down into the water. She could have sworn her body sighed its relief aloud.

Careful to keep her hands out of the water, she took the paperback from a black wicker table nearby. A whole afternoon and evening lay ahead of her — time to read, time to relax, time to remember being a woman outside of mommyhood. She briefly considered feeling guilty for finding this much joy in not having her kids around, but Joy had a point about every mom needing downtime.

And this mom hasn't had any in way too long.

She arched her back and felt the water

swirl around her. Settling into the contours of the tub, she opened a novel purchased eight months ago and held in preparation for a day just like today.

Even her headache — almost always present these days — eased up and began to dissipate.

See? Nothing serious is wrong with me. Just stressed out.

She lifted a foot out of the water and used her toes to lift the hot water faucet higher. Warmth a notch above the rest of the water flooded her feet and began crawling up her legs. She let it run for a few seconds — until the water line reached the overflow drain of the tub — then turned off the faucet with her feet.

The only sound that met her ears was that of rustling pages as she devoured the story in her hands.

I used to love reading. I should make more time for this somehow. She pushed the thought away and dove back into the pages in her hands.

Outside the bathroom window a high winter sun moved across the sky, noticed only peripherally by the woman lying beneath mountains of bubbles that fell into hills as the sun traversed its path.

Halfway through the book, Meg realized

the water had grown cold and sunshine no longer streamed through the window at her back. Instead it now came strongly through the panes on the opposite side of the room.

She stood and set the novel back on the black wicker table, then stepped out of the bathtub. Goosebumps formed along her arms as she wrapped a thick terry cloth towel — one the kids didn't get to use and that she normally saved for guests — around herself. It had to be dinnertime by now, but the house still sounded silent. Jamison must have decided to play eighteen holes rather than nine.

Which was fine with her.

She moved to the bedroom and slipped a nightgown over her head, not yet ready to give up the luxury of comfort. Real clothes — mom clothes — could be donned before the kids came home. Joy would call before she came; she always did. Meg would have plenty of time to make herself presentable again, to remove the vestiges of an afternoon totally devoid of productivity.

Picking up the novel once again, she settled into her bed's many pillows and clicked on a bedside lamp. Within minutes, she'd been transported back into another world, another story.

She stayed there until the sound of a car

in the garage pulled her back into her bedroom in Stars Hill. Jamison must be home. The thought of him made her smile. He was home and she didn't need him to take over the kids so she could fix dinner or pick up the house or breathe for a minute.

Rather than going to greet him, she stayed put. Let him come to her this time. He'd done that during their dating days in high school. No matter where she went, he'd come to find her and talk. He was the smartest guy she'd ever met, and she loved how they could talk for hours. She'd loved his desire to seek her out, to find her just to tell her something he'd heard on the news or some new thing he'd learned. The only "finding" these days was either for the car keys or one of the kid's socks/coats/shoes/toys.

"Well, hey there." A mixture of pleasure and surprise flowed in Jamison's voice. He stood in the bedroom doorway. "Playing the lady of luxury today?"

"Joy offered to keep the kids the rest of the day." She shifted and noted how his eyes followed her movement. "I just got out of the tub a little while ago."

He crossed the room in slow strides and stopped by the bed, his eyes never leaving her. The look that had driven her crazy during high school still kicked up her heartbeat now. A lazy smile spread across his face. "So you're telling me we're without children for the evening?"

The mattress dipped when he sat on its edge and her body turned to him as a result. "Oh, I'd say we have at least a couple of hours."

"Mmm." His eyes traced the lace edging of her neckline. "Nice nightgown. I forgot about this." He ran a finger down the light blue silk.

"I had too. Not very kid-friendly."

"No, but definitely husband-friendly."

She put her book on the nearby nightstand. When he leaned to kiss her, she met him halfway, more than ready to remember the wife part of womanhood.

TWELVE

While Meg began her day of reconnection and rest, Kendra and Tandy stood before Zelda's front door and rang the bell.

Zelda made them wait long enough to wonder if they had come all this way for naught. Just as Tandy opened her mouth to tell Kendra they should go, Zelda appeared behind the glass door. She didn't look happy, but she cracked it open. "You two making sure I'm far away from your dad?"

"No, Zelda," Tandy said. "We — that is, I — need to talk to you about that. If you could just give me — us — a couple of minutes, we'll leave you alone after that if you prefer."

Zelda eyed them both, and Tandy held her breath and focused on looking apologetic.

"If you came a thousand miles, I guess I can give you two minutes." Zelda opened the door wide enough for them to enter.

Tandy glanced around the foyer while

Zelda closed the door behind them. It only took a few seconds, but that was enough to see a home full of artwork, furniture upholstered in light blues and browns, oriental rugs, and a glass door at the far end of the room leading out onto a patio. Beyond, golfers were making their way along the fairway.

"Your home is lovely."

"Thank you." Zelda walked past them, and the sisters followed. She waved them to a long couch situated in front of a fireplace framed in marble. "Your two minutes are dwindling rapidly."

"Right." Tandy scrambled around for the right words, hooking her hair behind her ears. She clasped her hands in her lap to keep them from twitching about. "Look, Zelda, I messed up. I thought horrible things about you, and I refused to accept you into Daddy's life, and I was a total brat, and I talked about you behind your back, and I made assumptions about your character that weren't true and accused you of things in my mind that you had no intention of doing. I was wrong. I am so sorry, and I hope you can forgive me and come back to Stars Hill." Tandy's words came to an abrupt end, and she clamped her lips together. There, that hadn't been too bad.

"Hmm. I see." Zelda's shrewd gaze flitted

from sister to sister and back again. "And you, Kendra? What are you doing here? Or are you just a traveling companion for your sister?"

"No, I need to say I'm sorry too. I might not have thought or said all the bad things about you that Tandy did, but I jumped right on the bandwagon with her. I wanted to tell you though that most of this had nothing to do with you. Daddy's not had a serious relationship since Momma, and well, we just weren't ready for it. At least I know I wasn't."

"Me, either," Tandy chimed in. "She's right, Zelda. This was less about you than it was about our inability to deal with your presence."

Zelda nodded. "I can understand that."

"You can?" A bit of the weight that had settled on Tandy's chest in the driveway began to lighten.

"Sure I can, just like you two can understand that I've got a life outside your daddy, that I had a first love just like he did, and that I can choose not to have four meddling, hard-to-please daughters of a boyfriend in my life."

Tandy swallowed. "You could choose that, of course." The weight settled back on her chest. "But wouldn't you be giving up the man you love?"

Zelda looked away, and Tandy could see the muscles of her jaw working. "I've lost love before."

"Not by choice though, right?" Kendra scooted forward on the couch. "You lost your first husband to death, but Daddy's in perfect health so far as we know. I get that Tandy and I have made this harder than it probably should have been. But would you really hurt Daddy just because his daughters are hardheaded and protective of him?"

Zelda's quick smile preceded her pointed finger. "I thought this one was the attorney, not you, Kendra."

"She was, but she left her arguing skills in Orlando."

"If y'all were blood sisters, I'd say lawyering runs in your family. As it is, I guess Jack and Marian raised you to present logical arguments."

"You'd be right on that point."

"So will you come back to Stars Hill?" Tandy dared to ask.

Zelda sniffed. "I don't know, Tandy. Your daddy doesn't seem to have noticed that I'm gone."

"Oh, believe us, he's noticed. He just isn't sure what to do about it."

Tandy grimaced. "Other than yell at us so

loud the roof shook."

"Brought you down a peg or two, did he?" Zelda laughed. "I suspected he might be headed your way after I ran into him at Darnell's."

"He found us right after that. And I don't think he's been that mad since the night he found Ken and me parked uptown at midnight with a bunch of friends. And we weren't even smoking; *they* were."

Zelda threw her head back and laughed louder than a bingo caller in a roomful of deaf folks. Tears of mirth formed in the corners of her eyes. "Whew, me, child." She swiped at her face and got her breath. "I wish I had known your momma and daddy back when you girls were teenagers. I'll bet they were a sight to behold."

"I don't know about that, but they did manage to keep us in line. And that's no small feat for four girls whose own birth parents didn't want them."

Zelda rose and straightened her shirt. "I think what we could use here is a tall glass of iced tea. You girls thirsty?"

"As a hiker in the Sahara," Tandy answered, feeling the weight completely leave her chest.

"Then I'll see if I can't hurry before you thirst to death." Zelda bustled off toward the kitchen.

Tandy waited until Zelda disappeared around the kitchen doorway, then turned to Kendra. "That went way better than I expected."

"I know. You think we can get her to come back with us today?"

"Got me." Tandy shrugged. "I'm still trying to figure out what she moved down here with a U-Haul. This stuff looks like it's been here a while, not newly placed."

Kendra's spiral curls brushed her shoulders as she looked this way and that, taking in the furniture. "You've got a point. I wonder if she packed up because she didn't intend on coming back?"

"Gosh, I hope not."

"Here we are." Zelda walked around the corner, her hands gripping a white wood tray bearing three tall glasses of tea. She set it on the coffee table at Kendra's knee and handed each sister a glass. "And I should tell you this house transmits sound better than Ma Bell ever dreamt of." Zelda raised her glass to her lips, then winked before taking a drink.

Tandy sputtered and nearly lost the gulp she'd just taken. "Um, excuse me?"

Zelda swallowed and licked her lips. "Man, I love tea." She turned her gaze back to Tandy. "Look, if there's any hope of the three of us getting along, we're going to need to lay a ground rule or two."

"Sounds fair. Difficult, but fair."

Zelda held up one short finger made stubbier by the giant topaz cutting off its base. "Rule number one: Stop trying to figure me out. If you want to know why I did or said something, just ask."

The sisters nodded.

"Rule number two: If I do or say something that offends either of you, tell me as soon as you can. Don't talk about it amongst yourselves or pull the other two into it. Chances are pretty high I'm not even aware I've upset you, so give me the benefit of the doubt and ask. I'll do the same for you."

Ice clinked in the glass she held and she paused to swirl it around. "That's it. Think you can abide by those rules?"

They couldn't nod fast enough.

"Absolutely," Tandy said. "As a matter of fact, we'll start exercising them right now. Where's the stuff you brought down from Stars Hill? Homer told me you packed up a U-Haul, but this place looks like it's been furnished a while."

"That's because it has. I packed up the Stars Hill place because I wasn't sure if I'd be back. Truth be known, I doubted I'd ever be back. Got the furniture down here and had a boy put it in storage for me."

"So you still have your Stars Hill stuff?"

"Sure."

Tandy jumped up. "Then let's go pack it back up and head home!"

Kendra followed a half beat behind. "Yeah. If we start now, we can probably have it loaded by dark and then start toward Tennessee in the morning, right? What time does it get dark here?" Kendra consulted the lime green watch on her wrist. Sunlight caught its giant rhinestones and sent rainbows of color dancing off the walls.

"Dark doesn't matter. We're not packing up my stuff." Zelda sipped serenely from her glass.

"Excuse me? I thought you forgave us."

"Oh, I did forgive you, Tandy. And you too, Kendra. But I don't think I've forgiven your daddy yet."

Tandy sank back onto the couch. "Forgiven Daddy? What'd he do?"

"It's more what he didn't do."

Kendra balled her fists and put them on her hips. "Okay, what did he *not* do?"

"That's none of your concern. It's between me and your daddy. Y'all have done what you came to do. Now go out there and soak up some of that sunshine before you hit the road."

"Hit the road?" Tandy pulled back and squinted at Zelda. "Zelda, we came down here to apologize and take you back to Stars Hill."

"And one out of two ain't bad. I'm a grown woman. If I want to get back to Stars Hill, I know where the road is."

"Why wouldn't you just go back with us now? There's no reason for you to stay here."

"Have you gone blind *and* deaf? Look around you." Zelda waved her hand toward the back door. "I'm surrounded by warmth, sunshine, and quiet. I don't think I've got it half bad."

"Yeah, but you don't have Daddy. I thought you loved him." Tandy crossed one leg and peered at Zelda in the same way she used to peer at liars on the witness stand. "If you love him, then you would want to get back to him as soon as possible. Not sit down here alone — sunshine or not."

Zelda wagged a finger. "There you go again, breaking rule number one. Don't try to figure me out, Tandy."

Kendra threw up her hands. "She's not trying to figure *you* out, Zelda." Her loud voice bounced off the twenty-five-foot walls. "She's trying to make our daddy happy.

140

And he's happy when he's with you. Though for the life of me I can't figure out why right now."

Zelda smiled and studied her tea. "You don't have to know why, Kendra. Neither do you, Tandy. But you do have to leave this between your daddy and me. I said I forgive you both and I do." She looked up, then came to her feet. Sunshine pouring in from an overhead window provided the spotlight in which she stood. "I appreciate you girls coming all this way to say you're sorry. I'll pray for safe travels during your drive home."

Kendra stared, mouth agape, while Zelda walked across the hardwood floor and through a white wooden door. It closed with finality.

Kendra pointed a long, purple-tipped finger in the direction Zelda had gone. Her bracelets clanked together. "Did she just kick us out of her house?"

"I think so." Tandy shook her head. "What do we do now?"

"Storming her bedroom — at least what I assume is her bedroom — would just give us something else to say we're sorry for later."

Tandy chewed her lip. "I think we have to leave."

"Without Zelda? Are you nuts?"

"What's the alternative, Ken? She's made it clear she doesn't want to talk anymore. We got what we came for — her forgiveness. Let's do as she says and hit the road." Tandy stood and put their glasses back on the tray. "Come on."

Kendra followed her in stupefied silence through the living room and around the corner into the kitchen.

Tandy set the tray down on a black and brown granite surface. She had no idea why Zelda wouldn't come back to Stars Hill, but there were eleven long hours of driving time between them and Stars Hill. Suddenly that looked like a better option than going through airport security again.

Enough time to talk it out and formulate a plan.

Rules were made to be broken.

Thirteen

My hallway looks like a toy department exploded. I can't remember when I had this much fun.

"Aunt Joy, it's your turn!"

James has more energy than a six-week-old puppy. He's set the bowling pins up at least twenty times already, but the sparkle in his eye and laughter bubbling up from within haven't ebbed a bit. No wonder Meg's tired all the time.

Scott's hands are warm on my back as he pushes me out of our sitting position on the floor. "Go on, Aunt Joy. Knock 'em dead."

He's having a ball too. Years have disappeared from his face in the few hours we've had James and Savannah.

I take the plastic bowling ball from James and ruffle his hair. "Okay, go keep watch."

His sock-clad feet slip and slide, but James gets to the other end of the hallway and gives a triumphant grin that I can't help but return. "Aim good, Aunt Joy!"

We've rolled the oriental rug to one side, and light gleams on the hardwood floor. I close one eye and sight down the length of a few planks, then roll the ball toward the plastic multicolored pins at the other end.

James is dancing before the ball even makes contact. "Good throw! Good throw!" With a loud crash, plastic ball hits plastic pins and they all go flying. "Did you see that, Uncle Scott? Did you? I just think Aunt Joy is the best bowler ever!" He slips across the floor, retrieving pins and placing them back in formation. "Let's do it again."

Scott hauls himself up. His knee pops and I laugh. "Snap, crackle, pop, old man."

"Hey, watch who you're calling old." His arms come around my waist, and I wonder briefly if we should hug in front of James. But I've got thousands of pictures in my mind of Mother and Daddy hugging, dancing, kissing, laughing. It's good for children to know the adults around them love each other.

I hug Scott back, then push him over to where I had been. "Your turn, Uncle Scott. Show me what you've got."

He lowers his head, his big hand slides around the back of my neck, and he puts his forehead to mine. "That'll come after we take the kids home."

I giggle — me! giggling! — and step backward. "We'll see if either of us has any energy left or we end up sacked out like Savannah is right now."

"Come on, Uncle Scott!" James places the last pin in position. "You've got to hit 'em all or we'll know Aunt Joy's better than you."

Scott shakes his head, the smile never leaving his face as he aims and rolls the ball. All ten pins crash down and skid off in varying directions.

"YAY! Great job! Great job!" James jumps up and down, hopping from pin to pin and setting up again.

"Hey, James, how about a break from bowling?"

"Aw, but I want to bowl some more." He doesn't look up, intent on getting every pin just right.

"Even though I'm about to make chocolate chip cookies?"

The red pin in his hand clatters to the floor. "Cookies? Can I help? Mom lets me help sometimes, and I'm really good. I promise. You can ask her."

"I believe you, James. Let's go to the kitchen and get our aprons on."

"You're sure sugar this late at night is a

good idea?" Scott's putting pins back into their box.

"If this child is still awake in an hour, I'll give up my subscription to *Living*."

"Wow. What are you planning to do? Put Benadryl in his milk?"

"No. Everybody knows warm cookies and milk do the trick every time."

"And eight hours of nonstop playing." He puts the last pin in the box and hefts it onto his side.

"That too." I kiss him — a short, quick, happy-to-be-with-you kiss — as I head toward the kitchen.

Soon we could be playing with our own children. In the blink of an eye, the whole scene comes fully formed into my mind and stops my feet. Our little girl, sitting on the kitchen counter with flour on her nose and a wooden spoon in her hand, chattering away about the butterflies and bluebirds outside. She'll be fascinated with nature because I'll introduce her to it early on. I'll explain how the hummingbird hovers just outside the window and how a caterpillar becomes a butterfly. She'll laugh and lick batter off the spoon, then her fingers. I'll put her in a red corduroy dress because that will be so striking next to her black hair.

"Aunt Joy! I found my apron!" James's

voice dispels the image, and I feel a bit of sadness as it slips away. What if the doctor tells us tomorrow that we can't have children? What if I never have a little girl to teach about baking and singing and nature? Can I be happy without a child?

"Aunt Joy!"

I get my feet into gear and hurry through the entryway. James stands, surrounded by kitchen towels, holding up an apron. "Look! I found a blue one. Can I wear the blue one?"

"Sure you can." I kneel before him and slip it over his head. "Now, do you know the first thing we do before we make cookies?" I have to wrap the blue ties around him twice and tuck the bottom of the apron into the waistband so he won't trip.

"What?"

"We wash our hands. Do you know how to wash your hands?"

His little eyes are serious as he nods. "Yep. Mommy taught me when my nose was running away. I washed my hands so it would stay on my face."

Only creative Meg could make up a story about a running nose to impress the importance of washing hands on a seven-year-old. I pull a stool over to the sink.

"Right. Well, we also wash our hands so

the food stays clean while we work. Now hop up here and let's get to work on some cookies."

"Come on T, I'm exhausted and so are you. Let's enjoy a couple of days here in the sunshine, do some wedding planning, and then go home." Storefronts and strip malls whizzed by as they traveled down Pine Ridge Road. Kendra pulled a yellow bandana from her bag and tied it over her head to keep her hair down.

"Don't you want to get back to Darin?"

"Of course I do."

"Then why the full-court press on staying here a few days?"

"Didn't you just tell me you need some time to figure out why Zelda's not coming back to Stars Hill with us?"

Tandy nodded, stopping at a red light.

"Okay, then let's go sit on a beach and think about it. Maybe if we come up with something, we'll take another crack at getting her to come back with us."

This made Tandy nibble her lip, and Kendra knew she'd just been granted a couple of days in sunshine.

"You've got a point."

"I usually do."

"Yeah, but this time it's a good point."

Kendra stuck her tongue out before glancing back around them. "Pull in over there at that 7-11. I'll bet we can get a map and figure out where the beach is."

"The beach is this way." Tandy turned the car in the opposite direction of the convenience store.

"You know Naples?"

"I know the beach. Something about the way the sky looks over the beach." Tandy pointed out the windshield. "See that gorgeous blue? That's a beach sky."

Kendra squinted, then twisted in her seat. Nope, the sky behind them looked just like the sky Tandy pointed at. "I don't get it."

"Landlubber," Tandy teased. "Trust me." She turned the radio on and smiled when the bouncy notes of Bop poured from the car's speakers.

"You're kidding me. Bop?" Kendra wrinkled her nose.

"Oh, be quiet. You know you love it."

They giggled and bopped their heads back and forth in time to the music. Tandy steered the car another three blocks, then pulled into a parking space and cut the engine.

"Um, sis, this is a parking lot."

Tandy hooked her thumb behind them. "And that's the ocean. Come on." She was out her door before Kendra had time to tell her that a building lay behind them, not the ocean.

Kendra scrambled to catch up. "Wait a second. Wait just a second. Where are you going?" She hurried after Tandy, who now stood at the end of a sand-covered sidewalk.

"I thought you wanted to go to the beach."

"I do."

Tandy held out her arm and Kendra looped her own through its crook. "Then come along, sister dear."

People in various states of swimwear met them from the other direction as they strode down the long paved walkway. Kendra barely suppressed a giggle when a heavyset fortyish man came into their line of vision; his red spandex Speedo left little to the imagination.

When he'd passed, Kendra leaned over to Tandy and whispered, "If Clay or Darin ever does that, they will never be allowed to leave the house again."

"Absolutely."

A little girl with red pigtails and a bright yellow polka-dot bathing suit came bounding down the walkway, followed closely by a tall, lithe woman whose hair bore the same red hue.

"Sally! Stop right there until Mommy

catches up!" The woman hefted a turquoise beach bag higher on her shoulder. Her other hand gripped a matching beach lounge chair. "Do you hear me, Sally?"

"Yes, Mommy," came the tiny voice. "I waiting!"

Kendra glanced behind them to see that Sally had, indeed, stopped in her tracks. "You think Joy's kids will be that obedient?"

"I think they'd better."

They strolled further until, at last, just over a small rise, Kendra saw a slice of ocean.

"Ooh! I see it!" She pulled Tandy at a faster pace. "Come on!"

"What are you, two?" Tandy chuckled but let herself be hurried.

"Hey, you got to live near this long enough to take it for granted. I'm so Stars Hill, my bones are frozen for the winter." Kendra let go of Tandy's arm and jogged the rest of the way down what had now become a wood-planked boardwalk. "Ah! Warm sand!" Kendra dug her toes into the white powder and tilted her face to the sun. "Heaven."

"Not quite, but it's close." Tandy breathed in the salty air. "Feel better now that you're at the beach?"

"I'll feel better when we have a hotel room

and I know I'm going to get a whole day of the beach."

"Okay, okay. We'll stay a couple of days, long enough to figure out the next step with Zelda, and then hurry home. Sound good?"

"Sounds great. Hey, let's find one of those little mom-and-pop hotels that are here on the beach."

"No way. You know I'm a hotel snob."

"This is Naples, T. Even the little locally owned outfits are going to be fine. Besides, you can stay in your precious Hilton anytime."

Tandy sighed. "I'm going to regret this."

"No, you won't. Even if we have to fight off cockroaches all night, we'll have a funny story in the morning."

"Unless the cockroaches get us in our sleep and all they find in the morning are our bones."

"That's gross."

"That's the reality of staying in a motel."

"You really *are* a snob."

Tandy rolled her eyes. "It's not like this is a surprise."

"We let you stay in the city too long, sister." Kendra looped her arm back through Tandy's and tugged her back to the sidewalk. "You've forgotten the cultural ambience of locally owned establishments."

"Now *there's a* spin."

"Behold the skill."

"There's a name for that kind of skill."

"Watch it, lady."

Tandy laughed. "Okay, let's go see what locally owned establishment we're calling home for the night."

FOURTEEN

This office is frigid. Why do doctors' offices have to be so cold? I read somewhere that the point is to make the environment inhospitable to the growth of germs. Well, it's also inhospitable to the comfort of humans. Someone should tell them that.

Scott looks worried. I don't blame him, of course, but I wish there were something I could do to wipe those worry lines from his face. He's been concerned ever since he came in here and let them draw blood and other fluids to run tests on. I wonder how he'll react if there is something wrong with him.

I wonder how I'll react.

Perfect. Now *I* have worry lines.

I'll still love him. That should go without saying, though I felt the need to say it anyway. I wonder why? I'll still love him even if the doctor says that we can never conceive a child. We can always adopt, right?

I was adopted. I believe in adoption. I'm all right with that option.

I think.

"Hello, Joy, Scott." Dr. Goodman's white coat looks inhospitable for germs as well. I wish the door to his office wasn't behind us.

Scott stands, so I do as well.

"Hello, Dr. Goodman." Scott's hand is tan inside Dr. Goodman's pale one when they shake. Lots of hours on the golf course. I sneak a look at Scott's other hand and see that it's a shade or two lighter. Must be the golf glove. "You have news for us?"

Dr. Goodman settles himself into that leather chair. His face doesn't look as promising as it did the last time I sat before this desk, with Meg here as my support.

"The good news is that we've isolated the barrier to conception."

Which, of course, means there *is* a barrier to conception. Scott stiffens beside me, and I reach out to hold his tan hand. The coolness of his skin startles me. Shouldn't tan hands be warm?

"A barrier to conception?" I ask because it appears Scott isn't going to say a word.

"Yes. And it's a problem that can be easily overcome using today's technologies."

Oh, good. Technology to get pregnant.

That sounds . . . sterile.

"Scott, it appears you suffer from a condition called oligospermia."

The muscle in Scott's jaw is working. I'm fairly certain his teeth are clamped tighter than a street peddler's wallet.

Dr. Goodman keeps speaking into the silence. "That's simply a long way of saying you have a low sperm count. There are easy treatments — injections of hormones to increase the sperm count, or extraction of the sperm you have and IVF to bring about conception within Joy's womb, or a number of other options. The point here is, we now know what we're dealing with, and there are very easy ways to address the situation."

Silence stretches and I keep my eyes on my husband. I know this isn't easy to hear, but I also know he's a capable man who does not shy away from life's difficulties. Finally Scott clears his throat.

"All right. Where do we go from here?"

Just six words, but oh how my heart lifts with the sound of them!

"You'll need to see an andrologist, which is a doctor specializing in male fertility. Dr. Murray is excellent. His office is one hallway over from this one. If you'd like, I can get you an appointment this week."

"That fast?"

Dr. Goodman smiles. "I assume you two have had enough waiting to last a lifetime?"

"Oh, yes!" I can't help myself. Knowing the problem is key to conquering the problem, and now we've got a name for our problem: oligospermia. It's an awful-sounding word, but Dr. Goodman gives me hope.

"Then I'll have Tina set it up. Just wait right here."

I wait until Dr. Goodman leaves before turning toward Scott. "Isn't this wonderful news?"

"Wonderful news?" His eyes widen, and I realize my blunder too late. "I can't give you the children we want, and you call that wonderful news?"

"But you *can!* We might need a little help, but who cares about that?"

Storm clouds enter those eyes I love. "I care, Joy."

I rush to assure him. "I care too, Scott. I don't mean to say I don't care. I'm just so happy there isn't something wrong that we can't overcome, can't find a solution for."

His smile is small, but it parts the storm clouds a bit. "I know what you meant."

"And you know that I love you, right?"

"Right."

That will have to be enough for now.

Dr. Goodman returns to the office, and the optimistic look on his face keeps my hopes rising. "Good news again! Dr. Murray had a cancellation this afternoon and is willing to work you in if you'd like."

"We would!"

"Then 2:30 it is." He hands a white appointment card to Scott. My dear husband tucks that card of hope into his shirt pocket.

"Thanks, Dr. Goodman." Scott stands and holds out his hand.

"My pleasure, Scott." Dr. Goodman shakes the proffered hand. "I know this wasn't easy to hear, but trust me that it could have been much worse."

Scott just nods and I shoot a thankful look to Dr. Goodman as I follow my husband out the office door.

"So, we've got sun, sand, food, towels, wedding magazines, a pen, and a notebook. I'd say it's time we talked wedding plans."

Kendra stretched out along her newly purchased lounge chair and enjoyed the warm sun on her back. "Sounds good to me. So far, I've picked out music and colors. What's left?"

"Kendra, tell me you're kidding."

"I've got months and months to plan, T. Why rush?"

"Did you pay no attention during my wedding planning? Have you forgotten how long it takes to decide on cake flavors and decorations and arrangement of tiers and bridesmaid dresses and tux styles? And don't even get me started on the thousands of flower choices you've got to wade through."

"I was thinking about keeping it simple."

"Oh, please. Kendra Sinclair and simple go together like snowflakes and this beach. You're only saying that because you don't want to put the work in to have a bigger wedding."

Kendra opened one eye and looked over at Tandy. "Guilty. Does that make me awful?"

"Not wanting to devote a ton of hours to your wedding day? No, I wouldn't say it makes you *awful,* exactly."

"It's not that I don't love Darin with all my heart, and I definitely want us to have a dreamy day. But I get depressed when I look at those organizing books and see the thousands of little boxes that need to be checked off. I get overwhelmed and just put the thing down. I'd hire a wedding coordinator, but I'd rather spend that money on flowers or cake or food for the reception."

"It makes sense that you'd hate the planning books. That's too much forethought for you."

Kendra laughed. "Hey, I resemble that remark."

"I can't believe you bought a planning book in the first place. What were you thinking?"

"I was thinking a woman's wedding day is the biggest day of her life and I didn't want to walk down the aisle to Jimmy Buffet music and find Darin at the altar in khaki pants and a loud Hawaiian shirt and then reach up to find a lei around my neck and hibiscus blossoms in my hair."

"Lack of planning leads to a bad Hawaiian wedding?"

Kendra picked at the sand. "Evidently."

"You get that you're a nut case?"

"Yeah, but a lovable nut case, right?"

"Darin sure seems to think so."

"Isn't he the greatest?"

"I happen to think Clay is the greatest, but Darin is a close second."

"Ah, the blinding power of love."

"Back at you, babe."

"What do you think about a black-and-white wedding?"

"I think it'll look like your apartment did before you met Darin. Don't you think you need tons of color? Kind of like the color Darin brought into your life?"

"That's a great idea! Why didn't I think of that?"

"Because when you're freaked out, you pull color out of everything and try to make sense of it."

"Thank you, Dr. Freud."

"Anytime. So, colors? What about red?"

"I like red. I look good in red. You, Meg, and Joy all look good in red."

"And red's the color of love."

"But the carpet in the sanctuary is blue. We'll end up with a patriotic wedding."

"It won't be blue by the time you get married. They're replacing it with gray this summer."

"Seriously? Who says?"

"Daddy. He told me about it a couple of weeks ago."

"Gray, white, and red. I really, really like that. The gray and white is my life without Darin. The red is my life with him. I love the symbolism."

"The artist loves symbolism. Go figure."

Kendra smiled, envisioning the wedding of her dreams that had begun to take shape now that Tandy freed her from the tyranny of the organizing book.

They sat for a bit and listened to the gentle lapping of waves. A seagull screamed its delight over finding dinner. Snatches of chatter came to them on the breeze.

"I owe Zelda a thank you for interjecting a beach trip into my wedding planning."

"Speaking of Zelda, why do you think she won't come back to Stars Hill?"

"I thought we told her we wouldn't try to figure her out anymore."

"We did."

"Isn't that what we're sitting here doing?"

"Sort of. Think of it more along the lines of trying to help Daddy out."

"Situational ethics were never your thing."

Tandy sighed. "They're still not. I just don't like not knowing people's *reasons* for their actions. Doesn't it bug you?"

"A little. But Zelda's right. It's between her and Daddy now."

"You're probably right. I *know* you're right. I'm bugged though."

Beach sounds swept over them again and Kendra rolled over on her lounger to feel the breeze across her face. "Should we call Daddy and tell him how it went? We said we'd keep him informed, remember."

Tandy snapped her fingers. "That's a great idea. Let me find my phone." She rummaged around in their brand new beach bag bearing the name *Sandy Shore Motel* in pink letters. "Daddy can tell us what to do next."

"That's not what I said."

162

But Tandy was motioning her to silence as she dialed and held the phone to her ear. "Daddy? It's Tandy."

Kendra nestled further into her lounger and listened as Tandy gave Daddy a run-down of their previous day's activities.

A red wedding. That would be beautiful, if she did it right. Red roses were too cliché for her and Darin, but red Gerbera daises would be playful enough to reflect them. Could she get daisies in the fall? When did daisies come into season?

By the time Tandy flipped her phone closed, Kendra had added edelweiss — Momma's favorite — to the mix. They would be beautiful bouquets.

"Daddy has no idea why Zelda won't come home with us."

"Seriously?"

"That's what he said. I had to tell him over and over again everything she said to us, as much as I could remember anyway. And he said either she didn't really forgive us or there's something we can't put our finger on."

"Daddy can be so obtuse sometimes."

"About what? Zelda's being difficult."

"No, she's not, T. I think I figured it out while you were on the phone."

"Do tell."

"Well, I'm sitting here picturing my wedding day and thinking about how I want everything to be a reflection of this grand romance Darin and I have shared. Why wouldn't Zelda want the same thing?"

"Zelda can have the same thing, Ken. But she's got to go back to Stars Hill and get the ring before she can plan a wedding."

"I'm not talking about the wedding. I'm talking about the grand romance."

"I think I got left back at 'I'm sitting here picturing my wedding day.' "

Kendra sat up and met Tandy's gaze. "Where's Zelda's grand romance?"

"Eww." Tandy scrunched her nose and shook her head. "I am *not* thinking about Daddy in those terms."

"Stop being a baby and listen for a minute. Zelda is a woman, like us. She wants to be courted and romanced and, I don't know . . . wooed."

"Wooed? Did we transport back to 1950?"

"You know what I mean. You said it yourself. We came down here to apologize because we needed to make a grand gesture that emphasized our apology."

"But Daddy didn't do anything wrong."

"She said it wasn't what he *had* done but what he *hadn't* done."

Kendra let Tandy think for a minute.

"Wait, you think Daddy hasn't romanced her?"

"I think Daddy didn't come running after her when she went to Florida."

"Why would he? He knew we were coming."

"Yeah, but we're not the ones she's in love with. We're not the ones she wants to be romanced by."

Tandy chewed her lip, then nodded. "I get what you're saying. She wants the fairy tale where Daddy comes down here and tells her he can't live without her, that she just *has* to come back to Stars Hill or his life will never be the same."

Kendra lay back. She knew Tandy would catch on. "Exactly."

"Then let me call Daddy back and tell him."

"Don't you think we should let him get there on his own?"

"He's male, Ken. We'd be waiting until this sand became glass."

"Point well-taken. Dial away."

FIFTEEN

Dr. Murray's office isn't cold. I wonder if that means they are growing more germs in this office or they simply see patients with bigger problems than germs. Judging by the look on Scott's face, I'd guess the latter.

"Hello, Mr. and Mrs. Lasky." Dr. Murray's voice is smooth, sort of like John Tesh. "Dr. Goodman has shared with me your medical history and the problem we are facing today."

Scott shifts in his seat, and I know that he doesn't like Dr. Murray's use of the word *problem* with regard to him.

"Scott, I'll need to run through some questions with you to determine if any of the usual causes are present in your lifestyle."

Scott nods his head once. I begin to plan dinner, knowing about three courses will return him to a relaxed and happy state.

Dr. Murray begins to question Scott on

his use of nicotine, alcohol, and drugs. I try to concentrate, but I'm so happy that we've finally found the problem, I'm having a hard time shifting into solution mode.

". . . draw blood to test your hormones and, depending on the results we get, schedule an ultrasound to ensure no blockages in your system."

"You're telling me my hormones could be wreaking havoc on my ability to get her pregnant?"

Dr. Murray's smile is understanding. "I know — women are supposed to have the hormone problems, right?"

I briefly consider being offended, but Scott's grip on my hand has lessened and there's a smile creeping across his face. If Dr. Murray's jokes about female hormones help my husband get through this, then I can crack a smile as well. Besides, Dr. Murray knows better than I how to get men through this since he works with them all day.

"Anyway, that's our first round of activity, so unless either of you has questions, I'll direct you to an exam room and we'll get started sucking your blood."

I withhold my cringe, barely. The rigid line of Scott's shoulders has released back to the easygoing stature of a man confidently going into the world. Dr. Murray must know his stuff.

We enter an exam room that looks more like someone's foyer than a sterile facility. Hunting pictures grace the walls, and a leather club chair sits in the corner. I look around but can find no hospital bed or bed of any sort in this small room.

"*This* is an exam room?"

Scott sits in the chair and motions me to its cousin in the other corner. "Looks like it."

"I'm definitely having a chat with Dr. Goodman about his décor, then. You men have it much better than women when it comes to the sex doctor."

"I cannot believe you just said sex in a public place."

Scott is laughing at me, and I'm so happy he's still smiling that I don't care. "We're in an andrologist's office. I think they probably say sex quite a bit here."

"Yes, but *they* didn't say it. *You* did. Something on your mind, Mrs. Lasky?"

Honestly, do men ever stop thinking about that? Here we are, learning about what's stopping us from getting pregnant, and my husband is using innuendo while sitting in an exam room. Not that it looks like an exam room, but the principle remains the same.

"I only said it because it's the type of doctor he is, and you know it."

Scott pats the firm arm of his chair. "Mmhmm. Come sit here and tell me all about it."

Thank goodness the nurse comes in right about then. I'm not certain how I'd have gotten his mind onto something more appropriate to discuss in a doctor's office. The sight of the nurse's needle though took that problem right out of my hands. Her gray and brown hair was piled high on her head in a series of curls, the effect of which made one wonder how her hair exploded in such symmetry.

"Hi, Mr. Lasky. I'm Marinda. Dr. Murray says we need to get some blood from you today, so if you'll roll up your sleeve, I'll make this as quick and painless as possible."

I turn my head while the curly-haired Marinda performs her task, positive I do not wish to see my husband's blood filling those vials on her metal tray. I occupy my mind by attempting to determine how she keeps all that hair from falling down around her ears.

"There we go."

It doesn't seem as if enough time has passed for her to have four full glass tubes of blood, but then again hair issues have always been able to occupy me. Good thing since I spend my day working with hair.

"Marinda, do you know when we'll have results or what our next step is?" Scott's rolling his sleeve back down and buttoning the cuff.

"We have our own lab here in the office, so we'll probably call you tomorrow with the results."

"Wow, you guys move fast."

"Well, Dr. Murray knows by the time a patient gets to us, he's probably just about worn out his ability to wait anymore. So we've got pretty much everything we need right here to diagnose and treat quickly."

"Speaking of treatment, we didn't get to that with Dr. Murray. Can you let us know what we're facing here?"

Marinda holds up the vials. "Not until we see what's inside these. I know it's hard to wait, but give us a day and we'll have a plan of action for you."

Scott nods and I send up a prayer of thanks for a doctor's office that doesn't take weeks to see a patient, much less diagnose him.

We say our good-byes to Marinda and leave the office.

"I'd say today's been a productive day

170

thus far, wouldn't you?"

Scott takes my hand in his. "That it has. By this time tomorrow, we'll know what we're up against."

I love that he's using *we,* acknowledging that we're in this together. "I love you, Scott Lasky."

He squeezes my hand, then pushes the button for the elevator. "How about we see a movie and have dinner before heading back home?"

"We haven't seen a movie in ages. Is there something you wanted to see?"

"Not really. I just thought it'd be nice to spend some time in a darkened theater with my wife."

"Scott, we're entirely too old to do what you're thinking about doing."

"And definitely too refined."

"Precisely."

"Though I'm intrigued that you think you know what I'm thinking."

The elevator arrives and we fall silent as we step into the crowded chamber. Scott's grin telegraphs to anyone interested in looking what we were talking about though. I wait until we're in the parking garage before picking up the conversation again.

"Are you saying you're *not* interested in engaging in public displays of affection after paying an exorbitant sum to enter a darkened room with a floor covered in a sticky film of soda residue and popcorn from the last hundred people who paid that same exorbitant sum to sit in that same room and, at least for the few sitting in the back row, ignore the entertainment being afforded on the screen to better entertain themselves?"

"You're right. We should take a movie home."

"But the television in our bedroom has the biggest screen, and it's only four o'clock."

"Didn't you hear Dr. Goodman and Dr. Murray? I'm a weakened man who must have rest." He lays a hand across his chest and adopts a Scarlett O'Hara look of desperation. "I must have rest, I say, rest."

"Going to bed with me at four o'clock in the afternoon is not rest."

"No, rest is what I'll be doing by six."

It would be easier if the man didn't have such amazing powers of persuasion.

A few hours later, I find the remote control and turn off a screen that has long since gone to blue. *An Affair to Remember* makes for a better movie when you write your own ending.

I stretch, careful not to wake the sleeping bear beside me, and roll out of bed. A rumble in my tummy reminds me we didn't have dinner before our movie. I'm almost certain there are cold cuts in the refrigerator downstairs. I could whip up a ham and Swiss, press it in the griddle, and call it a panini in about fifteen minutes.

The house is silent as I make my way down the long staircase to the main floor. If Dr. Murray is able to help us, it won't be silent too much longer. Perhaps this time next year I could be hearing that sweet small cry of a newborn.

I almost can't fathom it.

The phone rings just before my feet touch the floor of the kitchen. I hurry across its cold surface before the sound can wake Scott.

"Lasky residence."

"Joy? Is that you?"

"Of course it's me, Tandy. Who else would it be?"

"I don't know, but you sound kind of, I don't know, sleepy or something."

"That would be because I just woke up."

"But it's early evening. How are you just now getting up?"

"You mean to tell me you and Clay are only active at night?"

173

"Eww! Yuck! I do *not* need that mental image of you, sister."

I laugh at her mock outrage. "You asked."

"Next time just tell me I don't need to know."

"I'll remember your wishes."

"Since we're already discussing it though, what did the doctor have to say?"

I fill her in on all we've learned today.

"Wow, so Scott was the problem."

"Yes, but it appears the problem is easily overcome once they learn a little more about it. But let's stop with all this talk of my husband's reproductive system. Are you and Kendra back yet?"

"No, we're still living it up in the Sunshine State. Kendra's decided to have a red wedding."

"Not surprising, given her love of color now that Darin is in the picture."

"That's what I thought. We're coming home tomorrow."

"With Zelda?"

"Without Zelda. We think she's waiting on Daddy to romance her."

"Come again?"

"Hey, if I have to endure mental images of you and Scott, you can consider the fact that Daddy is a man and has a girlfriend who needs sweeping off her feet."

"I suppose. Did Zelda tell you this?"

"No, we deduced it."

"Oh, dear." Tandy and Kendra deducing things rarely ends well for anyone involved.

"Stop it. We're right about this."

"So call Daddy and tell him to get himself down there and bring Zelda back to Stars Hill."

"Have you *met* our daddy?"

"You're right. He won't do it."

"Not until we show him how much it makes sense. How he's going to be alone forever if he doesn't swallow his pride and get down here."

"I assume you and Kendra have also planned how you will 'show' this truth to Daddy?"

"We were hoping you could help with that."

"Why do I hear the theme from *Jaws* in my head?"

"Because your sisters have spent the day sunning themselves by the ocean."

"Sure, sure. That must be it."

"Seriously, do you have any ideas for convincing Daddy to come down here after Zelda?"

"I don't, but I can think about it while you and Kendra are in the air."

"We'll call you when we land."

"I'll sit by the phone with bated breath."

"I think I liked you better when you were withdrawn and quiet."

"Then it's a sad day for you. Quiet me is out the door. We've got a diagnosis. A new day is dawning."

"It's nighttime."

"Can I have an umbrella for the rain?"

"It's raining there?"

"I was referring to the rain you just dumped on my parade. You two *do* need to get back here. You're losing your ability to converse."

"Easy to do when our only activity is to lie around in the sun."

"And get sunburned."

"That too. See you tomorrow, Joy."

I put the phone back in its cradle and survey the kitchen. For the first time I notice the sharp edges of each corner of the countertop. That would hurt a little toddler head. We'll need to get rubber bumpers or have the kitchen redone.

Oh, and the refrigerator will definitely need replaced. I cannot have my child pulling out our bottom-load freezer and crawling inside.

Except that it's customarily full enough to prevent the child actually closing herself into the compartment.

Maybe we'll keep the refrigerator and just replace the countertops.

Sixteen

"Joy says to sit Daddy down and have a talk with him." Tandy rolled her suitcase up to the table where Kendra sat eating a barbeque sandwich.

"Did she say in what universe she's operating?" Kendra wiped her mouth with a napkin. "Because I know *I'm* not having a conversation with Daddy about his dating life."

Tandy plopped into the chair opposite Kendra. "Tell me again why we're eating in the airport when we can get food for half the price as soon as we leave here?"

"Because Whitt's is in the opposite direction of the highway, and I'm not passing up a chance to have Whitt's barbeque before we get out of Nashville."

Tandy drummed her fingers on the table. "Fine. Whatever."

"Thank you. Did Joy have any other bright ideas?"

"Nope. She thinks if we have an adult conversation with him, he'll respond like a logical adult and book the next flight to Naples."

"She realizes that we're talking about *our* daddy here, right?"

"I think so."

Kendra shook her head. "She's left her problem-solving skills somewhere in infertility land. I think we're on our own here."

"We could at least give it a shot."

"You *want* to have that kind of conversation with Daddy?"

"No. I don't want to have any conversation with Daddy ever again about Zelda, but we said we'd keep him informed and this is keeping him informed. What he chooses to do with the information is up to him."

"I think you're taking *inform* a little far there. We don't know for sure that Zelda wants him to come down there and get her. We're assuming."

"We've been over this, Kendra. Two days of lying on a beach talking it to death in between bouts of wedding planning didn't give us anything other than this theory."

"Maybe we're not smart enough to figure it out."

"Bite your tongue, woman."

Kendra smiled and chewed, then washed it down with her sweet tea. "I'd feel better if we asked Zelda about this first."

"Not gonna happen."

"I know, just wanted to be on record as having made the suggestion."

"Duly noted. Can we get on the road now?"

"Two minutes." Kendra popped the last bite into her mouth and wadded up her sandwich paper.

"You know, we *could* try to get him to Naples without Zelda knowing and then arrange for them to be in the same room —"

"Tandy Sinclair Kelner, I will drop you where you stand."

"Right. Straightforward, that's the way to go. Let's get home and find Daddy."

Two hours later Tandy crossed her arms over her chest and sat back in the dining room chair that had served as her seat for nearly thirty years. "I don't get it, Daddy."

"What's there to get, honey girl?" Daddy spread his calloused hands wide. "Zelda didn't afford me the luxury of a conversation before getting out of town. I wouldn't have even known about it if I hadn't run into her."

"That's not a reason to just let her go, though." Kendra twirled one spiral curl around her finger. "Is it?"

"I'm just respecting her wishes, girls. She made it clear she wanted to be rid of me, and rid of me she shall be."

"Daddy, you sound like a teenager. You know she wasn't running from you. She was trying to respect your relationship with us."

"Be that as it may, she still left town without so much as a by-your-leave."

"What does that mean, anyway?"

"What?"

"By-your-leave. I've never understood it."

"It's a saying, Tandy, that's all."

"That makes as much sense as you not calling Zelda."

Daddy cleared his throat and got up. "I'm getting some more coffee since this is sounding like a circular conversation. Either of you want a cup?"

"No, thank you." Tandy slumped in her seat.

"I'll take a cup."

Daddy left the room, and Kendra turned to Tandy. "We're not making progress here, T."

"Don't I know it. Who knew Daddy was so stubborn?"

"Um, all of Stars Hill?"

"Yeah, you're right. I didn't think he'd be so stubborn about Zelda though."

"He's a lion with a thorn in his paw."

"You're breaking out Aesop's fables? Who's the mouse?"

"Wrong story. This is the one about 'hurt people, hurt people.' Daddy's hurt, so he's not exactly in a position to reach out to someone else."

"Not even when the someone else is the woman he loves?"

"Especially not then. She hurt him once already, leaving town overnight like that and not giving him the respect of a conversation except when she was caught at Darnell's."

"But she left because of us, not him."

"He knows that, but it doesn't change the fact that she left."

Tandy pushed her chair back and rose. "How long does it take to make a cup of coffee?" She walked into the kitchen and found Daddy staring out the window over the sink. "Penny for your thoughts?"

Daddy turned. "Make it a nickel and you have a deal."

Tandy pulled her jeans pockets out. "Empty. Guess you'll have to put it on my tab."

Daddy's smile was like watching a sunrise over a field of corn — timeless and hopeful.

"Daddy, I don't understand why you won't go down to Florida and tell Zelda how much she means to you."

"There's no sense in telling a woman what she already knows, honey girl."

"Maybe she's forgotten it."

Daddy shook his head. "Zelda's a smart woman. She knows just how I feel about her. By the state of her geography, I'd say it's not enough."

"Oh, Daddy, you can't think that."

"I can and I do."

"You *are* a stubborn old mule."

"Hey, watch who you're calling old, little lady."

"I missed the memo about moving to the kitchen." Kendra entered the room and walked across the worn linoleum to get her coffee. "Did I also miss where Daddy finally came to his senses and booked a flight to Naples?"

Daddy sipped his coffee, then turned his back to them and again gazed out the window. Tandy saw the sunlight shining strong on a field full of green winter wheat.

"No, I don't think I'll be booking any flights anytime soon, girls. Now y'all have men you best be getting on home to."

"But, Daddy —"

"That's enough, Tandy. Let me worry about my own affairs for a little bit."

Tandy closed her mouth and looked at

Kendra.

Kendra finished her coffee, then set the mug on the counter. She moved to Daddy and hugged his back. "If you change your mind, Tandy knows a good Web site to get a cheap flight."

"I'll keep that in mind."

Tandy followed Kendra from the room, certain that an answer lay just beyond their reach. Smart women could solve any problem so long as they put their minds to it. Daddy and Momma had taught that very lesson to all the Sinclair sisters, and it wasn't about to be proven wrong just because Daddy was being bull-headed.

They slid into the gray leather seats of Tandy's BMW, and Tandy turned the ignition key.

Kendra snapped her seat belt. "Got a plan yet?"

"Working on it."

"You realize there may not be a solution we can execute, right?"

Tandy shifted and increased her speed down the straightaway of their country road. "There's always a solution, Ken."

"I didn't say there wasn't. I said there might not be one within our power."

"I'll let you know when I'm ready to throw in the towel. What we need is a male perspective."

"Good thing we've got men in our lives then, hmm?"

"Yep. You go grill Darin, and I'll talk to Clay. I'll call you tonight or tomorrow, and we'll figure out where to go from here."

"What do we do if Darin and Clay tell us to stay out of it?"

"Simple." Tandy shrugged. "We ignore them."

"If we're going to ignore them, why are we consulting them in the first place?"

"Because there's a small chance they'll have good ideas."

"Ah."

Tandy rolled down Lindell and parked beside the diner. "Want to come up and call Darin?"

"I think I'll head in the diner and call him from there. I'm in desperate need of a Diet DP."

"If you see Clay, send him upstairs, will ya?"

"You bet." Kendra opened her door, then turned back to Tandy. "You won't do anything until we talk again, right?"

"Right."

"Okay. Thanks for the wedding help."

"My pleasure."

Tandy got out of the car and headed up

the steps to their apartment over the diner. Clay had said he wanted her to talk things over with him more often. Poor guy. He had no idea what she was about to dump into his lap.

SEVENTEEN

Tandy turned the key in the apartment door and walked in. "Honey! I'm home!" A deep *woof!* greeted her. "Cooper, I'm home!" she amended and headed to the bedroom. "Hey, Coop! Did Daddy take good care of you while I was gone?" She unhooked the latch on Cooper's crate and knelt down to scratch her beloved basset hound's ears. "Tell Mommy how many treats he gave you. Did he give you your vitamins?"

"Is that my long lost wife I hear giving her love to our dog instead of her man?"

"Clay!" Tandy jumped up and ran back to the living room. "I can't believe how much I missed you!"

His arms came around her and Tandy fell into his hug. Three days without Clay might as well have been three months.

"Next time you decide to take a Florida vacation, how about packing me a bag?" Clay smoothed her hair back and kissed her.

"Definitely."

"Kendra said I needed to come up here. I left Oscar on the grill. What's up?"

"We had a talk with Daddy."

"Oh, no." Clay pulled her onto his lap as he sank into the couch. "And let me guess. He didn't appreciate you meddling in his affairs and told you to leave well-enough alone."

"Sort of. He said he didn't see a reason to go get Zelda in Florida and that if she wanted to come back, she'd be back by now." Tandy finished giving him the rest of the conversation.

Clay rested his head on the back of the couch and stared into space. Tandy leaned into him and enjoyed the feeling of warmth from his chest while he thought out the problem. Having someone to share her thoughts and worries with made marriage rock.

"You told him he needed to do this to have a relationship with Zelda?"

Tandy nodded. "We did."

"And you told him that the only reason she left was because of you and Kendra?"

"Yep."

"Shoot, Taz, I'm not sure what to tell you."

Tandy smiled at her pet name, derived from her initials before they married —

TAS. "What if I left you? Wouldn't you have come running after me?"

"Depends on the reason you left."

"Are you serious?"

"Forget it. Never mind. I didn't answer that question. We are not making this about us."

"Too late. You really wouldn't come after me?"

"I'd follow you to the ends of the earth if I had to."

"That's better." She snuggled back into him again. "Which is why I don't understand why Daddy won't at least follow Zelda down to Florida."

"Your daddy never struck me as a beggar."

"He wouldn't be begging!"

"Yeah, he would."

"Oh, he would not, Clay. He'd be courting her."

"I'm pretty sure he did plenty of that right here in Stars Hill. And he's got a point. Whatever he gave her here wasn't enough to keep her or bring her back once you and Kendra apologized."

"But —"

"Stop and think about it for a second, Taz. Your daddy spent over a decade mourning your mom. He finally allows himself to care about a woman again, and she up and leaves him because of something his daughters said to her. Can't you see how he'd want to wash his hands of that? Shoot, the more I think about it, the more I wonder if Zelda doesn't *deserve* to be left down in Florida."

"Clay, you don't mean that."

"I might."

"But all she wants is some romance."

"She had plenty of that here in Stars Hill. And if she came back, I'm sure she'd have plenty more."

"But then she'd be the widow woman chasing after a man."

"No she wouldn't. She'd be the woman who came back to her man after his daughters apologized."

"You are *not* helping the situation."

"Sorry. Them's the breaks of the game when you force your man to talk about romance. Besides, I haven't seen my wife in three days, and now that I have her all to myself, there are much more important things to discuss than her daddy's love life." He tilted her back onto the couch and Tandy melted at the touch of his lips to hers. He slid a hand beneath her head and drew back. "You know I love you?"

"Yep."

"And that if you ever decide to hightail it

to Florida, I'll be right behind you?"

"You'd better."

He kissed her again and happiness flooded through her. The day she'd left Stars Hill, no one could have made her believe she would end up back in Clay Kelner's arms.

But that's right where I am. And I can't think of anywhere else more perfect for me.

Zelda must not feel this way about Daddy. If she did, Clay was right. She'd be back in Stars Hill the second Kendra and Tandy apologized to her. Which made Tandy wonder just what kind of trick Zelda was trying to pull.

"Hello?" Laughter bubbled across Clay's voice. "Welcome back to the room. I'm Clay, the man kissing you?"

"Sorry, sorry. I can't get this Zelda thing out of my mind."

"You realize this borders on obsession."

"I'm not obsessed. I'm concerned about Daddy." Clay rolled off of her, and the cold that swept in made her think Zelda and Daddy should figure out their own worries. "I'm over it now. Come back here."

Clay pulled back, his grin in place. "Not a chance. Go find the phone and call a scrapping night with the sisters."

"But I just got home. You want me to spend the rest of the night over at Daddy's scrapbooking?"

"I want you to do whatever it takes to work this out in your head so when you're here with me, you're *here* with me." He reached behind and plucked the cordless from its cradle, then tossed it to her. "Here. Start with Ken. I'll bet she's not paying any more attention to Darin than you are to me."

She caught the phone and looked at him over its top. "I love how you know me."

"Ditto." He stood and patted her knee. "I'm going to go see if Oscar's burned the place out from under us yet. Give me a call when you've figured things out."

"Thanks, sweetie."

He gave her a quick peck, then headed for the door. "Just remember this when I can't figure out a chord and Darin wants an extra hour of band practice!"

She chuckled and dialed.

"Hello?"

"Ken, it's me."

"Hey, me. Either Clay's at the diner or you guys have picked up speed."

"He went back down to the diner. I'm calling a scrapping night."

"Something happen with you two?"

"No! No, not with us. I can't get this thing with Daddy and Zelda out of my head."

Kendra's sigh buzzed over the phone line. "Me either. Darin told me if I didn't find another topic of conversation he'd turn on the game."

"Which explains the squeak of gym shoes in the background right now. Basketball?"

"Of course."

"So you're free to scrap?"

"Free as a bird. Who am I calling?"

"You take care of Meg. I'll call Joy."

"Roger. See you in thirty?"

"Yep."

She then dialed Joy's house.

"Lasky residence."

"I'm calling a scrapping night."

"You're too much of a newlywed to need a scrapping night."

"Not for me. For Daddy and Zelda."

"Oh, all right. I'll wrap up this dish then. Half an hour?"

"See you at Daddy's."

Tandy cut the connection and nibbled on the blunted antenna of the phone. Cooper came to rest at her feet, plopping his big basset head down on her shoe.

"Want to go see Daddy, Coop?"

Cooper woofed, his tail thumping the floor.

"I wonder if Daddy misses you as much as you miss him?"

Cooper turned mournful eyes her way.

"You're not fooling me, little guy. I know you're only in it for the treats."

His thumping tail picked up rhythm at the magic word.

"Come on then. We better get in the car before you beat a hole in my floor."

Cooper woofed again and waddled his way after her out of the apartment and down the stairs. Tandy tried to decide if this was a good idea. On the one hand, Daddy might not take too kindly to the sisters having a scrapping night about his relationship. Scrapping nights were normally reserved for issues the sisters couldn't face alone.

On the other, what he didn't know could help him.

"It has been entirely too long since our last scrapping night. I can't even remember —"

"Kendra's issues with Darin." Meg cut into Joy's musings.

"We had a scrapping night over that?" Kendra pulled her scrapping materials off the shelf and brought them to the big square table. "I don't remember."

"Well, we did." Meg dumped a bag of embellishments on the table. "Matter of fact, I don't know if any of us would end up with our happily-ever-afters without scrapping nights."

Tandy scraped her hair off her face and began twisting it into a knot. "Which is why we needed to have one tonight. Daddy should get his happily-ever-after, and unless we do something, he and Zelda are going to mule-head their way into a lifetime of loneliness."

"Mule-head?" Joy raised a perfectly plucked brow.

"You've got a better verb?" Little curls of copper escaped her hold and gathered around Tandy's nape.

"Not off the top of my head."

"Then don't knock mine."

"Touchy, touchy."

"Sorry. You're right. I'm tired and grouchy and want a fix to this whole thing since I'm the reason it's messed up in the first place."

"Hey," Kendra's tone scolded, "we said we were sorry."

"Yeah, but she never would have gone to Florida in the first place if she hadn't heard me outlining my Rude Plan."

Meg stretched her neck. "Water under the bridge, T. Focus on the here and now."

"Okay, here and now we have a stubborn old woman and an equally stubborn old man, both of whom are somehow in love with each other but determined not to be together until the other one caves in."

"And you think Zelda isn't coming back because she wants Daddy to come after her?" Joy leaned her chin onto a propped elbow. "That seems awfully manipulative for her. I ascertained Zelda to be a rather straightforward woman."

"I can't help what you *ascertained.* There's no other reason for her to sit down there alone unless she was lying about forgiving Kendra and me."

"She wasn't lying about that." Kendra's giant gold hoops swayed from her ears as she shook her head. "Sure as I'm standing here, she forgave us, free and clear."

"She didn't *say* though that she wanted Daddy to come to Florida."

"No, she said that it wasn't what Daddy had done, but what he hadn't done."

"Maybe she means he hasn't proposed."

"That can't be it. She knows he was about to. She heard us talking about the ring."

"You're certain? She heard your entire conversation?" Joy placed a picture in her cutter. "Think back, girls."

Tandy and Kendra looked at each other. Kendra spoke first. "I can't be sure."

Tandy shook her head, allowing a couple more tendrils to escape her hair knot. "Me either."

"All right, so perhaps what Zelda wants isn't an in-person appearance by Daddy, but a little box with a shiny rock inside."

"Here's an idea — let's call her and ask." Meg mumbled the comment, but all the sisters caught her words.

Tandy stuffed her hair back into its knot. "We did that already, Meg. She wouldn't tell us."

"Because she doesn't want us meddling?"

"That, or she's embarrassed, or she doesn't know herself what she wants, or she wanted to break up with Daddy anyway and this just gave her an opportunity. I don't know. I'm not a mind reader."

"Yet that's what we're sitting here trying to do."

"Hey, it's worked in the past."

"Yeah, because we've tried to figure out people we know. Darin and Clay and one another. But this time we're talking about a woman none of us has taken the time to really know. Which one of us has gone out of our way to be nice to her?"

Kendra arched a brow. "You think if we'd been nice she would tell us what she wants?"

"I think we'd be in a much better position than we are right now."

Tandy huffed. "Okay, Meg, if we can't define the problem, then how do we fix it?"

"Maybe we don't this time. Maybe we let Daddy deal with his own life."

"We do *not* have scrapping nights just to leave things alone." Kendra shook her head.

Meg shrugged, then talked around the slip of ribbon between her lips. "First time for everything."

"Okay, wait." Kendra spread her hands wide on the table. "We may not know Zelda, but we do know Daddy. Can't we come up with a plan of action based on him?"

Tandy distressed the edge of a piece of cardstock. "A plan of action to overcome what? We don't even know for sure what it is that Zelda wants."

"I still say she wants him to come down there and sweep her off her feet. He'd have done it for Momma."

"Momma would never have left like this, Ken." Tandy rolled glue onto the page.

"Yeah, well, I think we've established that Zelda is about as far from Momma as my bank account is from Donald Trump's."

Tandy held up her layout and eyed it critically. "You're right though about most women wanting to be swept off their feet. That's what we get for growing up watching *Cinderella* and reading romance novels."

Meg's head raised. "Hey, don't knock romance novels. Jamison and I happen to have just made a blissful memory with one not too long ago."

"Eww." Kendra held up her hand. "Save the details, please."

Meg gave a devilish grin and refocused on her work. "Fine, fine, but don't forget which sister to call after you and Darin are married."

"Duly noted. Can we get back to the matter at hand?"

Tandy slid a completed layout into its protective sleeve. "I think we'd decided there isn't much we can do."

Kendra tossed her handful of photos on the table. "There's always something to be done. The problem here is that we're working without fuel. I'm going to raid the pantry for chocolate. Anybody coming with me?"

"Sure." Tandy slid off her stool. "I'm at a good stopping point anyway. Joy?"

"Hmm? Oh no, you two go on ahead. I want to get this journaling done while it's fresh in my mind." She held up a picture of Dr. Murray's office door. "I plan to capture every detail of this process until I affix a picture of our little girl in here one day soon."

Tandy smiled. "Good idea. Meg?"

Meg's brow furrowed as she looked in

Joy's direction, peering at the layout Joy just laid down. "Nope. Bring back some for me, though."

"Will do."

Tandy and Kendra turned and made their way down the creaking old stairs. Tandy's mind was so focused on thinking through the Daddy/Zelda problem that she didn't see Kendra stop in front of her.

"Oof!"

"Shh!" Kendra held a finger to her lips and patted the air in a 'quiet down' motion. Then she pointed to Daddy's closed bedroom door.

"Zelda, you're not being reasonable." Daddy's muffled voice came through the heavy oak, and Tandy leaned forward over Kendra's back. "Tell me what it is you want and I'll give it to you."

Tandy pecked Kendra's back until her sister turned around. *"What?"* Kendra hissed.

"We shouldn't be listening to this."

"Says the sister who called a scrapping night to figure out how to get them back together. Now hush up." Kendra waved her hand and pressed her ear back to the door.

Tandy gave up and followed suit.

"I haven't ever been a mind reader, woman. I've told you that from the beginning. I've said I love you, I've asked you to come back. I'm hard pressed to know what it is I'm not doing."

Silence blanketed the hallway while the sisters held their breath.

"All right then, if that's what you choose, then all right. Not much I can do about it, I suppose."

Silence again. Shoots of pain rose up Tandy's lower back from her awkward position bent over Kendra. She nudged Kendra with her knee, but Ken wasn't budging.

"Good night to you too."

Tandy and Kendra straightened and shot down the hallway and final staircase as quickly and silently as possible. They didn't speak until they reached the kitchen and were staring into the refrigerator.

"You think he's giving up?" Kendra pulled pudding cups and Cool Whip from the refrigerator.

Tandy took down an Oreo cookie pie crust. "Sure sounded that way to me. We're doing Oreo pie here, I suppose?"

Kendra nodded and tossed more ingredients onto the counter. "I'm hoping it's enough to see us through the night. You pour the milk. I'll put all this in the pie dish. I think we should wait until we're back upstairs and see what Meg and Joy have to say about all this."

"It's not like him to give up."

"No, it's not."

They finished assembling the dessert and milk glasses as fast as they could, then placed it all on a white wooden tray and climbed the steep stairs to the scrapping room.

"Okay, we've got chocolate, milk, and more info to throw into the mix," Kendra announced and set the tray down. "Come and get it!"

"Ooh! Oreo pie!" Meg scooted around the table. "I haven't had Oreo pie in forever."

"You haven't taught your kids to make it for you by now?" Tandy cut a piece and licked the excess from her finger. "What kind of mother are you?"

"The kind who thinks my kids don't exist to be my slaves." Meg scooped up the pie and snatched a fork. "I'll take that, thank you."

Tandy cut another piece. "They may not be slaves, but they could at least be little servants for a day." She slid the plate down the table to Joy. "Here, sis."

"Thank you." Joy stopped the plate with her hand, then went back to her rub-on letters. "I need to finish this title before I give myself a break. Did you say something about information?"

"Yep." Kendra took the next plate and, holding it aloft, sailed around the table to her stool. "We overheard Daddy on the phone with Zelda."

"No!" Meg's mouth was full of pie. "And you *listened?*"

Tandy put a piece for herself on a plate, then settled onto her seat. "Of course we listened. How else could we figure out how to help Daddy?"

"First you go through his drawers; now you're listening to his phone calls." Joy shook her head, her ebony hair swaying like rich velvet curtains on either side of her pale cheeks.

"Yeah, yeah, we're awful. Can we focus on the important part here — Daddy talking to Zelda?" Kendra twirled her spoon in a "go on" motion.

"Right. Here's what we heard." Tandy filled them in.

Joy finally turned her eyes from her layout. "Daddy's giving up?"

"Sounded like it to us." Kendra nodded.

"That can't be right."

"That's what we thought." Tandy licked her fork. "But that *is* what he said."

Meg gulped her milk. "Then he has something else up his sleeve. Daddy doesn't give up on something he wants."

"Or someone he loves," Joy affirmed. "We're all proof of that."

"I only know what we heard, and we heard him tell her if that's what she wanted, then he'd say good-bye."

The sound of forks clinking on plates filled the sisters' shocked silence. Tandy finished her dessert and moved to cut another piece. *Thank goodness Kendra's wedding isn't for a long time. I'll have plenty of months to lose weight for a bridesmaid dress.*

"Ladies, I think we're faced with only one option." Joy's plate was perfectly clean in every area save the three bites of pie left. The woman even *ate* neatly.

Tandy set her plate back on the wooden tray. "What option would that be?"

"We have to send Daddy to Naples, of course." Joy's tone left no room for argument.

Tandy never had been good about honoring such things. "Joy, we've talked about that. First of all, we're not even sure that's what Zelda wants. And even if we were, there's the second of all, which is that Daddy won't go."

Joy shrugged. "Whether Zelda wants him there or not is no longer the issue. If you and Kendra heard this conversation accurately, then the situation has escalated and drastic measures must be taken to keep them together. The most drastic measure is Daddy's going to Florida to see Zelda. So that is what he will do."

"And your plan for getting our daddy to do something he doesn't want to do?"

"Logic."

"You're putting a whole lot of power in something that's failed us many times in the past."

"Kendra, go get Daddy and ask him to come up here for a moment." Joy held up a finger when Kendra opened her mouth to argue. "Get him, Ken."

Kendra closed her mouth and hopped off her stool.

Glad she chose Kendra and not me. Crossing Joy is about as smart as taking a knife to a gunfight.

In what felt like hours but could only have been a couple of minutes, Kendra popped back up the staircase with Daddy right behind.

"You girls got all of life figured out yet?"

"We're working on it, Daddy," Meg assured.

"Good, good. Nice to know the world will keep turning. Kendra says there's something

I can add to the conversation?"

Joy set her tape runner down and turned, squaring her shoulders. "Daddy, you need to go to Florida."

Daddy's face set harder than a glacier in the Arctic Sea. "I'll thank you to stay out of this."

"Keep your gratitude, Daddy. We've discussed this thoroughly and have decided you are being bull-headed, which, in some circumstances, is perfectly fine but not in this one."

"Now listen, little one —"

Joy was having none of it. "No, Daddy, you listen. You raised us to be decent, God-fearing girls with good heads on our shoulders and the ability to see reason, apply logic, and make a plan for attaining our goals. We've done exactly what you and Mother raised us to do, and I do not think it is fair for you to tell us we cannot apply the very lessons you taught simply because the application makes you uncomfortable."

"I didn't raise my daughter to speak to me in this way."

Joy leveled a look that Tandy knew would have sliced through a cement barrier. "You raised your daughter to love you enough to call you on it when you're being a dummy."

Forget pin, a dove's feather could have been heard falling on that floor. The crags in Daddy's face deepened so far the Titanic could have hidden in there and had room for lifeboats.

She may have gone a little far with that one. Though if one of them could get away with that line, it'd be Joy. Still, Daddy wasn't one to take direction from his children, right or not.

Tandy tensed, waiting for Daddy's anger . . . but instead his shoulders slumped and he reached a weathered hand to his face. Wiping away the misery there, he smiled and shook his head.

"Your momma would be real proud of you girls right now."

Joy came up off her stool and walked around to Daddy. Her tiny arms barely fit around his waist, but all the sisters could hear her say, "Well, that's what we thought."

Tandy, Kendra, and Meg joined them in the family hug, and they stood that way for a while. It'd been too long since a group hug — maybe since Momma's stool sat at the table?

Tandy leaned back. "I'll help you find a ticket, Daddy. We can get it tonight if you want."

Daddy just nodded, his eyes glistening a

bit. "I'm not too sure this is what Zelda is after."

Kendra propped a hand on her hip. "Daddy, if Momma had gone running off to Florida before you two got married, what would you have done?"

Daddy's answer came quicker than a frog's tongue on a housefly. "Your momma wouldn't have run off. She'd have stayed to fight it out."

"Then I say either you realize Zelda isn't Momma and make your peace with that or let her go and see if you can't find Momma again in some other woman." Kendra leaned in close and whispered, "Though we Christians have a thing about reincarnation — it doesn't happen. So I'd say your odds of finding Momma again are slim to none." She leaned back and adopted her normal tone again. "So, let's try that again. If Momma had run off to Florida, what would you have done?"

"I'd have gone down there and brought her home."

"Mm-hmm. Sounds about right. Tandy, go over there and find Daddy a ticket. Make sure he doesn't spend all of our inheritance on this silly woman who can't make this a simple process."

"Yeah, horrible woman." Meg rolled her

eyes and resumed her position at the table. "Wanting romance and grand gestures and all. What in the world is she thinking?"

"I'll grant you that, Meg." Kendra shoved her hair back from her face. "I was kidding."

"So long as y'all are handing out the advice and opinions, how about you tell me what you thought of the ring?"

"Ring? What ring?" Tandy kept her wide and innocent eyes focused on the computer screen.

Repressed laughter hummed in Daddy's tone. "The ring I bought for Zelda."

Tandy turned to face him at that admission, but kept her eyes wide. "You bought Zelda a ring?"

"I did, and you know it."

Tandy tossed a glance at Kendra. "How on earth would we know such a thing?"

"Because you make a better lawyer than you do a thief, honey girl. The box wasn't right where I had put it. Either one very kind burglar came through here, or my daughters thought they had a right to go through my things."

Kendra had the grace to look down at that. "We were just making sure of your safety, Daddy. Like with Tyrel back in high school?"

Daddy held up a gnarled finger. "One dif-

209

ference, Kendra, and it's a doozy. God didn't appoint you my parent to watch over me."

Kendra focused on the layout before her. "Yeah, you're right. Sorry."

"Me too," Tandy mumbled.

Daddy waited a beat, then said, "Meg? Joy?"

"We didn't have any part of that, Daddy." Meg couldn't sound more relieved if she tried. "They told us about it afterwards."

"Which isn't to say you wouldn't have joined in if you'd been with them."

Meg looked at Joy, who shook her head. "I'm not sure."

Daddy looped his thumbs in his pockets. "I'll keep that in mind then."

Meg rubbed her temple and let the photo in her hand fall back to the table.

"Your head hurting you again?" Daddy peered at her.

"Not much. I'm tired, is all. I should probably be heading back home pretty soon."

"How about I drive you? Wouldn't want you wrecking that van because your head was hurting."

"I'm fine to drive, Daddy. It's only a headache. It'll go away as soon as I lie down and close my eyes."

Joy poked a hole into the paper tag she held. "You know, you really should go see Dr. Brown, Meg. If you're experiencing migraines that frequently, there might be some change you can make to lessen their impact."

"I don't think they're migraines, exactly." Meg rubbed a bit more, then began packing up her supplies. "I can function with this. You can't function with a migraine, right?"

Kendra dabbed ink on a page. "Maybe there are different levels of migraines. I'm not sure. But I'm with Joy, you should see Dr. Brown and make sure you're okay."

"We can't have you keeling over or anything," Tandy piped up from her place at the computer desk.

"Gee, thanks, sis."

"Don't mention it."

"Hey, before I go, Ken, what's the latest on the wedding? Do you need help with any plans yet?"

"I made some choices while T and I were at the beach in Florida. Don't worry, we can talk it all over later when your head is done pounding."

Meg smiled her thanks and scooped a tote bag onto her shoulder. "Sounds good. See y'all later. Daddy, you let me know when you leave for Florida, and I'll come by and

211

check on the house."

"Will do. You be careful, little girl."

EIGHTEEN

I'm so excited I can hardly stand it. Dr. Murray says that men who suffer from oligospermia still have a chance — albeit small — of getting their partners pregnant naturally.

I don't like the use of this word *partner* rather than *wife.* When did society become so focused on each person doing his or her thing that we forgot we're here for each other? What is this obsessive need to reject commitment?

I do not have time for such rabbit trails, though. I intend to focus all of my mental energy on becoming pregnant, on creating a child. I read a book last week that said I could almost *think* myself into pregnancy.

As Kendra would say, *Yeah, right.*

But there is something to be said for the power of positive thinking. And if a few thoughts a day will make my ovaries more amenable to housing a child, then so be it.

Scott will be home any minute now. I took my temperature, just like Dr. Goodman told me, and it's up a degree and a half. That means I'm ovulating, and *that* means we could get pregnant tonight!

But I won't tell Scott this bit of information. No need to place more pressure on the man. I'm so proud of how he is handling his diagnosis. I wondered if he might lash out in anger or be embarrassed, but Dr. Murray put him at ease.

Thank the Lord for Dr. Murray.

And Frederick's of Hollywood.

I looked at Victoria's Secret, but too much of their stuff doesn't leave much . . . well, *secret* anymore. Plus I'm about a decade older than their obvious intended market.

But Frederick's came through. This red lace and I are going to do our dead-level best to make a baby tonight. I don't know why I think this time will work when it hasn't worked for over a year now. For the first time in many months though, I feel hope. We have a name for the problem we face. And Dr. Murray says if this doesn't work, there's always IVF. We'll try IVF next month if we don't see that extra pink line two weeks from now.

It's odd to have these thoughts in my

mind. They are so unlike me — thoughts of conception and lacy garments and the like. But when life throws a new experience, sometimes we're forced to learn a new lexicon, I suppose.

Daddy and Momma never shied away from topics like these. If Momma were alive, she would have had me at Dr. Goodman's for a frank conversation ages ago. She didn't mind the harsh realities of life and thought the ladylike thing was always to tackle them head on.

I loved that about Momma.

And now Daddy seemed to be following her lead since Tandy got him a ticket down to Florida. Time to tackle that problem head on!

Focus, Joy. Forget Daddy. Forget Zelda. Let everything else pause for this one night and focus on Scott.

Not just because you love him, though you do with all your heart.

Not just because he's wonderful to look at, though he'd give McDreamy a run for his money any day.

Not just because he's your husband, though he makes a terrific one.

But because if you focus on him, the two of you might have something else to focus on in nine months.

I hear his footsteps on the staircase now.

Lord, please don't let him be tired from a long day at the office. Please let him have had a good day that he wants to sit and tell me about.

And please bless what we're about to do.

Two weeks later Tandy and Clay and Darin and Kendra walked through the door of Joe's Jazz Place on a Thursday night. They settled in what had become "their" booth these past few months.

"I love that we have a booth." Tandy slid across the bench seat. "I feel like one of those people in a book or movie."

Kendra picked a piece of lint from the long, black velvet sleeve of her dress. "I know! Me too. And I love having an excuse to get dressed up every now and then."

"Yeah, that's not exactly something we can do at Heartland."

Darin threw his arm across the back of their booth. "Speaking of which, are we going tomorrow night?"

Kendra arched an eyebrow. "Better question — are Daddy and Zelda?"

"Yeah, when are they planning on coming back?" Clay pulled Tandy closer to his side.

Tandy shook her head. "He still isn't sure if she *is* coming back. I talked to him last night and he said he's making progress, whatever that means."

"Did he take the ring with him?"

"Yeah. If he's proposed though, I'd think they'd be back here already, not just making progress."

The opening notes of Harry Connick Jr.'s "I've Got a Great Idea" floated from the piano, and Darin stood. "If we're going to spend the evening talking about Jack and Zelda, let's at least start it off with some dancing." He held a hand out, and Kendra placed hers in it.

"I think that'd be a wonderful start to the evening."

Clay stood as well and affected a mock stance of seriousness — shoulders up, back ramrod straight. "I concur. M'lady, may I have the pleasure of this dance?"

"That is the worst British accent I have ever heard." Tandy laughed and took his hand.

"You expected better? I'm just a diner owner."

Tandy leaned in close as they walked across the dance floor. "You are so much more than that, sweetie."

Clay gave that lopsided smile that made her heart melt and put his arm around her back. "I love you, Mrs. Kelner."

"That's good. Works out well with my plans."

"You've got plans?"

"Oh, yeah." She swayed to the music and laid her head on his shoulder.

But Clay was having none of it. He bumped his shoulder so that she raised her face to him. "Yes?"

"We were talking about plans? Something I should know about here?"

She laid her head back down on his shoulder, keeping her smile a secret. "You're on a need-to-know basis, mister."

"I thought I did away with need-to-know when I left the marines."

"Wasn't it you who told me 'Once a marine, always a marine'?"

"I refuse to answer on the grounds —"

"Yeah, yeah. Just dance."

All too soon Joe played the final notes. Tandy sighed her contentment sound and walked back to the table with Clay, joining Kendra and Darin there.

"I love Harry Connick Jr."

"Hey, watch it, lady."

"Oh, I love you too, you goofball." Kendra gave him a quick peck on the cheek. "I just love Harry in a whole different way. Oh, and Al Green."

"So I've got *two* competitors?"

"Sounds like it."

They settled back into the booth, and Darin leaned across the table to Clay. "Remind me to write enough songs for an entire jazz CD and somehow engineer it to have five that will become part of the fabric of the entire jazz movement."

"Five?"

"I figure I'll never get to Al's level, but five might put me somewhere in his same stratosphere."

"Good plan, my man."

Tandy rolled her eyes, then looked around the room. "I wonder where Cassandra is tonight? I'm getting parched here."

"I'll go ask Joe." Clay left the booth and made his way back around the dance floor to where Joe still danced his fingers across the keys of the baby grand piano.

"Hey, Joe, where's Cassandra tonight? I didn't see her when we came in."

Joe grimaced. "She's got the flu. Left her shivering under a pile of covers with a box of Kleenex and the remote control for company."

"Man, that sounds awful."

Joe nodded. "It is. Only hope I don't get it too."

"Do you guys need some help tonight?"

"Jessica's picking up the slack."

"Jessica? Who's Jessica?"

Joe pointed his chin toward Clay's table. "That's her talking to your gang right now."

Clay turned and saw a woman who was 5'10" if she was an inch. Long jet-black hair hung straighter than the crease on his old dress blues down her back, all the way to her waist, which appeared to be smaller than the width of her hair. Shiny red heels that could double as weapons in a dangerous dark alley dove into the ground on which she stood. As Clay watched, she threw back her head and laughed at whatever Darin had just said.

Kendra didn't look too pleased.

"What's her story?"

"Came up this way from Atlanta about three days ago." Joe continued to play flawlessly while he related what he knew of Jessica. "Somebody downtown told her about me opening this club a few years ago, and she decided to come see for herself. You should have seen Cassandra when she opened the door and saw her standing there."

"Not a great first impression?"

"She was nice enough, but Cassie had that look in her eye like a new lioness was trying to enter the pride."

"Sort of like Kendra looks right now?"

Joe squinted at their table. "Yeah, about like that."

"Does she have a reason to worry?"

"Don't know." Joe embellished the song a bit, then went back to its standard version. "Still working out why she's here in the first place."

"Maybe she came to learn from the jazz master."

"She should head to New Orleans or Memphis then."

Clay patted Joe's shoulder lightly, so as not to affect his playing. "You sell yourself short, my friend." He loped back across the dance floor and arrived at the table in time to hear a voice that had one too many packs of cigarettes saying, ". . . came on up and Joe needed me, so here I am."

"Joe needed you?" Kendra's voice didn't leave her opinion in the realm of secrecy.

"Tonight. Cassandra is sick."

"Joe tells me it's the flu." Clay slid back into his spot by Tandy.

Jessica nodded and her hair swayed out from the sides of her back. "Yeah. She looks awful."

Clay tried to picture the statuesque Cassandra looking anywhere near awful and failed. Either Jessica was an idiot or after more than Joe's jazz knowledge.

"So, can I get you guys something to eat or drink? Joe told me to take good care of you." Jessica turned to smile in Joe's general direction, but her effort was lost as Joe stayed engrossed in the keys before him.

They placed their orders and watched as Jessica walked away.

"Can anyone say 'she-devil'?" Kendra pursed her lips. "Somebody better warn Cassandra."

"Cass is on to her already," Clay advised. "I doubt anybody needs to worry about how this will end up."

"Unless one of us cares about Jessica's hopes and dreams being quashed like a bug."

They looked at each other, but no one spoke.

"Well, all right then."

"Hey, forget her." Darin crossed his arms onto the table and leaned forward. "I think we need to focus on me for a second." His grin belied the joke behind his words.

"Why would we focus on you?" Clay gathered Tandy's hand into his own. "You know how I hate boring conversation."

"Ha ha. This is anything but boring. Unless a certain best man hasn't started planning my bachelor party yet?"

"Bachelor party?"

Clay almost heard Kendra's claws coming out.

Darin turned his head back to Kendra. "Yeah, bachelor party. Long-time tradition? Man goes out and has a grand old time with his buddies before he gets shackled to a woman who wants him home every night for the rest of his life? Ring a bell?"

"I'm gonna ring your bell." Kendra stuffed a curl behind her ear, which set her huge bangle earring to swinging. "You must not know who you're marrying if you think I want you home every night by my side. How am I going to get any painting done? Or sculpting? Or writing? You think I'm going to stop all that just because I'm marrying you?"

"Well, no."

Clay couldn't help but grin at his friend's back-pedaling — and idiocy. He'd have made the same mistake just a few month's ago.

"But when you become Mrs. Darin Spenser —"

"Mrs. Spenser? Who said I was taking your name?"

"You're not?"

Clay leaned in to Tandy's ear. "I'm so glad we're through this part."

Tandy's copper curls tickled his nose

when she nodded. "Yeah, now hush. Nothing on TV is this good."

Kendra ranted on about women's rights and being kept under a man's thumb and all the while Clay sat right beside Tandy, enjoying the warmth of her arm against his and sending up prayers of thanks that they'd made it through the wedding in one piece.

I cannot believe it. I simply cannot believe it. I wonder if my eyes are playing tricks on me? The mind can do that, you know. Thoughts are very powerful and — oh, I've told you about that book I read.

But I've blinked at least a hundred times and it hasn't vanished. It's shaking. I'm fairly certain that's my hand. Though how could I be still right now?

We've done it. Two pink lines.

Two!

No longer that single, solitary one, sitting by itself, waiting on its mate.

Two lines!

We're pregnant!

How should I tell Scott? I can't run into the bedroom screaming like a madwoman. He'll think I've lost my mind.

Besides, he went into the office early this morning. He wanted to finish his work so that we could enjoy the weekend together.

The weekend! Weekends were made for shopping, and I am going to shop at every baby store from here to Nashville and back. A baby. Finally!

I need to think this through, formulate a plan, but I can't get my mind to slow down long enough to even know for sure if this second pink line is real.

It is real. I know it's real. It's right here in my hand.

With two more just like it on the vanity. Of course, I wouldn't rely on one test's results for such a monumental occurrence. I had to verify.

Twice.

And all three of them are screaming double pink lines at me.

Perhaps those articles about getting rid of the stress were right. Less stress equals greater fertility equals greater chance to conceive.

Which makes me wonder how the human population has survived. Didn't the women of old have it much harder than we do today? They walked all over the place, made everything from scratch, and were demoted in the group if they didn't manage to give birth to males.

I'd say that is some serious stress.

I have to think here. Should I make a

special meal and announce our grand success to Scott over candlelight?

That doesn't seem special enough.

Make a reservation in Nashville and tell him across a linen tablecloth with silver utensils sparkling in the light of chandeliers?

He'll know before I tell him if I make reservations.

Oh, heavens, I can't think! I cannot wrap my brain around this! I need Meg. Meg will know how to do this right.

But how do I tell Meg?

Meg won't care how I tell her. She'll simply be happy to hear it. I pick up the phone — my hand won't stop shaking — then put it down. This isn't the sort of news to share on the phone.

I slip on my black Coach pumps — all grand news should be delivered in gorgeous shoes that have stood the test of time — and make my way down the staircase.

I must be extra careful not to trip and fall. I'm walking for two now.

Two!

The keys are there on the kitchen counter where I left them yesterday.

When I didn't know I was pregnant.

Pregnant! What a glorious word!

Hello, world! I'm Joy Sinclair Lasky, and I am pregnant. That's right. Pregnant. Preggo.

Knocked up. Bun in the oven and whatever other crass way people announce that they're growing a human being.

I have a little Lasky growing inside me right now!

The air is frigid when I step into the garage. If it's cold in here, it must be painful outside the garage door. I slip into my Lexus and start the engine, then breathe thanks for the luxury of seat warmers.

I have to keep myself warm. After all, I'm staying warm for two now.

As I drive the short distance to Scott's office, the sky seems bluer somehow. Birds are chirping. Why are birds chirping when it's ten degrees outside?

They must have heard the news.

I'm pregnant!

The clouds are giant and billowing. They look like cotton balls stacked on top of each other and falling over. Their exuberance is perfect. Everyone should be exuberant today.

Everyone!

It isn't long before I pull into the parking lot of Scott's office. He's inside, probably focused on a computer screen or fourteen pounds of closing documents. He has no idea how good his day is about to get!

I open the car door and arctic air rushes

into the compartment like fingers of ice, stealing their way across the leather and into the crevices of my coat. I don't care though. Let the iciness try to find a way inside me. It will melt the moment it hits my heart. A heart that beats above a womb that now has life!

My pumps clop across the pavement and my hand is shaking on the doorknob. This is it!

The receptionist isn't at her usual spot, so I breeze on down the hallway and turn in to Scott's office. He's sitting just where I'd pictured, shirt sleeves rolled up and tanned arms resting on a desk scattered with papers.

"Joy?" He stands and circles the desk, hands outstretched. "Is something wrong?"

I can't help it. A grin befitting a cheerleader besotted by the quarterback splits my face. "No, honey, something is definitely right."

It only takes him a millisecond and that light — so long dimmed in his eyes — begins to burn bright. He grips my elbows. "Are you sure? Are you absolutely certain?"

I nod, the tears starting again and pouring down my face. "We did it! I'm pregnant!"

He pulls me to him, and I wonder if the little one inside can hear the joyous pounding of my heart, of her Daddy's that flutters just below my ear.

"Oh, Joy," Scott breathes and, for the first time in a very long time, I think my name is just right.

NINETEEN

"Tandy Sinclair." Tandy ducked into a corner of Something by Sara and put one hand over her ear so that she could hear the caller on her cell phone. "Hello?"

"Hey, honey girl. Can you hear me?"

"Daddy! Hang on. I'm in Sara's shop and — hang on a second." She wound her way through the sales racks swamped by Stars Hill women on a mission — a bargain-hunting mission — and snagged an open changing room.

"Okay, can you hear me now?"

"Loud and clear. Can you hear me?"

"Like you were standing beside me. Which would be weird since I'm in a dressing room, but that's another story. Where are you?"

"I'm in a truck."

"A truck? That wouldn't happen to be a U-Haul truck, would it?"

"Well, now, let me see. It's white, drives

like a tanker with broken rack and pinion steering, and gets about two miles to the gallon. Yep, I'd say I'm in a U-Haul."

"Then I trust there's a red-headed lady at your side?"

"Present and accounted for."

"Oh, Daddy, that's great!"

Daddy's chuckle had lost the strain of the previous weeks. "You're right about that."

"How'd you finally get her to come back?"

"I'll give you the whole story when we get there. We're probably six hours away still."

"Six hours — how about dinner at Joy's?"

"Sounds good. We'll see you there around seven."

"Seven it is."

Tandy flipped the phone closed and punched the air. "Yes!" she whispered. "Yes! Yes! Thank You, Lord!"

"Do I hear some worshipping going on in my dressing room?" Sara's voice floated over the top of the door.

Tandy ducked her head and walked out. "Sorry about that."

"Never be sorry for telling God you're happy." Sara gave a knowing smile and adjusted the bun of hair at her nape. "Jack headed back home?"

"He is! And Zelda's with him!" Having everyone in your town know your business had its perks.

"And thank heavens for that. I think if he'd have grouched around here any longer, Tanner would have issued some sort of grouch ordinance."

"He *did* get bad before he went down to Florida, didn't he?"

"He passed *bad* when he stood up in the town meeting and told us we should cancel the Iris Festival parade because no fun was worth that much mess."

"I thought Tanner would come up out of his seat."

Sara winked. "He would have if I'd let him."

"Thanks for that."

"Don't mention it."

"I guess I better get back to those racks. If I sit back here much longer, there won't be anything left."

Sara shook her head. "I'm telling you, it gets crazier every year. You'd think these women had never seen a sale."

Tandy walked with Sara out of the fitting room. "Well, a dress sale at Sara's is an event no self-respecting woman should miss."

"Thanks, dear."

"Don't mention it."

Tandy left Sara standing at the entry way

to the dressing room and meandered across the gray carpet back to the spring-clearance rack. Dresses of every hue imaginable hung there — most of them now slipping off their hangers. What was it about a sale that made women forget their manners and let clothes fall to the floor?

Tandy adjusted the straps as she went down the array. Her fingers paused on a gold silk. It flowed from the metal hanger like lava down the side of a volcano. Thick — thicker than any silk had a right to be — and so perfectly gold it looked like light itself. Sara Sykes had always had an expert eye for beautiful clothing, but this was something else entirely. This begged for a night on Broadway, dinner over flickering candlelight at Tavern on the Green. Or better yet, a small, intimate restaurant lit only by wall sconces and blanketed by soft conversation and tinkling glasses. Or a charity ball on a warm Orlando night where partners from the old firm talked it up and, in the end, raked in millions for some deserving organization while holding crackers so delicate they might break under the weight of the caviar.

She couldn't think of a single reason to own this dress. Orlando dinners and New York arts nights were a part of her old life.

The life of an attorney who fought Orlando traffic each morning, worked out in the company gym, and sat at her desk drawing up briefs and answering clients' phone calls. This dress didn't belong in the closet of a small-business owner in the tiny town of Stars Hill, Tennessee. It certainly didn't fit the life of a diner owner's wife. Or a preacher/farmer's daughter.

No reason for this dress to find a new home hanging in her closet.

Other than its perfection.

Tandy picked up the hanger and held the dress before her. Maybe Kendra would let her wear it in the wedding. Its floor length would be formal enough for the occasion unless Kendra decided to get married outdoors or on a beach somewhere.

Even outdoors, the natural color of the dress would be beautiful against a backdrop of leaves and flowers.

She headed for the dressing area again, catching Sara's eye along the way.

Sara looked up from the customer at her side and gave a knowing smile with a little nod.

Tandy walked into the fitting room and quickly disrobed. The cool silk felt nothing like lava as she slid it over her body. It felt like a tall, cool drink on a hot summer's day. She stepped out to the three-way mirror.

Like the blue dress she'd found last year, this dress seemed made for her body. Every stitch sat in the most exquisite spot possible. The folds of draping from her left shoulder to right hip lay in gorgeous arrangement. Not a pull in place.

She returned quickly to her dressing room. Where in the world she'd wear such a dress she didn't know right now. But the fact that this dress would soon be hers had just become a given.

As Tandy arranged the dress back on its hanger, Kendra's voice floated over the door.

"Is she here? Tandy! Tandy, are you in here?"

Tandy opened the fitting room door and stepped out. "Yeah, Ken. What's going on?"

"A-ha! I knew you wouldn't miss this sale! What'd you find?"

"A to-die-for gold dress." Tandy turned back and snagged the hanger. "Look at this. Isn't it divine?" She laid an arm behind the dress and brought the fabric forward so that it caught the light.

"Wow, that's stunning."

"I kind of thought so."

"What am I saying? I didn't hunt you

down all over town to talk about a dress. I've got news!"

"I already talked to Daddy. That reminds me, I need to call Joy and arrange dinner at her house."

"Daddy's on his way home?"

"Isn't that your big news?"

"No! But that's great news too."

"Wait, I'm confused. What's the news?"

"Joy's pregnant!"

"You're lying!"

"Nope." Kendra jumped up and down. "Can you believe it? Meg called me and told me to come find you."

"That's incredible! She's pregnant? Really? For sure?"

Kendra's curls shook wildly as she nodded. "Yep! You know Joy, she wouldn't rely on one test. She took three."

"*Three* tests?"

"We're talking about Joy here."

"Who confirmed with three sources which pregnancy test gave the most reliable results before buying her first one." Tandy hung the dress back on the door hook so she could jump up and down too. "Joy's pregnant!" She grabbed Kendra's hands and they danced around the dressing room like eight-year-olds with new party dresses.

Sara peeked her head around the corner.

"Anything you'd like to share with the rest of the store, ladies?"

"Joy's pregnant!" The sisters blurted out in unison.

Sara's face lit up like the Christmas tree in Rockefeller Center. "Oh my stars, that's wonderful!"

Tandy's cheeks ached from the constant grin. "We think so!"

"Boy or girl?"

That put a stop to the jumping. "Do we know?" Tandy asked.

Kendra quirked her lips. "Meg didn't say. Call Joy."

Tandy tugged her cell phone from her jeans pocket and punched in the memory number for Joy's house.

"Lasky residence."

"You're pregnant!"

"I know!" Joy's voice rang more loudly than anytime Tandy could recall from childhood. Happiness infused it with such energy, it almost sounded like a different person. "Isn't it fabulous?"

"It's fantastic! Wonderful! Stupendous! Amazing!"

"And more!"

"Am I getting a niece or nephew?"

"We won't know for a few months yet. For now, I'm thinking green and yellow."

Of course Joy had already begun thinking through the color scheme for the nursery. "Okay. Oh, Daddy and Zelda are on their way back. Can we do dinner at your house tonight?"

"Sure! Invite the whole town, if you want. How many courses? I can conquer entire galaxies today! I am woman, hear me roar!"

Tandy rolled her eyes. "Just the fam, this time. But you get ready to be pestered for details, baby sister."

"You know, you'll need to stop calling me that once the baby is here."

"Um, no. Why would I do that?"

"Because you'll want to be a good aunt and reinforce my parental authority. Being called *baby* certainly doesn't give the illusion of authority."

"Oh, honey, what I call you in front of the little tyke is the least of your worries. I'll have Little Lasky addicted to chocolate before we celebrate the first birthday."

"No, you won't! Chocolate is bad for babies."

"Chocolate is a major food group. Accept it. Now back to dinner. Do I need to bring or buy anything?"

"No, I'm sure I have plenty here for us. Where are you?"

"Sara's shop."

"Feel like doing some baby shopping?"

"Absolutely. Hang on. Ken's right here. Let me see what she's doing." She held her hand over the mouthpiece and said, "Hey, Ken. Joy wants to go baby shopping right now. You in?"

"I'm more in than an Olsen twin on the cover of *Vogue*."

Tandy went back to the phone. "She's in. Want to grab Meg and meet us down here?"

"I need to do a little prep work for dinner. Let's see, it's about ten now. How about I meet you for lunch over at the diner and we'll go from there?"

"Sounds good. See ya soon, preggo!"

Joy laughed. "Enjoy it while you can."

"I intend to." Tandy flipped the phone closed and picked her dress up off its hook. "Come on, Ken. Let's see what else is out there and run over to the bookstore before we hit Clay's."

"The bookstore?"

"We're going to need baby books for Joy!"

"Oh, right."

Kendra followed Tandy to the cash register and waited while she paid for the beautiful gold dress.

"Where are you wearing that?"

Tandy shrugged. "I'm not sure yet. I just have to have it."

"I get it." Kendra nodded and fished a piece of gum from her giant red purse. "Never leave a perfect dress behind."

"They should make a bumper sticker out of that."

"Or a T-shirt."

"Speaking of which, we're running low on Sisters, Ink shirts."

"I'll order more when we get back to the office." Tandy signed the charge slip that Sara slid across the counter, then took her bag. "Thanks, Sara."

"My pleasure. You tell Joy I'm going through the maternity catalogs tonight."

"I will. She'll be thrilled!"

Kendra and Tandy left the store, turning left down the sidewalk toward Darin's and the bookstore. "I can't believe she's finally pregnant."

"Me either. How cool is this?"

"I wonder how many lists she's made already?"

"Knowing Joy, at least five." Kendra ticked them off on her fingers. "Nursery list, hospital list, pregnancy list, sister list, Daddy list."

Tandy stuffed her hands in her jacket pockets. "Why would we get lists?"

"You think she's going to leave our actions to chance?"

"Right, right." Tandy grinned. "Still, I can put up with lists for the next nine months.

"If it means I get to see a real smile back on Joy's face, me too."

They stopped at the corner, waiting on a car to turn onto Lindell. "She's finally pregnant." Tandy bounced on her toes.

The car pulled forward and Kendra hopped off the curb and into the street. "I know! We're going to be aunts . . . again!"

Twenty

Nearly an hour later Kendra stabbed her fork into a Caesar salad. "I am *so* ready to get married and quit dieting to fit in a wedding dress."

"Ooh, I remember that." Tandy licked the ice cream from her spoon.

"You ought to be dieting too, T. You've got a bridesmaid's dress to wear, you know."

"I know you're not sitting there telling me to lose weight."

"I would never dream of such."

"That's what I thought." Tandy scooped more ice cream onto her spoon. Closing her eyes, she dumped the load of sugar into her mouth and smiled. "Mmm."

"I won't tell you to lose weight if you don't enjoy your sugar quite so much in front of me."

Tandy swallowed and licked her lips. "Deal. But I don't think Darin will care if you've got five extra pounds on your frame."

"Oh, he won't. He's already told me he loves every square inch of me."

"Then why the diet?"

"We aren't married yet. That means there are a lot of square inches he has yet to see, and *those* inches tend to look a little better when they're thinner."

Tandy threw her head back and laughed while Kendra stabbed her salad again. "So it's not the wedding dress you're worried about."

"No, it's the wedding night."

Tandy dug her spoon into the ice cream. "Trust me, Ken. He won't be noticing five extra pounds of anything that night."

"In that case, hand me your spoon."

Tandy turned the handle toward Kendra and held it across the table. "Happy to contribute to your delinquency."

Kendra held the now-full spoon before her mouth. "As always."

"You two are hopeless." Joy unwound her baby-blue cashmere scarf and folded it over a wrist. "Kendra, I can't believe you're eating ice cream when you have a wedding dress to fit into."

"Old subject, sis." Tandy scooted over to make room. "How are you feeling?"

Joy's grin could have lit the midnight skies. "Excited! Nervous. Happy. Mixed up.

Elated."

"Sara said to tell you she's shopping the maternity catalogs tonight."

"Good. I don't want to go to Nashville every time I need a new maternity top or dress."

"And if Sara picks it out, you know it will be gorgeous on you." Kendra set her spoon in the ice cream. "If we're not shopping for maternity clothes, I assume we're finding nursery stuff?"

"Yes. I told Tandy green and yellow. I was thinking maybe *Wind in the Willows* could be our theme."

"Frog and Toad?"

"Toad, yes, frog, no."

"Toad is such an ugly word," Tandy mused. "I mean, think about it. Toes are ugly enough as it is. Then we tack on a *d* and it sounds like somebody either got hit by a foot or developed some deathly disease."

Kendra looked at Tandy and blinked. "You're weird."

"Thank you."

"As I was saying," Joy cut a glance at Tandy before focusing on Kendra, "I want to do a *Wind in the Willows* theme. That's yellow and green, which will work if I have a boy or girl."

"But if you have a girl, wouldn't you want pink?"

"No, I don't think so. Everyone does pink. I can dress her in pink, of course, and maybe add a pink ruffle to the bed-skirt of the crib. But yellow and green would be different."

"Then green and yellow it is." Kendra stood. "Ready to go?" Joy and Tandy joined her. "Where should we start?"

"USA Baby in Franklin."

It took Tandy a couple steps to realize Kendra and Joy had stopped walking with her. She turned back. "What?"

"It occurred to us that you're certainly up on your baby store knowledge." Joy wound the scarf back around her neck.

Tandy sniffed. "I'm not expecting, if that's what you're implying. But I like to be prepared, just in case."

"Translation: They're trying to get pregnant." Kendra buttoned her coat.

The little bell jangled over the door as they left Clay's.

"Are you, Tandy?" Joy crossed her arms to ward off the chilly blast of air. "Why didn't you say anything? We could have our babies together!"

"Whoa, slow down there. We're not exactly *trying.*" Tandy pulled her hands into her coat sleeves. "We're just not doing anything to prevent it."

"Ah, I see." Joy pulled gloves from her pocket that were the same shade of pale blue as her scarf. "Then today will be good research for you."

As if everyone researches things to death before taking action. "Are we taking my car?"

"Let's take mine. Bigger trunk." Joy pointed behind the diner. "It's back here."

The girls hunched their shoulders and moved down the sidewalk hurriedly. The car beeped its greeting when Joy pressed the unlock button.

"Good grief, it's stupid cold." Tandy jerked open the back door and escaped into the car.

Joy started the car and adjusted the heat setting to its highest. "Amen to that."

"Ugh, I can't think straight with that wind blowing up one side of me and down the other." Kendra rubbed her hands together. "It's February, for goodness sake, when are we set for warm weather?"

"I'll bet we see some pretty days by the end of the month," Joy comforted. "I usually plant my spring bulbs the first week of March, and the ground has to be thawed for that."

"Ooh! I hope you have a girl. You can

teach her all about spring planting."

"I could teach a boy that too."

"Yeah, but he won't care about tulips and daffodils. He'll want to grow stinkweed and moss."

Joy put the car in gear and backed out of the parking space. "Well, we won't be growing stinkweed anytime soon, but moss has a certain nostalgia about it."

"You're weird too." Kendra pulled her gloves off now that the car was heating up.

"Welcome to the club," Tandy piped up from the back.

"Thank you." Joy pointed the car in the direction of the interstate.

I am on my way to purchase items for my baby's nursery.

I am pregnant.

Every time I think that, I wonder if I've lost my mind. If I might be lying in a hospital bed somewhere, totally oblivious to the noises around me, ensconced in my own version of reality.

I wouldn't, however, make up stinkweed.

This must be real.

I'm having a baby! Scott is happier than he was the day we wed. So much joy lit his eyes when I shared the news that it almost hid the tinge of relief there as well.

Oh, let him be relieved. Let him be whatever he wants.

We're going to be parents!

I asked him if we should plan a trip to
China. I feel like I should see where I was
born so that I can tell my little one at least
a bit about her mother's heritage. At first
Scott looked skeptical — eyebrows raised
and that thought wrinkle going across his
brow. But I explained that a child needs to
know his or her heritage, and I think he
knows I meant me more than the baby.

The baby! I can see the finished nursery
in my mind already. I'll sew a yellow quilt
with pale green toads and white lily pads
trimmed in yellow. I'll make white curtains
with eyelet lace if it's a girl, and green polka
dot trim if it's a boy. Either way, the crib
will, of course, be white. Nothing but white
for this pure presence growing in me.

My belly is as flat as it was yesterday. Meg
says I won't begin to change shape for the
first few months. She had a small belly at
four months. That's two months away. Two
months and two weeks, if I've kept my days
of the month correctly.

And I know I've kept my days of the
month correctly. I've kept them flawlessly
for over a year. I'm six weeks pregnant.
There is a six-week peanut right now multi-

plying as fast as he or she can.

I wonder if this is how my mother felt. Not *mother* as in *Momma* here — but the one who gave birth to me. The woman who might at this very moment be walking a street somewhere in the massive land of China, wondering whatever happened to her little girl with the strange blue eyes.

I still do not know if my blue eyes caused her to leave me on that orphanage doorstep. Isn't that something I should find out if I'm about to give birth myself? This little one will want to know the medical history of my family. *I* want to know. Does my baby — baby! — have a risk of experiencing some awful disease because my body carries the genetic trait for it?

But China is teeming with millions of people — 1.3 billion according to my research. Surely hundreds of thousands of the women there gave up a little girl nearly three decades ago. Maybe even millions.

I should find her. Soon. Whoever she is, she's about to be a grandma.

TWENTY-ONE

"Do either of you ever wonder about your birth mothers?"

Kendra would have fallen out of her seat if it wouldn't insult the Lexus. "You're kidding, right?"

"No, why would I kid about such a thing?"

"Why would you want to go find a woman who left you crying on a doorstep?" Tandy met Joy's eyes in the rearview mirror.

Joy lifted a small shoulder. "I don't know. I've been wondering about her lately though."

"Because you're going to be a mother yourself."

"Maybe." Joy thought about it, then nodded. "Probably. I think it matters less why I'm thinking about her than that I'm thinking about her at all. Do you think I should find her?"

"Now I know you're kidding." Kendra turned the radio down. "You're going to comb through millions of people and hope one of them says, 'Yeah, I gave birth twenty-eight years ago to a little girl that I left at an orphanage with a note.' "

"It's over a billion people, Ken, and I thought I might start at the orphanage."

"But that place isn't even in operation anymore. Remember? We got the letter when you were in junior high."

"Surely someone who worked there is still alive. They've probably gone on to work for another orphanage."

"I think you're nuts." Kendra raised the volume again. "Let it go. Focus on your own kid and don't spend time thinking about a woman who's shown no sign for twenty-eight years of thinking about you."

She didn't mean that last part to sound so harsh, but birth mothers were best left alone.

Especially when the daughter is carrying a grandchild.

Ten minutes later the sisters stepped from the car in the USA Baby parking lot. Joy hefted her purse higher on her shoulder. Her lips compressed into a thin line. "Ladies, we are on a mission."

"To create the best baby nursery since Hannah was born!" Tandy lifted a foot to step forward, but Joy's hand on her elbow halted her stride.

"No, you and Kendra share the same mission. Don't let me purchase everything in that store."

Kendra laughed, tucking her arm through Joy's. "Come on, baby sister. We'll guard your checkbook."

They walked together into the store and paused in the doorway. Joy's eyes grew wide as she took it in. Painted white wood, oak, mahogany, cherry, walnut — at least seven trees were represented in the cribs lining each wall. Fleur de lis ran amok over one, crying out for a little girl in pink ruffles to take them home. Another with stark bars of missionary style under the clean line of an arch called for a little boy with a heart for baseball and dirt. Changing tables, diaper pails, bunk beds, cribs, rockers, strollers, curtains, rugs, and even matching wicker baskets to store clean diapers had been arranged in orderly fashion.

Joy crossed her arms. "I should have brought Scott. He should see this."

Tandy couldn't take her eyes from a painted white set in the far corner with a splash of red ladybugs in the curtains and fabric. "No, he shouldn't. If I'm overwhelmed, I pity the man who walks in here."

"Good point."

They were still staring when a saleslady in a long, dove-gray skirt, ivory cashmere sweater set, black boots, and pearls strode forward. "Welcome to USA Baby. I'm Noni. Is someone expecting?"

"That would be me." Joy stepped forward and held up her hand like a second-grader on the first day of school.

"Congratulations!"

"Thank you."

"When are you due?"

"September."

"Oh! You found out early then."

"We've been trying for a while," Joy admitted.

Noni looked between the sisters, a crease forming on her brow. "All right then."

"Not the three of us." Kendra rolled her eyes. "She and her *husband* have been trying."

Noni's hand flew to her throat, and Tandy couldn't help but notice the veins there.

"Yeah, we're the sisters." She tried to put Noni at ease for her mistake.

"I'm so sorry." Noni laid a hand on Joy's arm. "So, so sorry."

Joy placed her hand over Noni's. "Don't worry a bit about it."

Tandy kept a close eye on the veins in Noni's throat as she swept a hand across the store. "Well, what can I show you? Have you settled on a theme or colors?"

"I have. *The Wind in the Willows.*"

"How lovely!"

"Thank you. I thought I could go with a green and yellow theme, then highlight with pink if I have a girl or blue if I have a boy."

"How sensible of you. And creative! Let's see, I think we have just the thing. Follow me, please."

Joy walked alongside Noni. Kendra and Tandy fell in line. Tandy felt like a baby chick following the mother hen.

"Cluck, cluck," Kendra whispered.

Tandy whipped her head to the side. "That's what I was thinking!"

A grin split Kendra's face. "I know."

"Here we are." Noni turned into a mock nursery. A pale-green crib stood in the center of its back wall. The slats were straight, but each end rose in a French arch and sloped out on the corners in a manner reminiscent of a pagoda.

"It's exquisite!" Joy rushed to the crib like a hungry man to a Big Mac. "And green. I thought I'd have to settle for white, which would have been perfect from a purity standpoint, but maybe a little too girly if I have a boy, now that I think about it further.

Oh, Noni, thank you!"

The elderly woman's face broke into a series of smiles as her wrinkles mirrored the movement of her lips. "My pleasure, child. That's why I'm here."

Joy ran her small hands over the wood, caressing each inch of its top.

Tandy leaned over to Kendra. "I think Joy's in love."

Kendra nodded. "We should meet her new beau."

They walked forward and joined Joy, whose hands had stilled on the wood. "I have to buy this."

Tandy snagged the price tag and turned it over. "That's it, I can't afford kids. Look at this."

Joy and Kendra looked at the tag as well.

Kendra's eyes widened. "For a crib?"

"Hush, girls!" Joy slapped the tag out of Tandy's hand, and Tandy didn't know if she should be more shocked by the price tag or the fact that Joy had just slapped her hand like Momma. "Quality furniture costs money. Besides, I spent less than that on the bed I share with Scott. Shouldn't our baby have something as nice as we do?"

Kendra waved a hand in front of her nose. "Your child is going to stink."

"I beg your pardon?"

"Well, he's going to be so spoiled, we'll smell him coming a mile away."

"Oh, why do I bother with you two?" Joy turned from them and marched over to Noni, who stood waiting at the entrance to the nursery. "I'll take it."

"Wonderful!" Noni clapped her wrinkled hands together, and Tandy was reminded of Jessica Tandy in *Fried Green Tomatoes.*

"Idgy Threadgood would have been even more appalled at the price of that crib," she said from the corner of her mouth.

"Idgy?" Kendra looked lost for a moment, then snapped her fingers. "*Fried Green To-matoes.*"

"You're getting slow in your old age, sis."

Again, they fell in line behind Noni and Joy, whose heads were joined together in conversation as they walked back down the hallway.

"Is it me or do they look like they're planning a frontal?"

They waited with Joy at the counter as she made her purchase and arranged for delivery, which cost even more.

"For that price, shouldn't the thing drive *itself* to Stars Hill?"

Tandy almost laughed, but a laser look from Joy killed the hilarity.

They were almost out the door when

Tandy realized what they'd forgotten. "Stop!" She threw her arm in front of Joy and Kendra.

"What now? Find some new way to tell me how ridiculous and dumb I am to spend money on furniture?" Joy crossed her arms and tapped a foot.

Oh yeah, she had the mother thing down cold already.

"No, we didn't take a picture! How will you scrap this moment?"

"You're right!" Kendra dug around in her bag and pulled a digital camera from it triumphantly. "Aha! Back to the crib, ladies."

They all trouped back to the mock nursery, catching Noni's eye in the process. Noni hurried over as quickly as her wizened legs allowed. "Was there something else I could help you with, dear?"

"Yes, Noni. Could you take our picture, please?"

"I'd be delighted." Noni took the camera from Kendra's outstretched arm and the sisters positioned themselves around the crib.

Tandy saw from the corner of her eye the moment Joy laid a hand on her belly and gave a triumphant smile.

"Say *baby!*"

"Baby!" They chorused and Noni flashed the camera.

"Thanks so much." Kendra popped the camera back in her bag. "We almost had nothing to scrapbook!"

Noni waved to them as they dashed out of the store and back to the Lexus.

"Where to next?" Tandy pulled her seat belt around.

"How about Target? I heard the one in Cool Springs has a pretty good baby section."

"Okay. And after that we could hit the Bombay Kids at the Galleria."

"I thought they went out of business." Kendra buckled her belt and pulled the visor down to check her lip gloss in its mirror.

"You're right. I saw a sign up there the last time we were in." Tandy put a finger to her lip and tilted her head. "When was that? A few weeks? Maybe they're still having the going-out-of-business sale."

"Did someone say *sale?*" Joy's excitement vibrated from her being. "Let's do the mall first. Target is open later anyway."

Satisfied, Kendra snapped the visor closed. "Did you forget you're fixing dinner for the family tonight?"

"Oh, that's right. All right, it's one o'clock

now. I called Daddy and Meg and told them dinner at eight. So we have seven hours. An hour to get home, an hour to get dinner ready, that leaves us five more hours to shop. We can easily do the mall and Target in that time. We'll simply need to come back for the other stores."

Kendra watched cars out the window. "Twist my arm — you're asking for more shopping time?"

"I know. I'm a slave driver."

"Count me in too," Tandy said. "Maybe we can even get Meg to come with us next time. You know, if Jamison will watch the kids. Speaking of which, I'm worried about her. Don't you think she's getting those headaches a little too often?"

"She told me they're mostly from dehydration."

"I don't know, Joy. Meg's a healthy person. She shouldn't get migraines just from not drinking water for a while, should she?"

"Well, what else could it be?"

"I don't know." Kendra pulled her legs into the seat to sit cross-legged. "All I know is just about every time I see her, she's rubbing her temples or reaching for a bottle of aspirin."

"I hadn't noticed it that much," Joy admitted. "I've been so caught up in this baby thing —"

"As well you should be." Tandy reached over the seat and patted Joy's shoulder. "I may be making a mountain out of a mole-hill. I'll talk to her tonight after dinner and see if she's been to see the doctor."

"Let me know what she says."

"You bet."

"So you're going to be a dad." Clay grabbed one end of the golf club with his left hand, the other end with his right. He lifted the club over his head, pulling it back and forth to warm and stretch his muscles. "Think you're ready?"

Scott did some stretching of his own, holding a Big Bertha driver over his head. "You mean to tell me there's a way to get ready for this?"

"Probably not. I meant, have you read all the books, figured out what's going to hap-pen in the delivery room, that kind of thing?"

"Not yet. I figure I have seven months ahead of me. Plenty of time to read and prepare."

Darin pulled a 3-wood from his bag and walked up to the amateur tee. "You better enjoy those seven months. I've had buddies become dads before. This," he waved a hand to encompass the course laid out before them, "will be a thing of your past pretty soon." He knelt and drove a tee into the ground.

"Nah. I'm sure Joy's having a boy, so it'll be important to introduce him to the world of golf at the earliest possible age."

They fell silent as Darin took a couple of practice swings, then addressed his ball. Rearing back, he brought the club down, swung his shoulders and hips, keeping his head level all the while, and made contact.

The ball went sailing high into the air.

Clay whistled low. "Man, you've been working on your swing. That was pretty."

Darin waited until his ball settled about ten yards from the green. "Thanks." He sauntered off the tee.

"You been to golf school and not tell me?" Clay climbed the one-foot hill and took his place between the markers.

"Nope. Just read a *Golf Digest* article about common mistakes in a swing. Guess it took."

Clay addressed his ball, following the same motion as Darin, but his ball shot left rather than straight. "Hooked it," he muttered.

"You're still using that right hand too much," Scott advised.

"I know, I know. Get up here and see if baby news has rattled your swing at all."

Scott climbed the mound and settled his ball on a bright blue tee. "Watch and learn boys." He settled into his stance, cast a final glance at the flag flying above the hole 214 yards away, then focused on his ball and swung.

The little white dot sailed through the air, landing with a short hop and roll on the green to rest not ten feet from the hole.

"That's it, Darin. We've got to get out here more often. We're going to get schooled by an old daddy." He slapped Scott on the back as they walked back to the golf cart.

"An old daddy who's heading out of the country in a few weeks."

"What?" Darin sat down in the cart.

"Joy's got it in her head she needs to see her birth country, or something like that, so we're planning a trip to China next month. Nothing's set in stone yet, but you know how it is when Joy gets something in her head. We'll probably have tickets purchased before we go to bed tonight."

"Wow, that's *intense.*" Scott pressed the gas and the cart shot forward. "You sure that's a good idea?"

"Why wouldn't it be?"

"I don't know." Clay grabbed the side of

the cart as they cut across the fairway toward his errant ball. "I just thought women who were expecting shouldn't be traveling and all. And won't it stress her out to see the orphanage and stuff?"

"What is this, 1979?" Scott shook his head, bringing the cart to a halt by a stand of trees. "I'm sure it will be fine, but we'll check with her doctor just in case."

Clay nodded. "Probably a good idea."

"Knowing Joy though, she's already read fourteen books on the early stages of pregnancy and knows how many breaths per minute she should take to grow the optimum child. I love the woman dearly, but I have never met anyone in my life who plans things to the detail she does."

The guys chuckled as they exited the cart and began scanning the area for the telltale white. "Here it is." Darin picked up the ball and threw it back out onto the fairway. "Wow, that was a pretty stiff wind."

"Oh, so *that's* how we're going to play this." Scott swigged his Diet Coke. "Okay, I see how it is."

Clay pulled an 8-iron from his bag and took off for the ball. "Hey, not all of us have twenty hours a week to golf and call it work."

"And I have to pay for you not choosing a

career that allowed business meetings on the golf course?"

"We can't all be realtors. This town's got to eat, you know."

Darin and Scott sat in the cart and waited for Clay to make his stroke before heading off for their own swings.

Two strokes by Darin and Clay and one stroke by Scott later, they piled back into the cart to drive to the second hole.

"Seriously, man, not to beat a dead horse, but has it sunk in you're about to have a little one running around calling you Daddy?"

Scott steered the cart up a short incline and over a wooden bridge. "Sure it has. We've been trying for this for over a year. I can't believe it's finally happening."

"Oh, you'll believe it all right." Darin nodded. "Just wait until you haven't had a whole night's sleep in two months and you'd give your entire life savings for just twenty-four hours of no crying, feeding, or changing."

Scott twisted in his seat to glance back at Darin. "How do you know so much about this?"

"I have a sister. She has kids. Lots of them." Darin motioned to the cart path. "Watch where you're going."

Scott turned back and jerked the wheel to keep from running off the path. "Thanks."

"No problem."

"Maybe we should save kid talk until we get to the clubhouse."

"I'll amen that." They came to a stop, and Clay stepped out of the cart. "Tandy told me the other night that she thinks it'd be great if we started trying to have kids. I think the woman has lost her mind."

"You haven't even been married a year." Scott propped a foot on the front of the cart.

"Don't tell me, tell her."

Darin laughed. "Man, that's tough."

"Don't laugh." Clay pointed the business end of his club at Darin. "You're marrying her sister. And those two do *everything* together."

Darin's mouth closed faster than a catfish on a wriggling worm.

Not another word was said regarding children until they got to the clubhouse.

Twenty-Two

The sun had long since gone to bed when the various limbs of the Sinclair family tree — including Daddy and Zelda, who'd arrived not a half hour earlier — sat down to dinner at Joy's massive dining room table.

Joy surveyed the elegant array. Tall taper candles flickered from glass holders, which stood at attention in a march down the center of the table. They alternated in baby blue, soft pink, pale green, and yellow. The playful notes of Handel danced around the room, flowing in and out of the lighthearted banter across the white linen table cloth. Joy sighed, utterly content.

"Hey, Joy, have you two thought through names for the little one yet?" Jamison picked up a bowl of green beans and helped himself to a spoonful.

Joy cut her eyes at Scott. "That depends on which of us you ask."

"I think Scott Jr. if it's a boy, and Scotty if

it's a girl."

The sisters groaned. "You can't be serious," Kendra said. "Scotty? For Joy's daughter? That sounds more like a name for a kid of mine, who would inevitably be a tomboy."

"That's what I keep telling him." Joy cut her pork and speared a bite with the sterling silver fork she'd had since the day she married. "I love Madeline, Isabella, or Abigail for a little girl. I'm having a harder time picking out a boy name."

"I like Abigail!" Meg was cutting pieces for Hannah, who sat in a booster chair at her side. "We could call her Abby."

Tandy buttered a roll. "Yeah, but Isabella sounds so romantic." She batted her eyes at Clay across the table.

Clay grinned. "Joy, we get to use Isabella. You can keep Abigail."

"Okay, if you're going to steal my names, I'm not sharing anymore." Joy affected a mock injured tone. "Let's talk about Daddy and Zelda instead. You two want to share with the rest of the family what happened down in Florida?"

Zelda's face heated to the shade of a ripe tomato in June. "Let's just say we worked things out."

Daddy reached to her from his position at head of the table and held her hand. "And thank the good Lord for that miracle."

"Hear, hear." Scott held his glass of water up and each family member followed suit. "To happy times in the family."

"To happy times," they echoed.

Joy chewed her pork and took in the faces of her family sitting around the dining room table. God had blessed them, no doubt. Clay and Tandy with their happy marriage — even if it did take over a decade for them to admit their love for one another. Kendra and Darin planning their own wedding this fall. Meg and Jamison with three beautiful children of their own. Daddy and Zelda, together again. And now she and Scott with a baby on the way.

Life had never been this good for all of them at the same time. Joy took a deep breath and thanked God for His blessings. And hoped her next announcement wouldn't upset Daddy and Zelda's applecart.

She took a deep breath. "While we're all here together, Scott and I want to let you know we're planning a trip to China next month. I mentioned it to the sisters already, Daddy, but I wanted you and Zelda to know as well."

"To China?" Daddy's face tensed. "While you're pregnant? Are you sure that's wise?"

Joy nodded and patted the table. "I talked to Dr. Goodman this afternoon on my way back from Nashville, and he says travel in the first trimester and even into the second is fine, so long as I take it easy, nap often, drink lots of water, and take care of myself."

She waited through the beat of silence in which all the sisters watched for Daddy's reaction. She didn't realize she'd held her breath until its escape caused the candle flame to flicker.

"All right, then," Daddy finally said. "I assume you're going to Changsha?"

"That's our plan, yes." Joy kept her voice small, hoping not to inflict more pain than she'd already caused. "I don't want to disrespect you or Momma, Daddy." She reached across the table and laid a hand on Daddy's tanned arm. "I simply want to be able to tell my child about the country where her mother was born. Do you understand?"

Daddy's smile held decades of wisdom and patience. "Of course I do, honey girl. And don't you worry for a second about anything. Just do me one favor."

"Anything."

"When you go visit that place where we picked you up, you remember that your momma and I will always be thankful to

China for giving us a beautiful little girl."

Tears welled in her eyes and she blinked, feeling them fall down her face. "Thank you, Daddy," she whispered.

"Thank *you.*"

"Aunt Joy, what's for dessert?" James's tinny kid voice cut through the seriousness of the moment.

Joy turned and smiled through her tears. "We're having good, old-fashioned ice cream sundaes. How does that sound?"

"Oh, yum!" James bounced in his chair. "With cherries and everything?"

"Yes, with cherries and everything. Will you help me make them when we're finished with dinner?"

"Yeah!"

"Me too, me too, Aunt Joy," Savannah begged. "I wanna make sundaes."

"Absolutely, Savannah. You two will be my helpers. Now be sure to eat up your green beans so you can have some ice cream!"

Both children dug into their green beans with newfound excitement.

Meg snagged Joy's gaze and mouthed, *Thank you.*

Joy nodded, then turned to Kendra. "Settled on more wedding details yet?"

Kendra looked at Darin. "We're thinking

maybe a destination wedding."

"A what?"

"You know, where you go off to some island or exotic location and get married?"

Tandy joined in. "I thought you were getting married at Grace with gray, white, and red colors?"

"We thought about that, and I still like that idea. But wouldn't it be easier if all of us just hop a plane to the islands or something?"

Daddy set his fork down. "You'd rob Stars Hill of seeing you two get married?"

"Not exactly. We would have a reception when we got back and show the video of the wedding."

Daddy shook his head, but he was smiling. "Of course you'd pick an out-of-the-ordinary way to get married. I'm surprised none of us saw this coming."

"Did you have a particular island in mind?" Joy sipped her water.

"We've been looking at St. Thomas."

"In the Virgin Islands?"

"It's just a thought right now. We have a few weeks before we need to make a firm decision."

"Well, I'm totally in favor of jetting off to the islands for a few days." Meg steered a spoonful of carrots into Hannah's open mouth. "That sounds like heaven on earth with all this cold outside."

Zelda picked a roll from the bread basket. "Darin, what does your family say about this?"

"Keep in mind, my family's not nearly as large as this one, so it's not such a logistical nightmare. They love the idea, but they're cool whether we stay in Stars Hill or go to the islands. My parents will probably be the only ones from my side of the family to come since it would cost a fortune for my sister to get all her kids on a plane."

Kendra looked around the room. "So what do you guys think? Want to go to the islands this fall?"

Tandy slapped the top of the table. "I vote yes."

Joy nodded. "Me too — provided I can take a newborn on the plane."

"Daddy?"

Daddy looked at Zelda, who shrugged. "Why not?"

"Then it's decided. We're getting married in St. Thomas!"

"I've got to find a new bathing suit!" Tandy turned to Clay. "And trunks for you, and island wear for the both of us. How long will we be there?"

"I did a little research on the Internet,

and Darin and I will need to be on the island a full twenty-four hours before we can get our marriage license. So I'm thinking we'll go down three days before the wedding, get the license the following day, go to the beach with everybody the next day, and get married that fourth day."

Meg clapped her hands. "Ooh! The beach! I'll bet the beaches are gorgeous in the Virgin Islands."

"They are. Megan's Bay is rated as the fifth-best beach in the world."

"We're definitely going there then." Meg handed Hannah her Sippy cup.

"Oh, yeah. And there's this gorgeous little church, St. Frederick's. It's over on the resident side of the island. I'll call and see if we can get married there." Kendra clapped her hands. "This is going to be so fun!"

Joy put a pat of butter on her potato. "Do we get to wear island dresses and straw hats?"

"Wouldn't that be perfect? Let's do that! I hadn't even thought of what you would wear in the wedding. I'll bet Sara can find us island dresses."

"We'll go down and see her tomorrow."

"Forget the wedding. Let's get to the important part," Clay cut in. "Darin, where's the honeymoon?"

Darin grinned. "We found this resort on another island, Virgin Gorda. The resort is Little Dix Bay. Looks perfect from the Internet pictures, and it gets great ratings. I think we're going there. I've got to call and check dates and rates."

Zelda sipped her wine. "A baby *and* a wedding! This is going to be an exciting year."

Twenty-Three

I'm running down a hallway, but I cannot get anywhere. Doors are on either side of me, the kind you see in a mental ward — rectangles of glass on their upper halves with thin lines of wire that make a checkerboard pattern and prevent anyone from breaking the glass and escaping.

The floor is slippery and I'm not wearing shoes. Only socks. I can't seem to gain purchase on the tile that's been buffed to a shine. Fluorescent lights overhead are spaced about a foot apart, their hum growing louder every second.

I know the switch is at the end of the hallway, though I have no idea how I know this. The knowledge is of no use at any rate because, no matter how quickly I pump my legs, the switch seems to move further and further away.

My feet finally decide not to cooperate any further and I fall forward, throwing hands out to break my fall, turning my head to prevent a broken nose. I squeeze my eyes shut against the image of a hard white floor rushing to greet me.

I slide down the hallway. At least ten feet. I see two doors pass as I slide, slivers of light shining from under their doors. I hear laughter behind those doors. Not a child's uninhibited, innocent merriment and delight with life. No, this sound is of evil having its way.

I come to rest in a heap, breathing hard. Am I okay? Have I broken anything?

That's when I feel the warmth between my legs.

TWENTY-FOUR

"Clay? Clay!" Tandy flew through the back door of the diner. "Clay! Where are you?"

Clay burst through the swinging doors that separated the kitchen from the diner. "Right here. What's wrong?" One look at Tandy's face and he rushed to her and took her hands in his. "What's happened?"

"It's Joy. She's at the emergency room."

"Let's go."

Clay dialed his cell while they ran to his truck. "Oscar, it's me." Tandy heard him making arrangements for Oscar to take care of the diner, but it seemed as if he stood at the end of a very long tunnel. The sound was there, but muffled. Distant.

Joy in an emergency room. Joy losing the baby. This couldn't be. They'd bought a crib. This couldn't be.

"Hurry, Clay."

He reached across the seat and held her hand and she was grateful for its warmth.

Hers felt like blocks of ice. Useless and frozen.

Stars Hill flew by her window as Clay's hazard lights blinked and he broke every traffic law on the books. Red lights were ignored. Stop signs brushed away like a bad suggestion. They swung into the hospital parking lot six minutes after Tandy had run to the diner — which was six minutes and ten seconds after she'd left the receiver dangling against the wall on the upstairs phone — which was six minutes and sixteen seconds after Meg called to tell her Joy needed them.

She had the door open and her seat belt off before the truck came to a complete halt under the Emergency sign.

"Go," Clay said. "I'll park and come in."

Go she did. Through the double doors that whooshed open, down the long hallway tiled in white that had been buffed so hard it shone like wax on a hot summer's day, and around the corner to the nurses' station. Tandy skidded to a halt in front of the receptionist window, wondering in the back of her mind why the glass had wire crisscrossing it on the inside. Did a lot of people try to break into or out of the receptionist area?

Corinne Stewart, Stars Hill's emergency

nurse for the past thirty years, stood as soon as Tandy came into view. "She's in room 3."

Tandy didn't even stop to say thank you, just flew back down the hallway and turned right, down the patient room wing. She hadn't been in here since junior high, when Kendra had tried to jump from one tree limb to another — like a flying squirrel — and ended up flat on her back between the massive oak trees.

The sight of Daddy sitting on a bench outside room 3 finally slowed her mad flight.

"Daddy?"

He looked up and the anguish in his eyes made her heart break into a million pieces. Fifty new wrinkles had found a home in his face. The eyes that had danced with delight at dinner just a few hours ago now looked at her from a shuttered, dark place.

No niece or nephew Lasky. Tandy knew the truth before Daddy opened his mouth.

"Is she . . . ?" Tandy couldn't finish the question.

"She's in there. Scott's there and Meg. Kendra's on her way."

Tandy waded through what felt like a wall of water ensnaring her feet and stopped in front of Joy's door. "I don't know what to say," she whispered.

Daddy reached up from his bench and

took her hand in his. "You don't have to say a word. Just be there."

Tandy squeezed his hand, knowing his words were borne from the wisdom of a husband who sat by his dying wife's bedside for months. She pushed open the door and entered Joy's room.

Joy could never have been described as a large woman, but the bed made her seem like a child. The black of her hair lay fanned across a stark white pillow. Her face nearly matched the bed linens.

But it was the look in her eyes that caused Tandy's swift intake of breath. All hope, all life, all energy had escaped into a black void of nothingness. Joy raised her eyes to Tandy, yet nothing of Joy lay behind the startling blue pools.

Tandy stepped forward and took Joy's hand in hers. It felt colder than the glacier that hit the *Titanic.*

"Oh, Joy."

Her sister gave a mirthless laugh. "We'll be changing that soon enough."

At least she was talking, if incoherently.

"What, honey?"

"My name. I think those sisters at the orphanage either missed their message from God or weren't talking to Him at all. I'm changing it as soon as I get out of here."

Best to leave that alone for now.

Tandy cast about for something to say. Asking for details on how this happened seemed like it would cause Joy more pain than release. Talking about everyday matters though would be heartless and cruel. So Tandy did what Daddy said to do and simply stood there, holding Joy's tiny hand in hers, stroking it.

She looked over to Scott, who hadn't moved since she came into the room. He stood staring out the window, one hand across his abdomen, the other propping up his chin. His body had settled into the curvature of defeat.

Meg sat on Joy's other side, her legs curled up beneath her in the giant hospital chair. She held Joy's other hand. Tandy met her eyes and they shared a look of helplessness.

How could Joy have a miscarriage? They were all healthy as could be. Meg had carried all three of her babies with no problem at all. No one they knew had experienced this before — at least not that they'd shared with the sisters.

How could this be?

Tandy lost track of time as she shifted from foot to foot, alternately wishing for another chair and chastising herself for worrying about her own comfort at a time like this.

As the second hand swept around the white face of a large, round clock on the wall, Tandy entertained for the first time the thought of never having children. If this could happen, then perhaps motherhood wasn't for her after all.

She'd need to talk about that with Clay. Where *was* he? Probably outside the door with Daddy and Zelda. Clay would know to leave this to the sisters.

Scott, on the other hand, would benefit from Clay's presence right now. Staring out that window couldn't be doing him any good.

Tandy reached into her coat pocket and pulled out her cell phone. Typing a text message with one hand was laborious, but she managed. No way would she let go of Joy right now.

She finished the message in a few minutes and hit *Send.*

It took less than a minute for Clay to come through the door. He met Tandy's eyes, and she tried to tell him with a look what she felt right now. Which proved too difficult since she had no idea how she really felt. Everything mixed together in her heart and mind, and all she knew was that Joy no longer had a baby Lasky growing inside her.

And that truth changed a lot of what she thought she knew about the world and the way God worked.

An hour later Kendra, Meg, and Tandy sat at a table in the hospital cafeteria. Joy — with the blissful aid of modern pharmaceuticals — lay sleeping.

"How could this happen?" Tandy said for the fiftieth time. "I keep saying it, but I can't get past that. Did she fall or something?"

"I don't think so." Meg sipped her coffee, her hands wrapped around its soothing warmth. "Scott told me when I first got here that she woke up right after they'd gone to bed and there was blood on the sheets. They called 911 and here we are."

Kendra threw a handful of M&Ms into her mouth and handed Tandy some.

Thank heaven for comfort food. "What do we do now?" Tandy lay the buttons of chocolate on the table and began sorting them by color.

Kendra swallowed. "First things first. We've got to get to her house and change those sheets. Scott shouldn't have to, and Joy's definitely not going to be subjected to it."

"Oh, God, why is this happening?" Meg lay her head on the table.

283

Tandy considered chastising her for using the Lord's name in vain, then realized Meg was really asking God for understanding.

"We need to call USA Baby and cancel the crib."

"I never even got to see it." Meg's voice was muffled by the wood of the table.

Tandy shook her head. "I don't get this at all."

Meg sat up. "Me either. I don't think we're going to get a reason this side of eternity though. And we've got to buck up. Joy will need to lean on all of us to get through this, so we have to be strong." She swiped at a tear. "I'll go to her house and get the sheets changed."

"No, you stay here with her." Tandy tucked a curl behind her ear. Her hair probably looked like birds had nested in it. She'd been in bed with a good book when Meg called, waiting on Clay to close up the diner. "She'll want you when she wakes up. I'll go to her house."

Kendra crumpled the empty M&Ms bag. "I'll go with you. We can call Noni on the way and cancel the crib."

They looked at each other, then came together in a hug. "We'll get through this," Tandy promised.

"We always do." Meg stepped back and

pulled a crumpled Kleenex from her coat pocket. "Y'all go on. I'll find out about how many of us can stay the night and all."

"If they think they're kicking any of us out, they have another think coming."

"Ms. Corinne's on duty," Tandy said. "She won't send any of us home."

Kendra nodded. "Yeah, she knows us too well to have that fight."

"And she's too wise." Meg lifted a hand and gave a small wave. "See you two in a bit. Be *careful.* And wear your seat belts."

"Don't worry about us. One tragedy a year is plenty." Kendra threw her scarf over her shoulder and headed out the door with Tandy.

Twenty-Five

The house felt like a crypt when they entered, as if all the wood and marble knew a life had ended a few short hours ago.

Tandy crept up the stairs, trying not to disturb the shroud of silence around them.

"Do you think houses have feelings?" Kendra's voice came almost at a whisper.

"I think this one may."

Their feet sank into the plush hallway carpeting. Tandy tried to walk slowly, but she still arrived at Scott and Joy's bedroom door entirely too soon. She took a deep breath and looked at Kendra. "You ready for this?"

"No."

"Me neither."

"But it's got to be done."

"Yep." She pushed open the door.

The room looked like a hurricane had blown through. Sheets were twisted and falling off the bed, the telltale blood now disappearing over the mattress's edge. A light blue silk comforter lay crumpled on the far side of the room, where the bench seat that normally sat at the foot of their bed now lay on its side as well. The overhead light shone brightly on the scene, not leaving anything to imagination or shadow.

"Oh my," Kendra breathed.

Tears poured down Tandy's face. They didn't show this part in movies, this destruction of a personal space. As if losing a baby wasn't insult and injury enough, Joy would have come home to a ransacked bedroom. Joy, who prided herself on Martha Stewart-like rooms of order, peace, and relaxation.

Tandy swiped at the tears, but they kept coming. God's way of blurring the vision when reality painted too harsh a picture.

Too soon though, the tears stopped, leaving a small hiccup in their wake.

Tandy squared her shoulders and breathed deeply. "Okay, Ken, we've got to get this place picked up."

Kendra nodded, swiping her face with a Kleenex, then cramming the tissue into her pocket. "You're right. Joy doesn't need to see this."

They set about cleaning the room, righting the bench seat and stripping the bed linens.

"I think we burn these sheets."

Tandy nodded. "I'll go get new ones from the linen closet."

In short order the room returned to its serene vision. Tandy and Kendra stood in the doorway, surveying their handiwork.

Kendra slipped her coat back on. "I think that's as good as it's getting."

"It still feels sad in here."

"That's the house talking to you."

"You're right." Tandy sighed and flipped off the bedroom light. "Come on, let's get back to the hospital and see how she's doing."

My tummy never got round. I never got to feel him or her kick. Didn't get that flutter that Meg told me to expect in a few months.

Why, God? Why would You let this happen? I'm a good person. I go to church. I've believed in You since childhood. I trusted You. Loved You. Asked You to be Lord of my life. I followed the plan.

Why would You not protect the life inside me?

I don't know how to tell You I don't like You. I'm afraid You'll smite me too. But I don't like You right now. I don't understand You. How can I love what I don't understand?

Which isn't to say I ever completely understood You, but I thought I at least knew how You worked. I've abided by Your laws, loved Your word, and yet still You took my baby.

Could you not let me at least hold my child in my arms before bringing her back to heaven? Or was I to have a son? Will I ever know? They say there are no tears in heaven, and I know I would shed some if you introduced me to the child I didn't get to see on earth.

Does that mean I'll never see the child I shared life with for two months?

That stupid nurse told me one in three pregnancies ends in miscarriage. How about You smite her, God? How about You tell her that I don't care if every woman on the planet has had a miscarriage, that it doesn't make mine any easier to bear?

Oh, God, I'm losing my mind. I need You to somehow get me through this. I don't know how to lean on You when I'm so mad at You.

And Scott. Poor, dear, sweet Scott. He thought we'd triumphed. That we had beaten this infertility monster that had invaded our home. I'll bet he harbors secret anger toward me. After all, he conquered the problem. I couldn't see us to the finish line though.

I'm too young for this.

I'm too old for this.

I hate this. I hate not being in control of my own body. I hate the look of pity that nurse gave me. I hate these scratchy sheets. I hate this ugly hospital room. I hate the sound of ambulance sirens in my driveway. I hate flashing red lights that bounce off tree limbs and porch stairs. I hate dreams that tell me what reality is about to deal.

I hate everything. I hate it all!

I hate.

"Thank the Lord we made it back today." Zelda took Jack's hand in hers and leaned against him. "I don't think I'd have forgiven myself if this happened and we were out of town."

Jack kissed the top of her red, spiky hair. "I know. Thanks for coming home."

"My pleasure."

They sat without words for a bit, letting the squeak of nurses' shoes and beeping of monitors surround them. Had it only been a few hours since they sat around Joy's dinner table talking about nursery colors and raising children?

Zelda remembered the day the marine sergeant climbed the two porch steps to her front door and delivered news that Ray Jr. wouldn't be coming back from Iraq. She'd had years now to think through that, to let the scar form over the hurt. And until now, she'd never known to be grateful that she'd had eighteen years with her son.

Those were eighteen years Joy would never know.

Was it easier, letting go of a child you hadn't held — releasing a dream you never saw or touched? Zelda sighed and rubbed Jack's hand. "I love you, Jack."

"I love you too, Zelda Marelda."

"One of these days you're going to call me by my real name."

"Zelda Suzanne just isn't as much fun as Zelda Marelda."

"You take all the fun you need right now, love."

They let the hospital sounds wash back over them. Zelda counted the cracks in the tile one more time. Still thirty-two cracks in the thirty tiles she could see. Her eyes weren't what they used to be.

"I should go in there and check on her."

Zelda straightened and met Jack's eye. "Yes."

"I'm not sure I can yet. That's my baby girl in there hurting."

"Oh, love," she reached up and patted his

face, "you do just what you told Tandy to do. Joy needs to know her daddy is still here for her."

Jack nodded. "I wish Marian was here. She'd know what to do."

Zelda smiled, wishing again she could have met Marian. They would have been friends. "I wonder sometimes if those in heaven know what's happening on earth with their family members and friends they've left behind."

"Me too."

"If Marian knows, then I'm sure she's doing everything in her power to send love and comfort to Joy."

"Yeah."

"And her biggest asset would be you." Zelda nudged him with her shoulder. "Go on in there and tell your little girl that this too shall pass, but we all have a time for weeping."

Jack kissed her cheek and cupped her chin in his hand. "You're a mighty wise woman, you know?"

"I just say what comes to mind. Go on now. I'll wait right here for as long as it takes."

Daddy stood and, with a last look to Zelda, entered Joy's hospital room.

Twenty-Six

Three days later the moon had just begun to rise when Jack reached in front of Zelda and opened the door.

"Thank you." Zelda walked in front of him into Brick Tops Restaurant. "Did you talk to Joy before we left Stars Hill?"

"I talked to Scott. He says she's doing a little better. Even cracked a smile today. It's only been three days. She just needs some time."

Zelda hummed while Jack approached the maitre d' stand and confirmed their reservation with the tall German standing there.

"Certainly, right this way."

They followed the black-suited man through the room to a booth in the corner lit by a single overhead Tiffany lamp.

"This is to your liking?"

Jack nodded to the man. "Yes, thank you."

"Very well then. Your server will be with you shortly."

The maitre d' faded away while Zelda arranged herself on the bench seat. "This is so nice of you, Jack. You know how I appreciate a nice dinner out."

"I do. And I know how you love the symphony. That's why we're going to the Schermerhorn after dinner."

"You're kidding! For the Pops concert?"

"Is there another form of symphony performance you love more?"

"Not in all the world. Oh, you are a dear man."

"I try."

"You succeed. What a perfect night!"

"You think so?"

"I do."

"I don't know. I think it might be lacking something."

"Unless they don't serve chocolate in this restaurant, trust me, you haven't missed a thing."

"No, it's not the chocolate." Jack put a finger to his lips, his brows knit together. "What did I forget? Hang on, I'll remember." He looked around the room. "Oh, yes!" He slid from the booth and, before Zelda quite knew what was happening, knelt on one knee by her seat.

"Jack!"

"Zelda, I've loved every moment of my

294

life with you in it. While I know neither of us will be each other's first love, I know you are the love of my life after Marian. I hope you'll let me be the love of your life after Raymond." He pulled a white leather box from his inner jacket pocket. "Zelda, will you marry me?" He opened the box and a little light clicked on from its top, shining down on a circular diamond surrounded by a ring of rubies, all sitting atop a band of gold.

Zelda's hand flew to her chest. "Jack, it's gorgeous."

"Is that a yes?"

She pulled back a bit. "Do the girls know about this?"

"They not only know, they've each given their blessing. They've known for a while."

Despite the night outside, she would have sworn the skies split open with rays of sunshine and bluebirds sang on every branch of every tree. "In that case, yes."

"Yes? You'll marry me?"

"Yes!"

Jack tugged the ring from its nesting place and slid it onto Zelda's finger. "I love you, Zelda."

"I love you, Jack."

He kissed her, and she knew the amazement of second love. No, this wasn't that amazing, spellbinding feeling she'd shared in her twenties with a marine recruit bent on heading off to war. This was a peaceful, sure, brilliant feeling of knowing someone loved her unconditionally — enough to let her keep the memory of her first husband and know he could keep the memory of his first wife. This was perfect.

Jack went back around to his side of the table. "*Now* it's a perfect night."

Zelda held her ring up so that the light reflected off the stones' brilliance. "Yes, it is. Do you realize we're going to have *two* weddings in the family this year? I wonder if we'll make it to the end without losing our sanity."

"Since our grip on sanity is tenuous on a good day, I'd say that's doubtful."

Twenty-Seven

Scott's hand is warm in mine as I grip it and look out the tiny oval window at my right. The runway is as gray as the day, and I wonder again if we're taking the right course of action. Scott laid the tickets in my hand four days ago — tickets we purchased when we had looked forward to learning about China and then sharing that knowledge with our little one.

We don't have a little one anymore. Not this side of heaven. I do not know why I have told Scott we can go despite what's happened. All I know is that I cannot sit in my house for one more day and hear the echo of children's steps, wish for children's laughter, pass the door of the nursery, and wonder when or if our union will ever become the family of my dreams.

Giving something else up — this trip — well, I simply could not say no right now. I'll go to China and learn as much as I can about this land of my birth. If we decide to try again — and Dr. Murray says we can do IVF upon our return — then I have no intention of traveling outside the country or even further than a flight of stairs until my first trimester is successfully complete.

It's irrational, I know. I have become an irrational woman, willing to give up the normalcy of life to accomplish the normal act of womanhood. Irony shrouds the corners of my life.

Meg told me that this trip would be good for me, would give me something to focus on, something to move me past this time of loss.

I think she's tired of me and no longer knows what to do or say. I cannot help her in this. I do not know either what to do or say.

Scott's thumb brushes my hand and I turn again to the window. In nineteen hours my homeland will be within view. Will I feel anything when my foot steps on Chinese soil? Will some part of my genetic makeup rise up and say, "This is where I was made?" Or will it be like the numerous other trips Scott and I have shared over the years — interesting and enjoyable, but certainly not life-altering?

I do not know what to expect and that

unsettles me. I cannot fully plan for the unknown and that nearly unnerves me. I have no desire for life experiences that further question my beliefs of this world, of God, of myself.

And yet, here I sit, feeling my husband's thumb slide back and forth across my hand, breathing the recirculated air that blows overhead, hearing the engines rev as our speed picks up down the runway.

And wondering what on earth I'm hurtling toward.

The flight attendants are in their third wardrobe change on this China Airlines flight. They are remarkable women, all bearing the stature of a traditional Chinese woman — small, slender, with shining black hair. Some of them have chosen shorter haircuts. Those with long locks have all affixed their crowning glories into neat buns. They're so helpful, serving us a three-course meal during our flight. I had not expected such service here in business class but am thrilled for this small happiness.

We stopped in Anchorage for refueling. That was the second wardrobe change for the flight attendants. I think we had a crew change, but they all look so similar — with their high heels, flawless makeup, and identical hair — that I cannot be certain these are new ladies serving us.

By the time I awoke from my nap, the crew had again changed clothes. I think they changed in Tai Pei, our last stop before Hong Kong.

We're nearing touchdown in Hong Kong now. I did more research before we left, so I know that Hong Kong is at the same latitude as Havana and has the highest population density of any city in the world. We will only be in Hong Kong for two days. From there we fly to Beijing, which shares the same latitude as New York City. It's springtime at home, so it could be chilly in Beijing. Springtime in New York still requires a coat.

"Are you ready to meet China?" Scott asks.

"I'm not sure." I've resolved to maintain strict honesty on this trip. The temptation to hide is already growing, but I cannot succumb to its call. I must learn about this country and share that learning with my husband if there is any hope of us having a child and telling our little one where I'm from.

"Ready or not," Scott takes a deep breath just before our wheels lightly kiss the runway, "touchdown."

I smile, though I know it is feeble. I am

completely out of my element. Beyond that window lies a country crowded with people whose faces bear remarkable resemblance to mine.

And whose lives couldn't be farther from those in a little town in the southern United States.

"Where do you think she is right now?" Kendra popped a chip into her mouth and lay back into the cushions of the couch. The credits for *Top Gun* rolled up the screen.

Tandy checked the gold and silver watch on her wrist. "Should be in Hong Kong by now. She said she'd e-mail me if they found an Internet café."

"I still can't believe she did it." Kendra clicked the remote control to power off the TV.

"Went to China?"

"Yeah. Did she ever tell you she wanted to go?"

"Nope." Tandy swirled a straw around her water bottle. Light from the streetlights outside her window danced on the surface of the water. "I don't think it really mattered to her until she got pregnant."

Kendra scrunched her nose. "You can bet you'll never find me going after the woman who birthed me. I can't believe Joy would."

"She's going to learn about her birth *country.* Not her birth mother."

Kendra shrugged. "Same difference."

"Maybe. Maybe not. She said it was something she had to do. And after what she's been through, I think we ought to forego an opinion and just support her."

Kendra pushed up from the couch and popped another DVD into the player. "I hear you. Come on. It's nine o'clock already. Let's keep the movie marathon going."

"I'll go grab more popcorn."

I am in Hong Kong. I am lying in a bed in the central portion of downtown Hong Kong. It is noisy here, like any large city in America. I had expected to see bicycles. The tourist brochures had pictures of bicycles in the streets. But Hong Kong has embraced the idea of automobiles since those promotional pictures were taken.

Cars are everywhere.

Today we shall take the Star Ferry across the harbor to Kowloon. This is something hundreds of thousands of Hong Kong residents do every day to get to their jobs.

I don't want to do too many touristy things here in my birth country. I want to know the life that my fellow countrymen lead. So far, it isn't a life that calls to any part of me. It seems hurried and busy and rushed. And crowded. I miss the wide open fields of crops back home.

I must get up and get showered. The ferry waits for no one, we were advised, so I have planned to be there a full half hour before the one we wish to take is to leave.

"Good morning, sunshine." Scott's voice is smooth yet holds a note of question as he comes to stand beside the bed. He is already dressed for the day in pressed khakis and a golf shirt.

"Good morning." I assure him with my tone that I am all right in this land of millions.

"Ready to see Kowloon?"

"Just as soon as I experience a Chinese shower and find some breakfast."

"I spoke to the people at the front desk. There's a restaurant downstairs that has a breakfast buffet that includes Western foods like bacon, eggs, and sausage. I'm not holding my breath that their version of bacon is too close to ours, but I'll take anything halfway familiar and filling right about now so long as it's accompanied by caffeine."

"You're too good to me, Scott Lasky." I reach across the bed and he takes my hand.

"That isn't possible."

It's too early in this trip for so much emotion to clog my throat. I need to dole out my susceptibility to an onslaught of tears or I'll run dry before we even get to Beijing, much less Changsha, from which we'll drive three hours to see the orphanage that replaced mine.

I squeeze his hand and release it, then get out of bed and head for the shower. I'm not certain if Chinese showers are different than American ones, but in this hotel the shower offers hot water, a strong spray, and complimentary soaps that bolster my courage to face whatever this day may offer.

Less than thirty minutes later, Scott and I enter the dining area downstairs hand in hand. As the helpful hotel employees have advised, Western food is mingled among the traditional Chinese dishes of steamed dumplings and congee, a rice equivalent of grits. I choose more foods I'm certain of than not, needing the familiarity before braving the day. The bacon isn't much different than what I serve at home. They haven't yet conquered gravy, however.

After finishing breakfast we head out the hotel doors and into the never-ending stream of people. Shoulder to shoulder, pedestrians hustle and bustle, each person determined on his or her course. Cars roll along, some jerking out of a lane and into another with no warning at all. Hong Kong may have embraced the automobile, but their infrastructure certainly hasn't made the adjustment.

I'm admiring an enormous structure of at least sixty stories — one among many — when I hear Scott's warning. "Watch out!" He jerks my arm so that I fall upon his chest, flattened against a block wall. A compact car whizzes by, its horn blaring.

"Are you all right?" Scott looks me over for scrapes and bruises. "Did it hit you?"

"I'm fine." Fairly certain I am, anyway. "Did he just drive right up on the sidewalk?"

Scott puts an arm around my waist and we begin a more focused walk toward the ferry. "He did. I don't think the Chinese have quite figured out traffic control yet. Stay close to me and stay alert."

We confirm Scott's opinion just a few minutes later when we try to cross an intersection according to the directive of the light on the other side. Scott and I step from the curb and again he pulls me out of danger's way just before a small car races past. We wait until the clump of Chinese people behind us step off the curb and brave the traffic with the safety of numbers.

Hong Kong isn't as welcoming as Stars Hill. I'm glad I didn't come here while pregnant.

The ferry is as crowded as everything else in Hong Kong, but the sights are lovely. Giant, monolithic structures rise from the coastline like enormous fingers stretching toward the heavens. Everywhere I turn, I see newly completed skyscrapers and others in the works. It seems all of Hong Kong is on a building spree. They cannot accommodate the population fast enough.

The harbor is as packed as the streets and sidewalks, though this time with boats of every size and shape. From giant cargo ships to homemade vessels, each jockeys for position in the water.

As we approach Kowloon, I feel a bit more at ease. This space has the same bustle, but it's subdued somehow. I don't know why I wanted to come here, only that the desk clerk said many Hong Kong residents take this ferry to Kowloon each day, and I wanted that experience. It's hilly here — not mountainous exactly, though the hills are quite grand. They're covered in greenery, with lots of bougainvillea. I snap pictures, already seeing the layouts in my scrapbook. A scrapbook I will share with our child, if we are ever blessed with one.

If we ever choose to try again.

Right now I can only focus on this moment. On smelling the beautiful fragrance of these flowers, on enjoying a blue sky clear of smog, on listening to the chatter of thousands on their way to work.

From Hong Kong we board a China Southern Airlines flight to Beijing. We couldn't fly China Airlines again because it bears the flag of Taiwan, which isn't authorized to fly in country. Such strange political undertones in this country of my birth. So much to understand, such rich history to explore.

Beijing is only a few hours away by plane and before I'm ready, we again touch down. I haven't had time yet to fully process our two days in Hong Kong. I feel as if I'm spinning a bit out of control, unable to find the brakes.

Oddly I'm not certain anymore if I wish to find the brakes. Discovering new sights, sounds, smells, and feelings is a little intoxicating. I think Kendra must feel like this all the time.

Beijing is chilly, as I expected. We hurry from the airport to our hotel and unpack the light jackets I'd insisted we bring. I'm glad now for my preparation and planning.

Scott is unpacking our bags. We haven't spoken too much on this trip. He knows I need the space of silence to process so many new ideas and images. I love that he knows me that way.

Today we shall visit the Forbidden City, so named because the Chinese emperors lived there in another era. Commoners could not visit the emperors; they were thought to be deities themselves and therefore untouchable or see-able by ordinary citizens.

I don't think I could have followed a faith that didn't allow me access to my God. I don't feel worthy of that access, but, having been given it, I cannot imagine living without it. How does one worship a being that is untouchable, uncommunicative? I don't understand my country's three-thousand-year obsession with emperors, but I'm intrigued by it. We were told by the workers at this hotel to wear comfortable shoes, for the Forbidden City requires much walking.

I think a nap is in order before we hit those bustling streets again.

"Has she e-mailed you?" Meg settled onto her stool in the scrapping studio.

Tandy shook her head. "I think she's probably caught up in all the sights and sounds of China."

"I don't know, T. It's been days now." Kendra ran a glue runner down the back of a photo.

Tandy layered paper behind a picture. "She called Daddy."

Meg raised an eyebrow. "She did? When?"

"Yesterday, I think. I'm not sure when that was for her. What's the time difference again?"

"Thirteen hours."

"So it would have been about ten at night her time. She called him in the morning our time."

"And what'd she say?"

"Not much, according to Daddy. Just that they had made it safely, were seeing all the sights, and would have pictures to show us when they got back."

Kendra sniffed. "She can't find five minutes to shoot us an e-mail?"

"You know Joy." Meg affixed ribbon to the bottom of her layout. "I'll bet she's thought of e-mailing a thousand times, but isn't sure what to say, so she doesn't say anything at all."

Kendra walked over to the Cricut machine and began typing out words for the machine to cut. "Sounds like she figured out what to say to Daddy."

"She barely told him anything." Tandy

finished her layout and slipped it into protective covers. "I still say we give her some leeway and hope she finds whatever it is she's looking for over there."

"I agree."

Kendra kept her eyes on the blade of the Cricut as it sliced through the paper.

TWENTY-EIGHT

Did the woman who gave me life walk through these courtyards upon which my feet now tired? The Forbidden City is a sensory delight. Courtyard after courtyard, room after room, all designed and appointed with the idea of majesty at the forefront. The hotel clerks were right — my feet ache. And though I know this courtyard is every bit as beautiful as the first, my senses have been dulled with each new discovery of vibrant plants and architecture.

It's shameful to grow tired of such an enormous display of human effort. If I were a true Chinese citizen, would I still be ready to reach the end of this unending stretch of courtyard? Or would I gaze upon each one with worshipful awe and soul-stirring respect?

I hear a sigh behind me and turn to see who shares in my thoughts.

A Chinese girl stands a few paces from

what I assume to be her mother. Her hair is drawn back in barrettes, and she occupies herself with the buttons on her sweater. Her mother's gaze upon the wall of flowers before us bears the holy awareness I'd thought to have in this place. Does she know something I do not?

The girl looks up from her button and sees me watching. She smiles, inclines her head toward her mother, and rolls her eyes.

Disdain for parental display of affection evidently crosses cultural lines.

Relieved of the need to experience an awe I cannot manufacture, I offer a conspirator's grin, wink, and walk on to the next courtyard with a lighter step.

Tomorrow morning we will meet the parents-to-be. Scott arranged for us to ride along with several U.S. couples who have spent nearly two years completing the process of adopting a Chinese child.

I think this is a good idea. Though I dread it in many ways.

I am the girl these parents have come to save. Twenty-eight years ago, I sat in a crib — did we have cribs? — in an orphanage, in desperate need of a couple who would adopt me as their own. Do these parents know the inexplicable gift they will bestow upon a child tomorrow? Did they have any idea the ramifications of this one loving act on the life of another human being?

Could they?

Do I even fully grasp how much different my life would have been had Jack and Marian Sinclair not decided they needed me?

I would not know Stars Hill.

I would not know the bliss of sisterhood.

I would not have the strength of family.

I would not live the surety of faith.

I would not yearn to continue the cycle.

That thought is new. Do I truly long to produce a child? To hold in my arms a little one and shape his or her little world? Introduce new ideas? Teach new concepts? Answer millions of questions?

The parents we'll meet tomorrow — for they are already, in practice, parents because they have traveled thousands of miles and filled out mountains of paperwork and made untold financial sacrifices to receive their children — have answered yes to those questions.

They desire so strongly to build their families that they've overcome odds bigger than the Great Wall of China. They overcame. They answered the call of family that was placed on their hearts, even though they had to journey a path they may not at first have considered. I wonder how many of them had tried to get pregnant? And then to get pregnant with medical help? And then, perhaps, to adopt in the United States? How many different plans did they write? How many different steps did they check off before not attaining their goal?

How often did frustration make them yell at each other? Did they worry if they should just quit? Did they feel the concern that maybe they weren't meant to be parents after all? How many times did they erase their steps and rewrite them? Does it make the goal less worthy if you find another way to reach it?

I have much to discuss with Scott tonight at dinner.

For now, I must rest.

"Wake up, sleepyhead."

Scott's soft voice lulls me from dreams of bougainvillea and jade carvings.

"Mmm?"

"Dinner is in half an hour. Time to wake up."

I open my eyes and see his sweet face. "Hi."

"Hi. Feel better?"

I take stock of my body. It's tired, but the nap has done me good. "I do, yes. Did the group of parents arrive?"

"They did. I was in the lobby when they came in, bedraggled, every single one of them. Evidently flying United Airlines isn't the smartest way to get to Beijing. We had the lap of luxury compared to them."

I smile, thankful for the planning that led us to take China Airlines. "Let's not rub it in."

"Oh, I didn't. Just sent up a silent prayer of gratitude and came back here to wake you for dinner. They're excited about meeting you in the morning. Some of them are under the mistaken impression you have memories from your own adoption."

"How would I remember something that occurred before I was even a year old?"

"I think they're so excited, they aren't thinking very clearly."

"You're probably right. Where are we going for dinner?"

"I talked to the adoption group guide and he's lined up dinner reservations. We don't have to stay with the group, but if you want to go ahead and meet them tonight, we can join them for dinner."

I take a deep breath. "No time like the present, right?"

"You sound like Kendra."

"I'm beginning to wonder if that woman

doesn't have a good idea or two about approaching life."

Scott pulled back. "Who are you and what have you done with my wife?"

I swat his shoulder with a good-natured whack. "Very funny. I've just been thinking a lot, is all."

"You know I'm here to listen whenever you're ready to talk, right? I'm trying to give you space, but I'd love to know what thoughts are spinning through that beautiful head of yours."

"There've been too many to make sense of until this afternoon." I'm proud of myself for speaking so bluntly. "But I think I may have a few things to discuss during dinner."

"Then let's stick with each other tonight and join the rest of the group in the morning."

"I think that'd be best."

"All right. The restaurant downstairs is a lot like the one at the hotel in Hong Kong, so we should be able to find something to eat. Want to freshen up a bit before we go?"

"Are you trying to hint that my look needs some attention?"

He leans toward me and places a kiss on my forehead. "Your look always has my attention."

I love the way he loves me.

"Okay, Mr. Smooth Lines. Let me go assess the damage in the bathroom mirror and I'll be right out to join you for dinner."

Scott stands and offers me a hand. I put mine in his and let him pull me from the bed. "I'll be waiting with bated breath."

I can't help it. My eyes roll — so much like Kendra, it's a tad shocking — before I make my way to the bathroom.

TWENTY-NINE

I've selected steamed dumplings filled with pork and beef for dinner. Rather than the bok choy that we've seen offered at every single meal, we were offered green beans tonight. Steamed, of course, not boiled in tons of butter as we do at home, but still green beans.

I'm drinking Coke as I've grown weary of the bottled water we tote everywhere. Water from the tap in China isn't potable. I could not believe a society that calls itself modern cannot drink the water from its own tap. There are certainly cities in America where the *taste* of tap water sends me running for the bottled variety, but there is no city in which I would be concerned about the *quality* of the water running over my dishes and clothes and body.

But these thoughts take a backseat when Scott joins me at the table, his own plate piled high with Western and Chinese foods alike.

I smile and point at his plate. "It looks as if you found something to your liking."

"I thought I'd be a little adventurous tonight, try more of the Chinese stuff. We're only in the country for a couple more days. When am I going to get the opportunity to eat Chinese food in China again?"

"Probably never."

Scott sits down and spears a dumpling with his fork. "You don't plan to come back?"

"I think this is a one-time occurrence. I don't mean to say I'm not enjoying learning about Chinese culture. Seeing the land where I was born has been a wonderful experience thus far. But so much of who I am comes from the people who raised me that I don't feel any sort of longing to be back here. I'm a Southern girl at heart, I suppose."

Scott smiles. "That makes perfect sense."

It's time.

I'm unsure how to broach the subject. I toyed with several ideas while adjusting my makeup in our bathroom upstairs. I mentally rehearsed a few lines in the elevator on the way to this dining room. But I haven't yet settled on one.

So I simply blurt it out. "I think we should

try IVF."

Scott sets his fork down and meets my gaze. He doesn't say anything, which could either be a sign he's upset with my desire or waiting to hear how I reached it. I go with the latter because I don't know how to handle the former right now.

"I was thinking about these families I'm going to meet in the morning. They've all walked a long path to get to this day when they're given a child and allowed to experience parenthood. I doubt that any of them, when they first dreamt of parenting a child, thought this would be the route they'd follow, but it's nonetheless the direction God sent them. I believe that just as much as I believe God brought Daddy and Momma here to adopt me."

I pause to think and take a sip of Coke. Scott waits. He's such a patient man. "And so I got to thinking about how that applies to our situation. Neither of us knew what kind of roadblocks we'd encounter when we first started dreaming about a baby nearly two years ago. I'm sure we both thought, or at least I know I did, that we'd try for a few months, get pregnant, and have a baby. But that's not the story God's written for us. And for a while, Scott," I reach across the table and take his hand, fearful of the honesty, "I was really mad at Him for that."

Scott's thumb rubs across my hand as it did on the plane. "Me too."

His words embolden me. "I wanted God's story to be the one I had written for us in my head. And I couldn't get — I still don't fully grasp — why we can't have that story when we've followed all the steps for it. But I'm beginning to figure out that there may be steps we have to take that I don't know enough to write into our story."

"And you think one of those steps is IVF?"

"I'm not positive. And if you hate the idea, then let's talk about it. But I'm looking at our path so far and I'm seeing what we've been advised and allowed to know, and I think that's where we go next."

"Have you considered what we'll do, how we'll feel, if it doesn't work? How many times do we try, Joy? Once? Twice? Ten times? Fifteen? Dr. Murray made no promises."

I squeeze his hand. "Like I said, if you hate the idea —"

"I don't hate the idea. I'm a lot like you in that I like having a plan. This taking life as it comes, which seems to be about the only option when trying for parenthood, is new for me. It's hard. I don't like not controlling the outcome. I especially don't like that hard work and determination don't matter so much."

"I'm with you completely on that. I'm beginning to realize though that life might not be so rich if we're allowed to plan every step."

Scott's eyes widen. "Come again?"

I smile, liking this new ability to surprise him. Kendra's right. There is something to be said for not being predictable. "Well, think about it for a second. If I could have planned my life entirely, I'd probably never have come to China. Actually, I'd never have come *from* China. I wouldn't have the images of Hong Kong and Beijing and the Forbidden City that play on my eyelids as I sleep now. We wouldn't have these few days, just the two of us, in a strange new world experiencing new foods, tastes, and smells. So much of what we have wouldn't exist if we'd written our own stories.

"I mean, let's face it, Scott. We're intelligent, yes, and even in some ways creative. But we're not Kendra or Tandy. Put a paintbrush in my hand and without step-by-step directions I'm clueless and frustrated. I don't even scrapbook without a sketchbook. And you leave the development to Darin and enjoy selling the real estate. We're detail people and that's okay."

Clarity comes with each new word and I cannot help the torrent as I keep talking, waiting for that final clear picture to emerge. "We'd write stories that were interesting but gray. By not knowing all the steps, we introduce a little color, a little life, into our existence. We *live*."

Those sentences make so much sense that I stop. Do I believe what I just said? Do I really value the unexpected turns God has thrown at us these past two years? Would I choose differently if given the option?

I'm shocked to know I wouldn't. If God has taken the time to order our stories, then I want to live the story He's written. He's been doing this for millennia upon millennia, so I know He's better at it than I am.

The thought is freeing — and petrifying.

Scott is staring at me. I clear my throat. "Well?"

"I'm not sure what to say. I hear you, I do. And I think I agree with you. I think I've even had some of the same thoughts since we got here. But hearing you say them, hearing those words come from your mouth, it's just a shock to the system."

"I know." I laugh. "I'm surprising myself tonight." I break his gaze and release his hand, allowing him the gift of silence to process as he's given to me on this trip. I just threw a lot of thoughts at him that I'd never have associated with myself two years ago, so I cannot expect him to simply swallow them in two seconds.

I spear my green beans and taste the Chinese version. Not bad. Could use some seasoning. I try the pork dumpling. Its salty taste is layered with spices, and my taste buds receive it much better than the green beans. I wash it down with Coke, enjoying the fizzy burning in my throat.

The words I've spoken aloud replay in my mind. While I didn't know I thought all that, I'm pleased to find the ideas within me. I suspect the sisters have been spending some time in prayer on the other side of the globe, for those concepts couldn't have sprung from my psyche without divine help.

I'm finished with my pork dumplings and have begun on the two beef ones remaining on my plate when Scott's "Joy?" draws my attention.

"Hmm?" I look into eyes I love.

"What time is it back home?"

The question throws me. "Oh. I'm not sure. Why?"

"Well, I'm still processing and I reserve the right to discuss this some more," he winks at me, "but I think we better call Dr. Murray and make sure we have an appointment when we get back."

"Should we put a sign up across Lindell?" Tandy held the phone between her shoulder and ear, her hands busy washing Cooper.

Meg laughed. "For Joy? She'd never forgive us. I don't think they hung signs for Martha when she came home."

"Yeah, but Joy's more than a Martha Stewart lover. She's a Sinclair. If I had to endure the 'welcome back' sign, I think she should too." Tandy turned on the water and pointed the sprayer toward Cooper's droopy ears.

"That was different. You'd been living in Florida for three years. Joy's only been gone two weeks."

"But I didn't go across a gazillion time zones and a couple of oceans."

"Still, maybe we just put a sign across her door and call it done."

Tandy ran a hand down Cooper's back, pushing suds out of his fur. "Okay. Let's meet at Daddy's tonight and get it made."

"Can we do it here instead? I've got the kiddos tonight. Jamison's working late."

"Oh, sure. I'll call Ken."

"Great. See ya tonight."

Tandy pushed the disconnect button with a soapy finger and set the phone down on the rug. "Why, Cooper, you look like a brand new dog!"

Cooper woofed and wagged his tail, then shook his massive body. Water droplets sprayed in all directions.

"Agh! Stop!" Tandy rushed to throw a towel over him. "Eww, now I smell like wet dog."

Cooper leaned his head out of the tub and licked her full in the face.

"You know, dog, it's a good thing you're so cute."

As the dog panted and turned his big brown eyes her way, she would have sworn he was smiling.

THIRTY

Having made our decision, a weight feels lifted from my shoulders when my eyes pop open the next morning. Today we will fly to Changsha with the parents, who will then meet their children from the Hengyang Social Welfare Institute. This is the institute that took over from the orphanage in which I lived the first few months of my life. Hengyang is a three-hour drive from Changsha.

I'm no longer certain I need to visit the institute. I have learned so much, changed so greatly, in our few days here. I feel as if I've taken in the ideas that I needed to embrace. What good will seeing the institute do? I have no memory of it. It is not me.

I am a Sinclair. I am a blessed woman with three wonderful sisters, all raised by two loving people in a tiny southern town in America. I look Chinese, I even enjoy some Chinese food. But I am a Sinclair.

God knew I would be a Sinclair before my birth mother even knew of my existence.

I wonder, of course, why she left me. Was it my blue eyes? Did they reveal a parentage of which she was ashamed? If my birth mother was Chinese, then my birth father could not have been. Blue eyes are not in the genetic code of Chinese people. Or was my father Chinese and my mother of some other genetic makeup?

At the end of the day, I must accept that I will never know. And that not knowing doesn't have a bearing on my identity. I choose to believe my blue eyes directed the story of my life to merge with Jack and Marian Sinclair's story.

My mother could have given me up because I was born right at the beginning of the One Child Policy here in China, which is still enforced in some areas of the country. When families learned they could only have one child, they naturally wanted a male. Chinese males are expected to care for the elderly in their families, not females. Females are only for marrying off.

It's a modern country in many ways. Cars everywhere. High rises littering the landscape like trees in Montana. But the culture, oh the culture. So much of it hangs on tightly to the past.

I too had an idea of how life should work. Make a plan, follow the steps, reach the goal. But I'm learning that there are other ways to look at life. And that new doesn't necessarily mean bad.

These are heavy thoughts for so early a morning. I must shower quickly, awaken Scott, and meet the parents downstairs.

I'm anxious to see their faces when they're handed small children and given parental authority. I know I'll see in their eyes the emotions Daddy and Momma felt when they were given me to parent. I don't remember anything about that day. I have stories that Daddy and Momma shared with me, of course. Those are wonderful tales.

But today I'll see firsthand how a human being feels when she reaches the end of a journey she didn't know she would have to walk.

I approach the group, hesitant, Scott's hand firmly grasped in my own, aware that I am an outsider here. This group has traveled thousands of miles together and no doubt formed a bond along the way.

"Hi, you must be Joy." A woman in her forties turns from the group and reaches out her hand. "I'm Claudine, and this is Richard."

I shake Claudine's hand, letting her Southern accent fall comfortingly on my ear. "Yes, I'm Joy. This is Scott."

Scott shakes Richard's hand. "I think we met in the lobby yesterday."

"I can't imagine how excited you must be," I tell Claudine. "How long has it been since you started this journey?"

Claudine begins telling me their story of twenty-nine months of paperwork — the weight made more emotionally wrenching by the earthquake that devastated the region last year — obtaining notary signatures, sending in fees, talking to consulates, and praying through the silent weeks. Momma and Daddy's journey didn't take as long as it does today, but I imagine them filling out paperwork all the same.

Claudine's story draws comments from other parents in the crowd, who share their tales as well. They've come from all over the U.S. — Washington, West Virginia, Texas, Idaho, Florida, South Carolina. All of them for the sole purpose of being given a child.

The awe I could not find in the Forbidden City finds me here. It shines through the eyes of these men and women, so intent on a call to parenting that they traversed the globe. I receive their stories deep into my soul, knowing they are the stories of my own mother and father as well as thousands upon thousands of other parents who walked this path.

I am overwhelmed.

I listen and I feel the strong, sure presence of my husband at my side. In two days we will board a plane and head back to our lives to continue our own journey toward parenthood. Perhaps we'll end up here. Perhaps the IVF will work and our story will be completed in a hospital delivery ward.

One thing, however, resonates in my being. No matter the story God writes in our lives, I choose to follow His plan.

THIRTY-ONE

The cold of winter is beginning to lift. We have days of seventy degrees and sunshine now. Late March in Tennessee can change on a dime though, so seventy degrees on Monday may mean forty degrees on Tuesday.

Still, the ground is no longer frozen. I'd planned to plant yellow tulips along the front bed. The green stalks with their yellow flower cups would have been a wonderful harbinger of the new life to come. But between the trip and all that came before, I still haven't planted them and now it might be too late.

I think I'll still plant them. Nothing else to do with the bulbs but throw them out, and the thought of tossing anything aside these days seems callous and cruel.

I walk through the kitchen and into the utility room. The sign that my sisters hung on the front door is folded up on the counter. The sight of it was so welcoming when we pulled into the driveway in the middle of the morning. Much better than having them all gathered there, waiting. This way, I get to settle back into my Stars Hill life.

The bulbs are in a drawer in here. I pull them out and slip on my gardening shoes, sitting at rest on their mat beside the back door.

Today I'll plant these bulbs.

The air outside is pleasant. It smells of turned earth, a sign that others have had thoughts of planting, of cultivating new life. The grass has just begun to grow again, tiny shoots of green bursting through the dark earth.

The bed along the front part of our circular driveway is in need of attention. I thought of calling a gardener, but putting my hands in the soil is more appealing right now than it seemed a couple of weeks ago.

Birds are singing. I find comfort in that. In knowing, regardless of what attacks my life, the birds will still sing. The sun will still rise. The earth will still bring forth life.

I still don't understand completely why all this has happened, why our life's story was written in this manner, but I've mostly made my peace with that. It doesn't seem a wise use of time to emotionally resist things I cannot change.

And if I've learned anything this past month, it is that I do not have control over when and how I will have a family with Scott.

That's terrifying and gratifying at the same time. If I'm not in control, then I can't be held accountable for the outcome. But if I'm not in control, then I can't create the outcome. It's a paradox I'm still working through.

Having a miscarriage seems a cruel way to teach a lesson though. And, despite all this, I don't think He's a cruel God. I think we live in a cruel world, but I don't think He's a cruel God.

Peace does not equal understanding. Actually I found a passage in Scripture that says it perfectly: "peace that passes all understanding." Isn't that a lovely notion? At first I thought it must be a fairy tale. But no, I'm experiencing that peace on an hourly and daily basis. I have a peace that defies my own understanding.

I reach the flower bed and kneel down. The dirt will have to be worked first. It's become a solid mass over the hard, cold months of winter. I dig a cultivator into it, turning the tines and working until the soil loosens.

I can't help but see a picture here of my life. I'm a person who sees the world in pictures and allegories — in paintings and music and works of art that I cannot create myself but in which I find explanation and exploration of this world in which I live. It's the bond that Kendra and I share. And as I watch the dirt break apart, I realize that it wouldn't be ready for planting unless I stabbed it with sharp-ended instruments and twisted. Unless I pain the soil, it won't reap the harvest it could.

My womb has certainly been pained. Is it ready now to receive the seed that Dr. Murray will place there this Friday? Has my inner soil been turned and made ripe to grow a harvest? Or am I seeing hope when none exists?

I went to a few message boards online and read of experiences other couples have had. I know enough now to realize that Scott and I were very fortunate to have conceived at all. That doesn't make it any less painful that I couldn't carry our child to term. But it helps me feel less alone in all this.

I dig a shallow hole and drop a bulb inside. In a few short weeks, a yellow flower should spring up. It will herald the dawn of a new season. It will shout to us that winter is finally over and spring has sprung.

I cannot wait.

"Scott, hurry, honey! We don't want to be late!" Three days have flown by since our plane touched down on U.S. soil, and now we're going to be late for our very first IVF treatment. I'm not looking forward to this procedure at all.

Dr. Murray has explained it in depth. I would share the details, but I cannot imagine a way to give them without shedding my status as a lady. Suffice to say Scott will provide them, *ahem,* the necessary material. They'll analyze the material, extract the appropriate components, and insert them into me.

And that is as graphic as a Southern lady can get.

I'm not concerned about the procedure or about Dr. Murray's performing it. I'm not even worried that it will fail.

I'm halfway worried it will succeed.

Because haven't we proven that getting pregnant is only half the battle? Then you have to make it to that magical second trimester, when miscarrying is a distant worry and the mom- and dad-to-be can go purchase baby clothes, bottles, bibs, burp cloths, a crib, booties, and all kinds of baby stuff with nary a worry that their child won't come to fruition.

I sorely wish someone had told me about the magical second trimester that first time around. I might not have let the entire town know I was pregnant. Then I wouldn't have had to endure their looks of pity when I walked in Darnell's or Sara's or sat down at a table in Clay's. I know they mean well, but I've never been the Sinclair sister who failed.

It isn't a nice position in which to be.

I know, I know. This is the path we've been given to walk. That doesn't mean I have to love it every second, does it?

"Scott!"

"I'm here, honey." Scott looks dapper in his black pants, white Oxford, and baby-blue golf sweater.

"A sweater? It was seventy degrees yesterday."

"And fifty today. Didn't you watch the news last night?"

"I fell asleep before it came on."

"Grab a jacket. It might be a little nippy out there. Besides, I picked the color on purpose."

I pull my jacket from its hanger in the coat closet. "You're gunning for a boy?"

"Hey, you can't blame a guy for wanting

his namesake running around."

"No, I can't."

We walk down the long hallway, through the kitchen, and out to the garage. China has brought us closer, healed those fissures that had been created.

"Yours or mine?"

Scott steers me toward his vehicle. "Mine. That way you can rest the whole way home."

I nod, hoping that all this preparation and energy will have been expended for good reason. We won't know for two more weeks if today's work will bear fruit.

Two long, grueling weeks.

I've grown to hate the calendar again.

A little over an hour later, we're walking into Dr. Murray's office. It hasn't changed much. New issues of the same magazines litter the tables. A little boy with blond hair and blue eyes is playing in the corner with a dump truck. He's totally absorbed in his make-believe world and doesn't look up when we walk in.

For a brief moment I consider going to him and entering into his world, where the greatest concerns are what to load in the truck and where to dump it.

Scott alerts the receptionist of our presence, and I settle into the couch to wait until we're called. If all goes well, I'll be designing make-believe worlds with my own child in a few months.

Scott joins me and pats my knee before picking up a *Golf Digest* and thumbing through it. I wonder if he's anywhere near as nervous as I find myself.

No, probably not. He has no reason to be nervous. The only performance needed here is my own, my body's. Before my nerves get the best of me, Marinda is at the door calling us back to an exam room. Except there will be no exam today. No, the test comes in two weeks.

I take a deep breath, pray my womb is ripe for a harvest, and enter the door.

"Tandy?"

Tandy held the cell phone closer to her ear to hear over the thump of country music and twang of a fiddle. Heartland was rocking this Friday night. "Hello? This is Tandy."

"It's Zelda, dear. Can you hear me?"

"Zelda?" Tandy threaded her way through the dancers. "Hang on a second. Let me get somewhere quieter." She waved a hand at Clay, who was just turning back from the concession stand, and held up a finger. He nodded.

"Okay, I'm outside. What's going on? I thought you and Daddy were coming dancing tonight."

"We were, but we sat down with these bridal magazines and I'm about to pull my hair out."

"Help, honey girl!" Tandy heard Daddy's voice in the background.

Tandy grinned. "Overwhelmed?"

"That's the understatement of the century. I don't remember my first wedding being this difficult to plan. Then again, I was twenty years old and had twenty times the energy back then."

"Well, this time you've got four soon-to-be-stepdaughters to help. Now, you'll need to say the magic line."

"Magic line?"

"Yep. You might as well learn it now. Being married to Daddy and step-momma to us, I'm guessing you're going to use it a time or two. Ready for it?"

"I've got a pen in hand."

"Just say, 'I'm calling a scrapping night.'"

"I'm calling a scrapping night."

"All right, then. I'll call the girls. We'll see you at Daddy's house in about an hour."

"Oh, I don't want to interrupt your dancing time. How about two hours?"

"Sure you won't self-combust and leave a pile of bridesmaid dress material and fake flower petals behind?"

"I'm sure. I brought over *Casablanca*. Your daddy and I can forget we ever said the word 'wedding' and lose ourselves in Bogart for a bit."

"Good enough. See you in a couple of hours. Enjoy the movie."

"Thanks, Tandy."

"Anytime. You're nearly a Sinclair. That comes with backup."

Tandy flipped the phone shut and stepped back into Heartland. A steel guitar whined its way into her heart, and she glanced around the room for Clay, Kendra, and Darin. All three sat at a tall, round table in the corner. The room was so full of people, it took Tandy twice as long to get back across as it had to exit earlier.

"Whew, this place is more packed than a can of Spam."

"That's disgusting." Kendra wrinkled her nose.

"Who was on the phone?" Clay used the toe of his boot to push a chair out for Tandy.

"Zelda. She's going into wedding overload and threw up a call for help. She called a scrapping night."

Kendra set her cup down. "Let's go. Did you call Meg and Joy yet?"

"Sit down, sit down. She's watching *Casablanca* with Daddy first, so we've got a couple of hours."

Kendra sat. "She called a scrapping night and then said to wait?"

"She hasn't quite got the hang of it yet."

Kendra nodded, swirling her straw in her glass. "She'll get there."

"I figure."

They sat and listened to the music for a second, watching the dancers swirl and twirl around the floor. Dusty cowboy boots glided and stomped in rhythm to the steel drum.

Tandy felt Clay's fingers on her shoulder and turned.

"Feel like getting out there with them?"

"You bet!" Tandy hopped off her stool and followed Clay out to the dance floor. She placed a hand in Clay's offered one and smiled. The band broke into a country waltz, and she stepped in time with her husband. The noise lessened and it felt as if the entire room had taken a breath of fresh air. Only the sound of the keyboard could be heard. That, and the squeak of the door. Tandy turned to see who had come in and busted out laughing.

"Oh my word. Look!"

A giant momma sow made a beeline for the dance floor. Peals of laughter broke out around the room as everyone caught sight of the pig snuffling all the dancers' boots.

"Violet, get back here!" Edgar Smithfield came racing through the door a few steps behind the pig. His faded overalls vied with the John Deere cap for best placement of dirt and dust. "I said get back here!"

"Mr. Smithfield, how are you tonight, sir?" Tandy couldn't help asking.

Edgar tipped his hat. "Mighty fine, Mrs. Kelner. Be a sight better soon as I grab holda that there pig."

"How'd she get here?"

"Had her in the back of the truck. Didn't figure it'd bother anybody any if I left her there while I enjoyed the dancin' for a minute, but Violet had other plans."

"Violet?"

"I bought her at auction today. Man I got her from says her name is Violet."

"But, Mr. Smithfield, you don't name animals you're going to slaughter and eat."

"Oh, I ain't going to eat her. She's Della's birthday present."

"I see." Tandy bit her lip to keep the laughter inside.

"That child's been pestering me for weeks. 'Daddy, I want a pig like Charlotte. Daddy, Charlotte had an excellent pig. Can I have a pig for my birthday? An excellent pig?' It's dang near all I've heard about."

"Mm-hmm."

"Cussed librarian giving that child *Charlotte's Web* to read, and now I had to go and buy a pig named Violet that's done run up in here among all these fine-dressed dancers."

Tandy looked around Mr. Smithfield to see Violet, who had made herself comfortable underneath a table, licking up spilled soda.

Clay pinched Tandy's arm and stepped forward. "How about I help you get Violet back to your truck?"

"I'd be much obliged, Mr. Kelner, much obliged."

"All right. Do you have a rope or something we can tie around her neck?"

"Got me a rope in the truck. I'll be right back."

Edgar left and Tandy finally let go in gales of laughter. "Good grief, I thought my side would split!" She wiped at tears rolling down her cheeks. "There's a pig in Heartland!"

"Named Violet." Kendra slapped Tandy on the back, joining her in the hilarity.

"This is crazy." Darin stood with hands on hips.

"Definitely not something you'd see at Joe's."

Mr. Smithfield came lumbering back to their group. "All righty, now, got me a rope. Let's get this pig on home."

Clay took off across the floor with Edgar. Tandy, Kendra, and Darin watched as they wrestled with the pig, who obviously had no intention of returning to the back of Edgar's truck.

"I suppose I should go help them," Darin said.

"Probably."

"I don't think I've ever wrestled a pig. Surely not in cowboy boots."

"First time for everything, darling." Kendra pecked his cheek. "And cowboy boots are the perfect pig-wrestling attire. Go get 'em." She pushed him down the dance floor.

Darin, Clay, and Edgar proved a better match for the recalcitrant pig than Clay and Edgar alone. A cheer went up from the audience as they finally tugged Violet across the floor.

As she passed by Tandy's feet, the smell of pig mud rose up, bringing a wave of nausea that sent Tandy staggering back a few steps.

"Whew!" Tandy lay a hand across her stomach and the other across her face. "That pig smells awful."

Kendra nodded. "I'm not so sure she'll be an 'excellent' pig."

"Ugh. I think I'm going to throw up."

"Oh, it's not that bad. Come on, let's go sit down a minute and you'll be fine."

The girls settled back onto their stools at the corner table. "I never thought I'd see the day Darin Spenser wrestled a pig to the floor."

"In Coke, no less. Don't forget the Coke smearing all over the floor as he got his arms around Violet." Tandy shook her head. "This is better than cable. I *so* hope somebody got a picture of that for me to scrapbook."

"Aren't you glad you moved back here?"

"Thrilled."

"I mean, where in Orlando could you be in the middle of a romantic dance and be interrupted by a pig named Violet?"

"Thanks for all your help, ladies." Clay arrived back at the table with Darin.

"Didn't you see? We were the cheering section."

"Yay, guys!" Kendra shook imaginary pom-poms in the air.

"I love a supportive woman." Darin laid an arm across the back of Kendra's chair.

Clay reached to do the same with Tandy, who drew back and held her nose. "Eww, yuck, you guys smell like pig."

"You know what they say," Clay reminded. "You lie down with pigs —"

"You get mud and Coke on your clothes," Tandy finished and shooed him toward the door. "Go on, pig wrestler. Let's get you home and cleaned up. Ken and I've got a scrapping night to get to."

THIRTY-TWO

"Daddy! Zelda!" Tandy walked through the front door and down the hallway.

"In here, hon!" Zelda's voice carried down the corridor.

The credits were rolling on the TV screen when Tandy stepped into the living room. "Hey, you two." *At least she's not sitting in Momma's recliner.* Daddy and Zelda were nestled together on the big, comfy couch. "How was *Casablanca*?"

"Divine, as always." Zelda stood. "Is scrapping night starting?"

Tandy held up a bag of products she'd purchased the day before from Emmy's. "I brought supplies. You've done this before, right?"

"I'm not a complete beginner, but it's been a few years since I picked up a glue runner."

"They've added chipboard and a few other things, but the general idea is the same — capture your life's story."

"Good, then I should be fine." Zelda walked toward the hallway. "How's about we grab some snacks before heading up-stairs?"

"Sure." Tandy did a 180 and followed Zelda into the kitchen.

They met Kendra coming in the front door. "Hey, you two." Kendra shrugged off her light jacket and hung it on the hook by the entry. "Ready to scrap?"

"Zelda thought we should fortify first."

"I love the way you think, lady. Lead on." Kendra trailed behind them.

Zelda opened the pantry door. "How about Oreos?"

"Got milk?"

"Just went to the grocery today."

"Then Oreos it is."

Zelda tossed the bag to Tandy, who caught it and raised an eyebrow at Kendra. Momma would have put the cookies in the cookie jar the second she took them out of the grocery store bag. And that's only if she hadn't had time to make some from scratch.

Kendra rolled her eyes and went to the refrigerator. "I'll grab the milk. What else, Zelda?"

"I've got those cheese-and-cracker things."

"Ooh! With the little red sticks to spread

the cheese?"

"Yep."

"I love those!"

"Your daddy thought I'd lost my mind when I threw them in his cart at Darnell's, but he's been eating them up ever since. I told him, at our age you go for convenience."

"Good point."

Tandy set the Oreos and Handi-snacks on a tray. "Popcorn?"

"Already on it." Zelda tore into a plastic bag and tossed it into the microwave. "Be ready in two to three minutes. Y'all go on up. I'll wait down here for Meg and Joy. They're coming, right?"

"There's no excuse for missing a scrapping night other than death. So yeah, they'll be here."

"Ooh, and I'll bet Joy's bringing her pictures from China!"

"That'll be fun." Zelda waved toward the stairs. "See y'all in a few."

Tandy and Kendra left the kitchen, Tandy with a tray full of carbs and fat grams, Kendra with another tray of glasses and milk.

"You know, I think I'm going to like having Zelda around."

"Me too. Except one of us is going to have to make the brownies and buckeyes. I don't think the kitchen is Zelda's favorite place to spend time."

Kendra chuckled as they made their way up the extra flight of stairs to the scrapping studio.

"Have you finished your wedding album yet?" Kendra set her tray down on the table.

Tandy put her tray next to Kendra's. "Almost. I lack about four layouts and it'll be done."

"I can't wait to see the finished product."

"Honestly, neither can I. I've been working on it so long I've nearly forgotten what the first layouts looked like."

"Oh gosh, I wonder if Joy bought paper yet to scrapbook for the baby?"

"I don't think so. We'd know, wouldn't we?"

"Should we go through her stuff?"

Both sisters eyed Joy's spot on the shelf. Neither of them spotted green or yellow paper.

"I don't see anything, do you?"

"No, but it might be in a paper holder or something."

Kendra threw up her hands. "We can't protect her from everything. If there's something in there, she'll have to take care of it."

"Yeah, you're probably right. Besides, she

seems to be doing a whole lot better these days."

"Have you talked to her since she and Scott did the IVF today?"

"I tried to call, but she didn't answer her cell or home phone." Tandy pulled her scrapping supplies from the shelf. "I assumed she was resting or something."

"Probably. She'd have called if something went wrong. So is she coming tonight?"

"Meg said she'd go over there if Joy didn't answer her phone."

"Ah."

They began laying out their scrapping supplies when the sound of footsteps on the stairs stilled their hands.

"All right, ladies. I've got popcorn and a couple of Sinclair sisters. Are we ready for scrap night?" Zelda's red spiky hair appeared above the stair rail, followed closely by blonde and black.

"Hey, girls!" Tandy went to the stairs to help Zelda with her tray. "Y'all ready for a scrapping night?"

"You know me — any excuse to scrap." Meg's smile didn't quite make it to her eyes.

"Hey, you okay?"

Meg sighed. "I don't know anymore. These dumb headaches won't stop no matter how much water I drink or sleep I get."

"You've got to go see Dr. Brown."

"I know, I know. I'll call on Monday and make an appointment."

"Should we be worried?"

"No." Meg waved away the concern etched on everyone's faces. "I'm sure it's just some vitamin imbalance or hormones run amok or something. Gosh, I love being a woman. It's such fun."

"Don't get me started." Joy held a hand to the small of her back. "My back is killing me from lying flat in a bed all day. Scott thinks I'm made of porcelain and will crack if I dare to bend over and put on a sock."

"I can't believe he let you out of the house to scrap."

"He didn't. He was over at Clay's playing with the Wii by the time Meg got to my house."

"And he thinks you're at home in bed?"

"We called him on the way over here." Meg took Joy's stuff from the shelf and brought it to her. "We promised she wouldn't overdo and that she'd be better off surrounded by sisters than trying to find something worth watching on TV on a Friday night."

"So, Zelda, this scrapping night is yours." Tandy cropped a picture, then looked up. "Tell us what you need."

Zelda took in a deep breath. "It's hard to know, really. Jack and I have been looking at bridal magazines since we finished at Darnell's this morning, and I don't mind saying I'm in way over my head here. The first time I got married, it was pick a flower, pick a color, pick a date. Now there are thousands of dresses and color combinations and music choices and times of day, and my head is just spinning. The only thing we could decide on was the date — July 12."

Kendra picked a three-inch flower from its glass jar and laid it on her paper. "I totally understand being overwhelmed by choices. That's one of the reasons Darin and I decided to just run off to the islands. Takes care of a lot of the details and lets us focus on each other."

"I envy you a bit. But with your daddy the preacher of Grace Chapel, I think we'd end up tarred and feathered if we tried to get married anywhere outside that church."

"You're right about that." Meg measured a piece of striped pink paper. "They'd have you hanging by your toenails before you could so much as say 'I do.' "

"Which means, of course, I need my future stepdaughters' help so I don't put on the worst wedding those women have ever seen and have it talked about for the rest of my days."

"No problem," Tandy layered ribbon on top of her polka dot paper. "What are your favorite colors?"

"Turquoise and brown."

"We can definitely work with that. Do you prefer white or ivory?"

"Ivory."

"Do you have a favorite flower?" Kendra joined in to the discussion.

"I love flowers — all kinds. Peonies and roses, pansies and petunias, sunflowers and stargazers, African violets, and daisies."

"Wow, that's a lot of flowers."

Zelda tilted her head. "I couldn't begin to narrow it down to one or two right now. They're all so lovely."

Meg punched a brad through her paper. "Okay, skip the flower choice for the moment. Do you own a go-to dress?"

"A what?"

"You know," Joy explained, "a dress you go to when you're in a hurry and feeling horrible about your body. Every time you put it on you feel like a million bucks even though you didn't have to spend an hour putting the ensemble together."

"Ah, I get it. Yes, I have a go-to dress."

"Tell us what it looks like," Meg commanded.

"It's a long jacket with a row of buttons down the front and a V-neck that sort of sits up in the back, kind of like a cape but not that dramatic. The skirt comes to my calves and has a ruffle around the bottom. It's a suit made for a woman my age, but that collar and kick of fabric at the bottom remind me of being a young woman."

"Do you have that suit here in Stars Hill?"

"I sure do. But it's dark purple. It won't work if we're sticking with turquoise and brown."

"No, but we can take it in to Sara's shop and have her find something like it in ivory. And that will take care of your wedding dress."

"Good grief, you girls know how to make short work of a wedding."

"It's easier because you already know what kinds of things you like." Tandy cut a glance over to Kendra.

"Hey, I resemble that remark." Kendra smiled.

"Okay, let's see, we've got the dress, the colors, holding on the flower choices. What else?" Tandy tapped her chin.

"Music." Joy held up two pictures and eyed them. "Do you and Daddy have a favorite piece of music?"

"I don't know if it's our absolute favorite,

but for our first date we watched *When Harry Met Sally,* and we both love the theme song from it, 'It Had to Be You.' "

"That's perfect! You could walk down the aisle to that."

"You don't think the older women would run me out of town?"

"They might, but then again you might as well communicate to them now that you're not a woman to mess with."

"You girls have been dealing with those women longer than I have, so I'll take your word for it."

"You could also have your first dance at the reception be to that song and have the announcer explain to the crowd that you and Daddy have shared a love of it since your first date," Kendra suggested. "That'd smooth any ruffled feathers."

"You know, I like the way you think."

Kendra twisted an Oreo open and licked the icing off. "Back at you, Z."

"Speaking of the reception, let's discuss the cake." Joy directed them back to the planning. "Daddy's favorite is chocolate, so you probably want a layer of that. What's your choice, Zelda?"

"I like marble cake. You don't have to pick between vanilla and chocolate — sort of like having your cake and eating it too."

"Marble it is. You could do the entire cake in marble and have the groom's cake be chocolate."

"I like that idea," Meg affirmed.

"I'll make Daddy's cake, so don't worry about ordering that," Joy volunteered.

"You bake too?" Zelda turned to her, eyes wide. "What do you *not* do?"

Joy ducked her head. "Play golf, knit, or crochet."

Zelda stole an Oreo from the tray. "I'll try to make my peace with having such a limited stepdaughter," she joked, then bit into the cookie. When she'd washed it down with milk, she stood. "All right. I'm feeling much better about this wedding. I know we haven't figured it all out, but y'all have gotten me far enough down the path that I might be able to take a few steps myself over the next couple of weeks. Now, would anyone care to reintroduce me to the world of scrapbooking?"

"Oh, Z, we thought you'd never ask." Kendra came around the table with a gleam in her eye. "Now over here is a Cricut machine . . ."

THIRTY-THREE

Tandy rolled over in bed and slapped the buzzing alarm clock. "Ugh. I hate hearing an alarm clock on a Saturday morning."

"Then don't set it, sweetie." Clay came out of the bathroom with a towel wrapped around his waist. "I can't believe you agreed to go shopping this early on a Saturday in the first place. What'd you girls do last night? Bond?"

Tandy buried her face in the pillow. *Something like that.* Scrapping with Zelda was fun — way different from scrapping with Momma, yet still fun. Sort of like kissing a new boyfriend. Not necessarily bad. Just new.

And Zelda had gone out of her way to make the transition as easy as possible, letting them tell stories about Momma, even telling some stories about her own mother. *I'm more okay today with this whole wedding thing than I was a month ago.* When had that happened?

Before last night she was pretty sure.

Probably the night Daddy and Zelda came home from Florida. Sitting around Joy's table as a family, with Daddy holding the hand of a woman, felt right. It felt whole. And Momma would approve. Daddy wouldn't have asked Zelda to marry him if he thought Momma wouldn't approve.

Tandy rolled her head to the side and watched Clay get dressed for the day. "I'm going to have a stepmother in July."

"You okay with that?"

"I think so."

"Good, since I think your daddy isn't going to allow anything different at this point."

"She's really okay." Tandy flipped to her back and pulled the covers up to her chin. "Except for being a morning person. We're going to have to break her of that, and soon."

"You could have asked her to go later today, you know."

"It's already April. July will be here before we know it. Besides, her wedding, her day. If she wants to shop at a horrible hour of Saturday morning, then I should let her. And this way we've got more time, so more shopping."

"Ah, the truth comes out."

"Anything I should pick up for us while I'm in Nashville?"

"I need more of that shaving cream from the Body Shop."

"Got it. Anything else?"

"No, I think that's it."

Tandy pushed the covers back and got out of bed. "Alrighty, then. Guess I should get in the shower."

"It might help to wake you up."

"A gallon of Diet Mt. Dew will take care of that."

"I'll pop one in the freezer for you so it's nice and cold when you get out."

"Aww, he loves me." She gave him a peck on the lips on her way to the bathroom.

"Yes, he does."

With the image of a tall, cold bottle of liquid caffeine in mind, Tandy stepped into the shower. She ran through the day ahead of her, then began planning out the week. April already. Where had March gone?

Wait, where *had* March gone? Or more to the point, where had March's time of the month gone?

She counted back. This was the second week of April. Her period should have been two weeks ago. In all the craziness of dealing with Joy, and then worrying about Joy over in China, and helping Kendra and

Zelda with these weddings, she'd lost track of the calendar.

She rinsed as fast as a tornado and jumped out of the shower. Scrounging under the bathroom sink, she snagged the pregnancy test she and Clay had purchased right after their honeymoon while they were in a joking mood.

The directions were simple. "Wow, even picture descriptions for those illiterate mothers-to-be." She stumbled over the word *mother* but managed to follow the directions anyway.

The box said to wait two minutes.

It took twenty seconds before the second pink line began to appear.

THIRTY-FOUR

Two minutes later, with a pink line more pink than any flamingo dared dream, Tandy raced down the stairs and through the back entrance of the diner. She stopped short at the swinging door that stood between the kitchen and dining area. If she ran out there and blurted out their good news, the entire town would know in as long as it took for her to see the pink line.

And no way could Joy hear this from anyone but her.

Shoot, after what Joy had been through, they might not tell anyone until they'd made it to the second trimester anyway.

She walked through the door as casually as if she planned to consult Clay about their grocery list.

He stood across the room, joking with Ms. Corinne.

Tandy watched him for a moment. When she got herself out of the to-do list in her head and let the moment fully invade her mind, Clay still took her breath away. Would their little one have his daddy's strong back and easygoing way? Or be headstrong and stubborn like her? Would they have a little girl with long red curls, or a little boy with wavy black hair?

She stepped across the dining area and tapped Clay on the shoulder. "Honey, can you come to the kitchen for a second?"

Clay turned. "Hey! I thought you were going to Zelda's?"

"I am. I just need to see you for a second before I go."

"Oh. Okay." He looked back at the customer and grinned. "Be right back with your breakfast, Ms. Corinne."

"Take your time, Clay." Ms. Corinne waved him away and went back to her morning paper.

Tandy walked behind her husband to the kitchen, certain if he got a good look at her face, he'd know their news and blurt it out for all of Stars Hill to hear. Hours passed — entire civilizations crumbled and rebuilt themselves — in the time it took them to cross the dining area and stop in the kitchen.

Safely ensconced behind the swinging door, she grinned. "Guess what."

Clay's crooked smile warmed like summer sunshine and she hoped their child would get that feature. "What?"

"No, no, guess."

"Zelda and Jack eloped."

She swatted his arm. "Of course not! Be serious."

"I'm never serious."

What if their child got *that* trait? "I know. You might have to figure out serious though."

"What?"

"Well, we don't want our child thinking life is all play and no work."

Tandy counted about three milliseconds before understanding dawned on his face. "No way! We're p—"

"Shh!" She clamped a hand over his mouth and looked around the kitchen, but no one had come in. Oscar must be scheduled for the dinner shift today. "We don't want the entire town knowing."

Clay moved her hand and laced his fingers through hers. "But that's what you're saying, right?" he whispered. "We're pregnant?"

She bobbed her head. "Yep!" Digging in her pocket, she pulled out the test. "Check it out. Two pink lines!"

Clay took the test from her and looked at it for himself. "I can't believe this. We haven't even been married a year yet! This is — I mean, I'm thrilled. It's awesome. It's just —"

"I know. I'm with you." She leaned against the counter. "I'm so excited, but I don't know how we're going to tell the family. Especially Joy. Especially after all that's happened."

Clay's brow creased. "In light of Joy, should we even say anything right now?"

"I've been thinking about that ever since that line popped up," she waved toward the test still in Clay's hand. "I can't decide. I think the first thing we need to do is get a doctor to confirm. Those tests can be wrong, you know."

"Right. Okay." Clay ran a hand through his hair and blew out a breath. "Let's call the doctor and find out if we're right. If we are, then my vote is to tell everybody. If the roles were reversed, wouldn't you want Joy to tell you?"

"Yeah, but Joy and I do things different."

"A fact for which I am most grateful." He closed the distance between them in a short step and enveloped her with his arms. "Oh, honey, this is awesome."

She felt his heartbeat — galloping like a wild herd of horses — through his soft cotton shirt. "I know! Just think. We're gonna be parents!"

He kissed the top of her head and squeezed her arms. "Go see how fast you can get in to the doctor's office. I want to know for sure before we start celebrating."

"You're right. I'll call on my way to Zelda's. If I don't get there soon, they're going to know something's up."

Clay released her and stepped back. "You be careful on the road. You've got my kid in there."

Fifteen minutes later Tandy pulled into Zelda's driveway. Homer sat on his porch, a newspaper folded open and obscuring his face, but she could tell from the rumpled pants that it was him.

"Good morning, Homer!"

The paper rustled as he folded it down to see. "Morning, missy!" He gestured to Zelda's apartment. "I see you worked yourself a miracle."

"That'd be God, sir."

Homer chuckled. "I'd say you're right about that. Did I hear there's a weddin' in the works?"

"You heard right. We're going shopping for it today."

He rustled his paper again. "Then I'll be saying good day to ya," and the paper came back up.

Guess one wedding was more than enough for Homer.

Tandy walked down the driveway and up the porch steps and knocked on the door. "Zelda! It's Tandy! You ready to go?"

Zelda opened the door, her red hair sticking up in an even odder assortment of spikes and valleys than usual. "Morning, hon. I'm just about ready. Are Meg and Kendra outside?" She peered around Tandy, checking out the driveway.

"Nope, not yet. Want me to just hang out here and wait for them? You could just come on out when you're ready."

"That'd be great. I'll be ready in a jiffy."

Tandy turned on her heel and made her way back down the porch steps. She crossed the driveway, settled back into her car and turned on the radio to wait out the few minutes until Kendra and Meg decided to make an appearance.

I wonder if the sisters will be able to look at me and tell I'm pregnant. I'll be so glad when Joy knows if their IVF worked and then gets to that second trimester. I hate leaving her out of this stuff. She should be here today, helping us plan this wedding. But no, Scott's got her laying down and taking it easy until the calendar says it's okay.

I hope I'm not supposed to be doing the

same thing. Meg didn't.

Joy had shared all kinds of tips and tricks about event planning with them last night, and Meg had dutifully noted each one of them in a spiral-bound turquoise notebook they'd found in one of the desk drawers. Now all they had to do was remember to consult the thing throughout the day.

The tires of Kendra's red Rav4 crunched gravel as she pulled up beside Tandy's Beemer.

Tandy waved a hello and got out of her car to get into Kendra's. "Hey, you." She plopped into the passenger's seat.

"Hey, yourself. Zelda not ready yet?" Kendra swigged a Diet Dr. Pepper.

"Nope. She'll be out in a few minutes. Have you talked to Meg this morning?"

"She's on her way — had to run by Clay's for a decent cup of coffee and a donut this morning."

"She better be bringing enough for all of us. I could use more sugar this morning."

"I hear ya on that."

"What do you think we should conquer first today? The dress or the flowers?"

Kendra looked out the windshield, considering. "I think the dress. That will set the tone for everything else if we can find it without having Sara order it."

"Do you want to look around for your dress today too?"

Kendra shrugged. "It can't hurt. I haven't decided if I need the traditional wedding gown or something a little more suitable to the islands."

"Like a tank dress?"

"Yeah. That's what the women in the pictures for the resorts down there are wearing. But some of them are in full-on wedding garb too — veil, train, gloves, the works."

"Are you getting married in that church you talked about or on the beach?"

"Darin's supposed to call the church here in the next few days and find out if we can even get married there. It's the oldest Lutheran church in the western hemisphere and neither of us is Lutheran, so I'd say our odds are pretty slim. But if we get married on the beach, then we'll have to go over to the resort side to have a pretty setting."

"What about that place Darin was talking about for your honeymoon? Can you get married there?"

"We could, but I'd rather not have the entire family at the resort where we're honeymooning, know what I mean?"

Tandy nodded. "Totally. I guess we'll just hope that St. Frederick's overlooks your heathen nondenominational status and lets you in."

"Darin's family members are Lutheran, so we stand a chance."

"You know, it's crazy how we Christians have divided ourselves up so completely."

Kendra stuffed a wayward spiral back into her wide scarf headband with purple paisleys on an ivory background. "I hear you on that. I wonder sometimes if the whole denominational system wasn't set up by the devil himself."

"Hmm, that's something to think about. I don't know how much good has come out of it, and I can tell a host of evil that has."

"Guess that's your answer."

Kendra glanced in the rearview mirror. "Here's Meg."

Meg's minivan came to a stop behind Kendra's Rav4. Kendra and Tandy moved from it to Meg's vehicle.

Tandy climbed into a mid-row seat. "Did you bring enough donuts for everyone?"

"And chocolate milk." Meg handed a Clay's sack back to Tandy, then tossed her a plastic bottle of chocolate milk. "And good morning to you too."

"Hey, where's mine?" Kendra whined.

"Keep your britches on." Meg handed her another Clay's bag. "I had them keep yours separate because I know how Tandy hates goop on her donuts and that's all you seem to like."

"Aww, she loves us, Ken."

Kendra tilted her head and batted her eyes. "You're the bestest sister a girl could ever ask for."

"Yeah, yeah, yeah." Meg rolled her eyes and chomped down on a cinnamon and sugar twist. "So where's Zelda?" she asked around the mouthful of bread and sugar.

"Coming." Tandy pointed out the windshield.

Kendra and Meg turned to catch a glimpse of Zelda huffing and puffing her way across the lawn to the minivan. Meg reached up and pushed the button to automatically retract the side door.

"Morning, ladies." Zelda climbed into the van. "Y'all ready for a day of shopping?"

"Can't think of another thing I'd rather do." Tandy realized that was the truth. "We think dress first, then everything else will mold itself around that choice. What do you think?"

Meg backed the minivan out of the driveway while Zelda considered Tandy's suggestion. "Hmm, sounds logical to me."

"Dress it is then. There are a couple of bridal shops in Franklin, a couple more in

Cool Springs, more in Green Hills, and then there are the department stores."

Zelda sighed and laid back in her seat, her lime-green quilted purse in her lap. "This is all so surreal, shopping for a wedding dress at my age. I wonder sometimes if we're making too big a deal of this."

"Too big a deal of a wedding? You've got to be kidding." Meg sounded appalled.

"No, I'm serious. Jack and I have both had dream weddings once in our lives. Shouldn't that be enough?"

Tandy pulled another donut from her bag and offered it to Zelda. "I guess God didn't think so. That's why He brought the two of you together." She reached into the bag again, then bit into a yeasty glazed donut. It melted in her mouth and she closed her eyes to relish the flavor before it could dissolve completely.

Zelda chomped down on her donut. "You've got a point there, I'll admit. Yet I can't help but wonder how many ladies will be talking about us behind their hands for making a big to-do over this." She swiped at a bit of glaze stuck to the corner of her mouth.

"Don't you worry a second about the blue hairs," Kendra said. "We'll keep them under control."

"On this issue at least," Tandy hastily amended. No need promising something they couldn't deliver. As soon as they found out about this baby, they'd turn their focus from Zelda and Daddy anyway. And if Joy was pregnant too, then the blue hairs were about to make the phone lines in Stars Hill hotter than an August day at Daytona Beach.

"Blue hairs — that's hilarious. I'm going to think of that every time one of them walks up to me to complain about that day's song selection or sermon topic, as if I have any say over either. I'm not going to get mad though. Nope, I'll just remind myself that I could be walking around here with a cloud of *blue* hair." Zelda let forth a loud guffaw, and it wasn't long before the sisters joined in.

"Oh my." Zelda regained control first. "Are shopping trips always this fun with you three?"

"Not really, no. Perhaps it's that you came along today."

Zelda patted Tandy's knee. "Well, that was a mighty nice thing to say. Thank you, Tandy."

Tandy bit into her donut again and nodded.

THIRTY-FIVE

Raindrops sluice down my window, turning the world into rivulets of color. The tulips are up, the grass lying like a new green carpet on the lawn, and baby birds are flitting back and forth testing their new wings. April has flown by, drenched in the showers of its fabled history.

According to Dr. Murray, those April showers will fulfill their promise to bring May flowers.

Pregnant. Again. I can't believe our very first try with IVF worked! Dr. Murray says it's not entirely uncommon, but I feel as if we're the luckiest, most blessed people on earth right now.

My task is simple: make it to July, when that magical second trimester begins. Scott and I debated telling the family the IVF was successful, but they're all waiting to know. I don't think we should keep them in suspense for three months. That seems rather unfair. Besides, this whole pregnancy question has already taken a toll on my relationship with Tandy. She's barely spoken to me for three weeks now, nearly the entire month! When I call, she says she's just rushing out the door or has to go help Clay with something. I wonder if she simply doesn't want to talk.

No matter, with our new baby news, everything will be all right again.

So long as I can make it to July.

I need to get downstairs and begin preparations for dinner. The family will be here in a few short hours, and I haven't even set the table. I wonder if I should use a blue or pink theme? I have yellow napkins with white daisies stitched into the corners. I believe I'll use those. I might fool them into thinking this really is just a dinner with the family and not a special occasion where Scott and I will announce that we've jumped on the roller coaster again.

Clay opened Tandy's car door, and she stepped out onto Joy's driveway. "I really, really hope we're here to find out Joy's pregnant." She adjusted the hem of her spring dress. "I don't know how much longer I can keep our news quiet."

Clay's hand enveloped hers, and he led

them to the grand staircase ending at the front door. "I know what you mean. Darin's getting tired of me not wanting to go out with him anymore. He says I've been whipped by marriage."

Tandy chuckled. "So if she announces, you want to share our good news too?"

"Absolutely." He squeezed her hand.

They rang the doorbell, then stepped into the house. "Joy! We're here!" Tandy's voice bounced off the marble floor, and they crossed it to enter the large hallway. Tandy peeked into the dining room on their way to the kitchen, noting the yellow napkins with daisies. "Hmm, that could either mean she's celebrating spring or a pregnancy," she muttered and kept walking.

"Are you talking to yourself?"

"Just trying to figure out why we're here, is all."

"Well, it's about time you two got here," Kendra admonished when they entered the kitchen.

Clay checked his watch. "Hey, we're, like, ten minutes early."

"Yeah, but everybody knows Joy's got odds and ends to eat at least half an hour before the meal." She held up a sliver of turkey. "See?"

Joy pulled the oven door down and

reached inside with a mitted hand. She retrieved a pie with meringue as high as the Eiffel Tower. "Those are not odds and ends, Kendra; it's the main course." She set the pie on a cooling rack and turned to Tandy. "Could you get her out of my kitchen, please?"

Tandy laughed. "Sure thing. Is there anything else I can help with?"

"Nothing. Just take Ken to the other room before we run out of food."

"We can always call for pizza," Kendra offered, and Joy gave a scandalized look.

"Bite your tongue, sister."

"Come on, Ken. You know better than to mess with a Joy dinner."

"Oh, all right." Kendra reluctantly got up from her chair at the bar. "But there better be something good on TV to keep me out of here for the next ten minutes."

"We'll find a rerun of *Jon and Kate Plus 8* for you." Tandy threw an arm across Kendra's shoulders. "Or maybe even *Mythbusters*."

"Now you're speaking my language."

"Hey, where's Darin?" Tandy led them out of the kitchen and back down the hallway to the living room, Clay trailing in their wake.

"He's outside with Scott, talking lawn

maintenance."

"You're kidding."

"I wish. I had no idea the man — either of them — knew so much about grass. I don't think it's healthy to discuss greenery that much. They've been out there for a while now."

"I'll go see what's going on," Clay offered. "You ladies park yourselves in front of the TV."

"Roger that," Tandy said. "Have fun talking weeds and send Meg inside when she gets here, okay?"

How I'm going to sit in a room alone with my sister and not tell her I'm pregnant is beyond me. Tandy forced baby thoughts from her mind as they entered the living room. She began casting about for the remote, ready to find a source of conversation other than themselves.

"I haven't seen you much lately. Everything okay?" Kendra settled onto the paisley-patterned couch and picked up a striped pillow.

"Oh, sure. It's been a little nuts at the diner and everything, but you know I'd tell you if anything was going on."

"I think this is the least I've seen you since you lived in Orlando. You sure everything's fine? Look me in the eye and tell me everything's fine." Kendra sat up straight on the couch and leveled a gaze at Tandy.

"I'm fine, Ken. Call off your attack dogs. Sheesh."

Kendra sank back into the cushions and pulled her feet up underneath. "Hmm, I'm not sure I'm buyin', but I'll let it go for now."

"Thank you."

"Uh-huh." Kendra didn't sound convinced at all, but Tandy took an inward sigh of relief anyway. At least Ken wasn't hounding her to death. All she had to do was make it to dinner.

And pray Joy and Scott were pregnant.

She took a deep breath and pushed the remote button. *Please, God, let them be pregnant.*

"You realize that, whatever it is, I'm going to find out eventually."

Kendra's tone sounded so much like Momma's that Tandy smiled in spite of her worry at being found out. "Yeah, I know."

"So why don't you just tell me and get it over with?"

"I thought you were letting this go."

"I did. I've decided to pick it back up. I'm female; I can change my mind. It's among the rights we're given at birth."

Tandy tore her eyes from the television to

380

take in her sister's face. "Let it go for just a little while, Ken. Just until tonight."

Kendra stared at her for a full minute — a minute in which Tandy wondered if she shouldn't just go ahead and tell the best friend she'd ever had in life — then said, "Okay."

"Okay," Tandy echoed and turned back to the screen. "Tell me about the wedding. Were you able to get into St. Frederick's?"

"I think we might just pull it off. I told you Darin's family members are all Lutheran, right?"

"Mm-hmm."

"Well, evidently the mother church of the denomination in the western hemisphere will allow us into their church since Darin's family has devoted their lives to Martin Luther. I don't get it since Luther himself told those who agreed with him specifically *not* to form a separate denomination."

"Will you have to do anything during the service that you wouldn't do here?"

"It doesn't look like that, no. We'll have prayers, communion, vows, the normal wedding day stuff. Oh, and we've found this fabulous organist who's known all over the island and has even performed here in the States at some prestigious concert halls. He's going to play at our wedding."

"That sounds cool!"

"I know! Darin's totally jazzed about it." Kendra twirled a spiral curl around her finger.

"Have you talked to Sara about the dresses?"

"Yep. She's combing through the catalogs and finding me an island-type dress this week or next. We should be able to order them, alter if necessary, and pack them up in plenty of time for the trip in October."

"You make sure I see those dresses before you go placing any order." *Since certain styles aren't exactly flattering to the pregnant female form.*

"You bet."

"I'm really glad you decided to do the island thing. It'll be fun to take a vacation with a purpose!"

"Yeah, and it makes the honeymoon even easier since we'll already be there in the islands. Darin found a resort over on Virgin Gorda that's spectacular. White sand, private cabanas, open-air dining, even dining right there on the beach!"

"They've got a restaurant on the beach?"

"They do, but they've also got this option where they bring out a table onto the beach at night and set up an intimate, personal dinner right there."

"Wow, swanky."

"Yep. I'm totally stoked about it. Darin's parents went there a few years ago and say it's the most relaxing place they've ever been."

"Maybe Clay and I should head over there at some point."

"And crash my honeymoon?" Kendra drew back, mock outrage painted across her pretty face. "You wouldn't dare."

"You said 'private cabanas,' right? You wouldn't even know we were there. And when am I going to get the chance again in my life to go to the islands and enjoy some relaxation?" *Especially with a baby on the way. Do they even allow babies at resorts like that?*

"I guess it would be okay if you stayed in a cabana down the beach from ours." Kendra flipped the curl over her shoulder. "You know, it could be kind of fun having you there. We could maybe have dinner together one night and go snorkeling or something. Clay and Darin are friends anyway, so they probably won't care."

"So long as you keep your nights free for Darin."

"And middays."

Tandy held up a hand. "TMI, Ken. I don't want to hear about that much detail of your honeymoon."

Kendra laughed and threw a pillow across the room. "You're just jealous that you won't be the only one enjoying newlywed bliss anymore."

Forget newlywed bliss. I'm in for morning sickness now. "Yep," was all she could muster.

"You ladies having fun in here?" Joy's lilting voice came from the doorway. "Dinner is nearly ready. Can you round up your men, please?"

Tandy stood. "Is everybody else here?"

"They are. Meg's in the kitchen with Daddy and Zelda. James, Hannah, and Savannah are all upstairs playing with Play-Doh and watching *Lord of the Beans*."

"You let Meg near the food?" Kendra shot up from the couch and made a beeline for the doorway. "She's eating the odds and ends!"

"For the thousandth time," Tandy heard Joy say as she trotted after Kendra, "there *are no odds and ends*."

Tandy chuckled and went to get the boys.

THIRTY-SIX

They all sat down around Joy's massive dining room table. Steam rose from various bowls, artfully placed at strategic intervals along the white-linen-covered surface. Silver forks and knives gleamed in the light from the overhead chandelier. Lyrical piano notes fell from the speakers hidden in the corners of the ceiling. Daddy and Zelda settled into "their" spots, sharing the warm gaze of an engaged couple.

Tandy couldn't envision a better setting to share her news with the family.

Please, please let her be pregnant. I don't think I can wait any longer. She studied Joy's face, which seemed lit from within by a serene glow. *That could either be a pregnancy or a new facial cream.* Tandy bit her lip. It looked an awful lot like pregnancy glow.

Family chatter swirled around her as Tandy circled the table to take her place by Clay, who had begun amassing his salad.

Lettuce leaves bowed beneath the weight of cherry tomatoes, onions, egg bits, bacon, croutons, carrot slivers, snow peas, and red cabbage shreds.

"Think you've got enough salad there?" Tandy chided.

"I'm just getting started, honey." Clay leaned over and whispered, "Sympathy weight — remind me to explain it later."

Tandy wrinkled her brow and made a mental note to find out about sympathy weight later. She had just reached for the lettuce when Scott tapped the side of his glass with his knife.

"Sorry to interrupt your salad-building and conversation, but I wanted to make certain we start this meal off right. Jack, will you say the blessing, please?"

Daddy bowed his head as forks scraped against plates and settled.

"Heavenly Father, we thank You for this gift of family and the privilege of coming together to share a meal. Please bless the food we're about to receive as well as the hands that prepared it. In Your Son's name we pray. Amen."

"Amen," echoed around the table.

Again Scott stood. "And in the interest of staying on the right track for a perfect meal, Joy and I would like to make an announcement." He gazed down at Joy, who only had eyes for him as well.

Yes! That's pregnancy glow if ever I saw it.

"Dr. Murray informed us today that the IVF procedure was successful. We're four weeks pregnant now, so it appears we're once again riders on the pregnancy roller coaster."

Immediately the sisters jumped up and surrounded Joy in hugs, while the men slapped Scott on the back and shook hands. Tandy's heart felt as if it would pop right out of her chest with joy and excitement, both at hearing Joy's news and being freed to share her own. She squeezed Joy, then hurried back to her chair and snagged Clay's hand under the table.

He squeezed and nodded once while they waited for the words of congratulations to subside. Then he stood and tapped his own glass as Scott had done. "Since we're off to such a fabulous start this evening, I thought we might keep the ball rolling and let you know, Jack, that you'll be getting *two* grandbabies next year. Tandy and I are expecting as well."

"You sly dog!" Kendra jumped up so quickly her chair tipped over. "I *knew* something was up!" She was around the table before Tandy knew it, enveloping her in a sister hug. A second later, Joy and Meg's arms joined Kendra's.

Clay enjoyed the back slaps and hand-shaking that, seconds before, had been bestowed upon Scott.

"How far along are you?" Meg let go and headed back to her seat.

"About six weeks. We didn't want to say anything until we knew about Joy and Scott's IVF." She met Joy's eyes. "I so wanted your IVF to work. Clay and I have been praying every day that you and I would get to walk this road together. I can't believe we're actually pregnant at the same time!"

Joy shook her head. "Me neither. This is wonderful!"

"For you two, maybe," Zelda broke in. "Having one hormonal pregnant woman in the family is hard enough. Having *two* might just be the end of the rest of us."

Tandy stuck out her tongue. "Yeah, yeah, you're stoked about being a grandma and you know it."

Zelda ducked her head and stabbed her fork into her salad.

Zelda's going to learn sooner or later to share her emotions with us.

Things quieted back down, and talk of cribs, nurseries, and making it to the magical second trimester soon completely overshadowed all other topics.

She's pregnant too. I cannot decide how I feel about that exactly. Of course I'm thrilled. Tandy and Clay will be excellent parents, and it's incredible that God has blessed their marriage in this way in such a short time frame.

But I also feel a little cheated. Is that as selfish as it sounds? I won't be the pregnant sister as I'd assumed. I'll be *one of* the pregnant sisters. I've never been the prominent one of the four of us, and that's been all right with me for my entire life. Let Kendra have the spotlight with her beautiful artistry and kaleidoscope of colors. Or Tandy, with her expert opinions and zest for life. I've been content to be a Sinclair sister.

Yet I admit I looked forward to standing apart from them for a few months. To being the one everyone wanted an update from. Sharing this experience with Tandy . . . hmm. I think sharing it with Meg would have been easier.

But God works everything for good in His timing, and He knew this would happen before Tandy or I entered this world. He has a purpose in this, whatever it may be. Which means I need to make my peace with it and enjoy sharing this experience with my sister rather than seeing her as robbing me of something.

She's also farther along than I am, which means she'll make it to the finish line first. Her child will get attention before mine.

Oh, I do not like feeling this selfish. Why can I not simply be grateful that we're both being blessed by God with children?

And if I allow my inmost fears to be voiced, I'm scared to death that Tandy will be able to get to that second trimester and I won't.

I cannot help but clutch my stomach and hope it is enough to hang onto this child — that, and the faith and petitions that Scott and I send toward God constantly. *God, please, please allow me to carry this child to term.*

And please allow the same for my sister.

THIRTY-SEVEN

Southern sun beat down on the blue hairs as sparrows and swallows swooped through a clear blue sky. The women moved stiffly, shuffling along as quickly as possible from car to church door.

"Whew." Zelda fanned her face. "July in the South is nothing to mess with, girls."

Tandy turned away from the mirror and patted her small belly. You're telling me. Thank heaven I'm only fifteen weeks. I can't imagine being hugely pregnant in all this humidity. That'd be torture."

"And your dress wouldn't fit," Kendra teased.

"By the way, I haven't told you, but you girls look lovely today. I'm honored you would stand beside me at this wedding."

"Oh, hush now. We wouldn't have it any other way." Meg inspected the back of Zelda's wedding dress — a fitted ivory suit with a long skirt that had a kick of ruffle at the end. The ruffle was edged in slender beads that sparkled as they caught the light. Her pearl pumps were edged in the same beads.

"That's right." Joy smoothed a wrinkle in her skirt. "We may have taken a while to come around, but you should know by now that once you're a Sinclair, you're always a Sinclair."

Tandy slipped on her shoes. "And that means you've always got us at your back."

"Well," Zelda smiled at each of then in turn, "I'm grateful and excited to be a part of your family."

"And here I thought you had gotten to know us." Kendra wagged a finger. "Don't forget being a Sinclair means you've gotta put up with us too. It ain't all sunshine and roses around here all the time."

Zelda nodded. "Oh, don't you worry. I distinctly recall two girls determined to get rid of me with a rudeness campaign."

Tandy ducked her head. "Not one of my brighter moments."

"No." Zelda reached over and put a finger under Tandy's chin, lifting her face. "But it did show me how much you love your daddy. And being that loved by your children is a blessing in and of itself. You'll find out soon enough when that baby gets here."

Tandy patted her stomach. "I suppose I will."

The church bells rang, spurring them to action.

"There's my cue!" Zelda pulled her veil over her eyes — a short piece, only a few inches long, a la Jackie Kennedy. "Let's go have a wedding!"

The sisters filed out of the bride's chamber at Grace Church and down the blue-carpeted hallway to the sanctuary doors.

Tandy remembered the day — not so long ago — she'd stood in front of these doors herself, waiting to become Mrs. Clay Kelner. And now here she stood again, carrying Clay's child. The thought rocked her. Life's relentless, faithful path continued, no matter the circumstance. Whether she chose to live in Orlando and allow her intended life to pass her by, life would have gone on. Whether Joy's IVF had worked or not, life still would have gone on.

Even though Momma worshipped forever now with the saints in heaven and today Daddy married another woman, life goes on.

Maybe I do have a little wisdom to share with this tiny one.

Ushers pulled the doors back, and Tandy caught a glimpse of Daddy waiting at the end of the aisle in his navy-blue suit. Happiness bathed his face like sunshine on a spring day. Tandy winked at him, blew a kiss over her shoulder to Zelda, and stepped into the sanctuary.

The blue hairs had turned out in full force, fanning themselves with paper fans from Ransom Funeral Home. Most of them wore disapproving looks, but a few bore genuine, if small, smiles. Tandy briefly wondered if the frowns came more from jealousy — not everyone got a second love in life — than outright disapproval. She dismissed the thought almost as soon as she'd had it.

She made it to the front of the sanctuary, took in Clay's smile from beside Daddy, and cut left to take her place on the bride's side.

Kendra, Joy, and Meg followed the path she'd blazed. Savannah followed Meg tossing flower petals along the aisle.

Tandy clutched her bouquet of mixed wildflowers and daydreamed about the nursery. They'd find out in two weeks if she'd be investing in pink or blue paint. She hoped it was blue. Clay would be a thrill to watch, teaching their son how to throw a ball and slide into first base without breaking his leg.

She *hoped* without breaking his leg.

Not that a little girl wouldn't be perfectly fine as well. It's just a boy would be rough and tumble, playing in the dirt, jumping in mud puddles, chasing after frogs — all the things Tandy wished she could have done during childhood. And the nursery could be decorated in a baseball theme. Or a complete sports theme! Footballs, soccer balls, baseballs, basketballs. They'd amassed quite the collection of Pottery Barn Kids and Land of Nod and Hanna Andersson catalogs. Tandy lost entire hours paging through them, loving the little rugs and toy bins and diaper changers.

As soon as they knew whether this baby was a boy or girl, they could register too. Meg said that was one of her favorite things during pregnancy, being handed the UPC scanner gun and set loose in the aisles of Target.

Tandy had focused so much on the nursery planning, she nearly missed Daddy's "I do." She blinked and listened to Zelda follow suit, amazed she'd spent the entire wedding planning the nursery.

"I now present to you, Mr. and Mrs. Jack Sinclair." Dr. Acree from nearby First Baptist Church turned the couple to face the crowd. Applause rippled through the room as Daddy took Zelda's hand and led her back down the aisle.

Tandy met Clay at the middle of the stage and followed Daddy and her new step-mother out the doors to the reception area. The time for celebration had begun!

"Ugh, my feet are killing me." Meg pulled her high-heeled sandal off and dropped it on the floor. "Who told me those would make good wedding shoes?"

"I believe that was Kendra." Zelda forked a last bite of wedding cake.

The fellowship hall lay in party-remain purgatory with empty punch cups and glass plates bearing crumbs and swabs of icing littering the table tops. Only family members remained, picking up and setting things back to rights before calling it a night.

"The reception was beautiful, Zelda." Joy stacked plates as she walked from table to table. "We need to tell Athena the cake was divine."

Tandy followed behind Joy, a tray in one hand holding dirty punch cups. "I'll amen that. I ate three pieces myself."

"Put me down for three too." Kendra swiped a wet rag across the cleared tables. "I think I'm on sugar overload."

"Well, I only ate one piece, but I put two more to the side to take home with me." Joy headed toward the kitchen with her tower of plates. "I thought they might come in handy during my next middle-of-the-night sugar craving."

Tandy made room for one more cup on the tray. "Ooh, good idea. Save me some too, will you?"

"Can do."

"So, Zelda, when are we going to scrapbook all the pictures from today?" Meg folded up the chairs and stacked them in the corner.

"I think as soon as we get back from Florida would be good. Surely I won't forget too much between now and then."

"I can't believe you aren't going off somewhere exotic to honeymoon," Kendra said for what Tandy guessed was the thousandth time in the past three weeks. "It's your honeymoon, for goodness' sakes."

"And like we've told you a million times, we *are* going somewhere special — to the islands for your wedding. Until then, I have a perfectly good home in Naples that I enjoy being in and that your daddy enjoys as well. We can have fun and be together at my home — *our* home now — for a whole two weeks and not have to worry about maids coming in while we're still asleep or kids running up and down the hallway at two in the morning. It's just what both of us want."

"Which makes it somewhere special." Meg gave Kendra a reproachful glare on her way to the corner with two more chairs in hand.

"Yeah, yeah," Kendra said. "I suppose you're right."

"And on that happy note, I think I'll go find your daddy and head on home. We need to get a good night's sleep before hopping on a plane early tomorrow."

THIRTY-EIGHT

"I love the beach." Zelda settled onto her chaise lounge and pulled her floppy straw hat low to ward off the sun.

Jack looked up from his Dean Koontz novel. "What do you love about it exactly?"

"Everything, I guess. The constant breeze, the sound of the seagulls, the kids laughing, the hum of conversation, the crash of waves — it all just calms my soul."

He patted her leg and returned to his book. "Then I'm happy we came here."

Zelda gazed out across the water, taking in the two sailboats moving like small dots of color off to the right. Between her and the ocean sat a half-finished sand castle, a little girl with red pigtails and a bright orange bathing suit working diligently to finish it, her tongue sticking out and face screwed up in concentration.

They had enjoyed a blissful week here in Naples, and truthfully, Zelda didn't know if she'd be ready to go back to Stars Hill once this week had passed. Stars Hill was a wonderful little town — nothing in the world wrong with it and many aspects of it right as rain. Yet the pull of the beach remained, and she didn't want to leave.

At least Jack understood when she brought it up. Fearful he would want to sell the Naples house, she'd hesitated saying anything those first few days. Yet Jack was thrilled to have a house in Naples to which they could escape when the weather turned wintry in Stars Hill.

If she remembered the past winter in Stars Hill correctly, that would put them back here at the Naples house around the first week of December or so. Would Jack want to spend Christmas in Naples? Probably not. They wouldn't want to be away from the family during the holidays.

And that would take them into January before they came back to Naples. Five months without the Florida sun, three of them probably freezing under a winter sky leaden with the threat of snow.

Zelda sighed.

"Something wrong, love?" Jack peered at her over the top of his novel.

"I just love the beach."

"Struggling with the idea of Stars Hill again?"

"A little." She shifted to face him. "You know it isn't that I don't love Stars Hill. I do, and I want us to be near the girls and their families — especially now, when Joy and Tandy are about to gift us with grandchildren. I guess I'm being selfish and wanting it all, wanting to transport this —" she waved a hand to encompass the sand and surf all around — "back to Stars Hill."

Jack waited a few moments, she supposed to see if she had finished. When she held her silence, he gave a small nod.

"I'm not sure what to say, love. I enjoy the beach, though it's not in my blood like it seems to be in yours. I need the change of seasons to mark time for me, and I need the community and family of Stars Hill in my life. We'll be back down here after Christmas, once the babies are born, and in the meantime we'll be going to St. Thomas so you'll have some beach time there as well."

His hopeful look made her realize how selfish she sounded. "I know, dear. I'm just being a difficult old woman."

"Oh, now, stop that. You start saying you're old, then I'm going to have to acknowledge I'm right there with you, and I'd prefer to stay in my blissfully ignorant of age world right now."

She chuckled. Marrying Jack had changed so much of her life, brought loads of happiness and purpose. So what if she had to spend some months in Stars Hill? She *liked* Stars Hill. She mentally shook off the funk that had settled upon her like a dark storm cloud on this bright, sunny day. "Okay, I'll talk no more of age if you agree to put that book down and walk with me to get some lunch. All this sea air makes a girl hungry, no matter how old she is."

Jack stuffed a bookmark into his book and set it aside. "You're on."

They rose and strolled down the beach, hand in hand. Zelda was grateful for the built-in shorts feature of her bathing suit. She'd tried on all the latest ones with little skirts across the front to hide the post-fifty bulge, but skirts seemed entirely too girly for the beach. The beach was about walking and running and playing volleyball and building sand castles and *doing.* Who could do all those things in a skirt?

Kendra had wholeheartedly approved of the suit. Kendra would, of course, being the most healthy and active of all the daughters. Despite their rocky start, Zelda thought she probably identified most closely with the passionate and artistic Kendra.

"Penny for your thoughts," Jack said.

"I was just thinking about the girls and which one I understand more than the other."

"Did you come to any conclusions?"

"I think Kendra's the easiest for me to know. She's got a passion and zeal for life that I can identify with."

"She and Tandy both do — that's what made them harder to raise. They'd storm through the house, slamming doors and generally behaving like a tornado if things weren't going well."

"That *does* sound hard to deal with."

"On the other hand, they were balls of sunshine and joy if their lives were working out well in their eyes. We vacillated between thrilling happiness and utter despair for each day of high school. Marian used to say we'd all perish from the drama."

Zelda laughed, enjoying both the conversation and the feel of sand between her toes. "I can believe that. So were Joy and Meg any easier as little girls?"

"I don't know if 'easier' is the right term. Quieter, yes. But sometimes quiet can be more dangerous and difficult than a child who lets all of her emotions out in a maelstrom. We worried over them, unsure if they'd tell us their troubles and triumphs or simply keep life events to themselves."

"And did they share?"

Jack nodded. "Most of the time. We had to force conversation sometimes, especially with Joy, who can crawl so far into her head she loses sight of the world around her."

"They sure are an interesting bunch." She sidestepped a broken sea shell. "The restaurant is right up here." She pointed to a seaside eatery and they left the hard-packed, wet sand to cross the powdery expanse.

"Zelda, I want to thank you for taking such an interest in my girls." Jack huffed a bit as their feet dug into the deep sand. "I know they're grown women and don't need raising anymore, but they sure will like having a step-momma around, I think."

She brought their clasped hands to her face and kissed his. "It's my honor and privilege to be their step-momma. I'm just happy they've accepted me, accepted *us*."

Sacrificing a few months of the year's beach time was worth the love of a new family.

Remember that.

A stifling August blanket of humidity and heat had slowed Stars Hill citizenry to nearly a crawl. They sat around the diner, lazily bringing glasses of iced tea to parched lips, the old-timers telling stories of past droughts and baked earth.

Clay went through double his usual complement of ice, but was so grateful to have any at all, he didn't complain. He dumped another scoopful of the refreshingly cold cubes in a glass and filled it with water.

Crossing the dining area, he set the glass down on the table. "Here, sweetie. Drink this before you leave. I can't have the mother of my shrimp getting dehydrated out there."

Tandy looked out the big plateglass window. "Ugh, it is *so hot* out there. I forgot how hot we would get before fall. I can't wait for the seasons to change. Look out there — the air is literally shimmering with all the heat."

"It *is* stifling," Kendra agreed. "I hope Zelda's got the wall unit going in the scrapping room because, while I love my scrapping, I'm not about to sit up in a hot room and try to be creative."

Tandy turned back to the table and smiled up at Clay. "Burgers for us all, yes. You know Zelda, she's not about to cook, much less a meal for four extra mouths."

"I'll have 'em ready in a jiffy. You just sit and drink that water." Clay sauntered back to the kitchen and Tandy took the opportunity to appreciate his retreating frame.

"Pregnant women should not ogle like that," Kendra teased, adjusting the bright white kerchief around her head.

"We can ogle the guy who fathered our child, can't we?"

"Well, I suppose. I'm not sure about the rule there."

"Then let's make it ourselves."

"Makes sense. We don't like playing by other people's rules anyway."

"Exactly. I say, henceforth, every pregnant woman has the right, maybe even the *duty,* to appreciate the physique of the man who got her in the family way."

"Appreciating his physique is what got you *in* the family way, sister."

"So for consistency's sake, I should continue doing so."

"By all means, we want to be consistent."

Tandy took a drink of water and swallowed. "Have you talked much to Zelda since they got back?"

"Not a whole lot. The Sisters, Ink stuff has been keeping me pretty busy. We got a hundred new memberships this month."

"You're kidding! A hundred? Wow! We're going gangbusters!"

"I know, pretty soon we'll have a good

portion of the scrapping community signed up in Sisters, Ink."

Tandy looked off into the distance. "Just think, all those women out there making connections and forming friendships. Imagine how much more easily they can get through the tough times when they've got sisters to lean on."

"And enjoy the good times," Kendra added. "Most everything is better when you have somebody to share it with."

"Amen to that."

Clay approached the table, plastic bags full of Styrofoam boxes in each hand. "Here's your dinner, ladies. Tell Zelda I said, 'Hi and welcome back.'"

"Will do." Tandy stood and gulped down the rest of her water. "Love you."

"Love you too."

The sisters left the restaurant and piled into Tandy's car for the drive out to Daddy and Zelda's.

"You know, you're not going to be able to fit a baby into this car." Kendra looked into the backseat. "At least it won't be easy."

Tandy turned the air conditioner to high, shifted into first and pulled out of the parking space. "I know. Clay says we need a minivan, but I'm not sure. A minivan? We're only having one child, not four. Besides, I

don't think I'm old enough to own a minivan."

"You could get an SUV."

"And spend hundreds every month in gas?
No, thank you."

"So you're back to the minivan."

Tandy sighed. "Looks like it. We looked at
a Town & Country, and they're pretty cool.
They've got built-in DVD players, and if
you get the leather option, they're a nice
ride."

"You in a minivan. That's definitely a
scrapbook moment."

Tandy rolled her eyes and shifted again.
"It hasn't happened *yet.*"

"Mm-hmm. We'll see." Kendra adjusted
the vent so that the cool air hit her neck. "I
can't believe how hot it is and it's barely
lunchtime."

"It's getting ridiculous, but it'll have to
break soon, right?"

"I worry about the farmers if it doesn't.
The crops aren't looking too hot right now."

"They said on the news if we don't get
rain within a week, the corn harvest will be
significantly affected."

"Have you seen the weather forecast?"

"Yeah, there's a slight chance in a couple
of days that we'll get some scattered showers."

"Well, I guess we know what to pray for then."

Tandy slowed and pulled the car into Daddy's driveway. She scanned the rows upon rows of corn, standing proud and tall in the fields surrounding the house. Their giant leaves were folding inward in a desperate attempt to conserve water. "For Daddy's sake too."

"Mm-hmm."

She parked the car and they piled out, heading toward the house. "Looks like Meg and Joy beat us here."

Kendra held up the bags of food. "Well, they didn't have to stop for dinner."

"Does it feel weird having to bring our own food to Daddy's house?"

"Kind of. But it's not like we didn't know Zelda has nothing in common with Momma. The woman doesn't have a domestic bone in her body."

"It's strange, right? I mean, I've accepted Zelda and all that, but it's hard to figure out how Daddy could have loved Momma so much and then fallen for a woman like Zelda."

Kendra shrugged, rustling the plastic sacks. Their sandals slapped on the worn wooden porch steps. "No accounting for love, you know?"

"Yeah."

They made their way to the third-floor scrapping room.

Meg hopped off her stool and took the bags from Kendra. "We were beginning to wonder if something had happened."

"Nope, just waiting on food." Tandy went around to her side of the table and began arranging photos.

"And I, for one, am glad you did." Zelda began pulling the Styrofoam boxes from the bags and distributing them to each sister.

Meg opened her container. "What's Daddy doing for dinner tonight?"

Zelda waved a hand in the air. "Oh, I'm not sure. He's a big boy though, and he knows his way around that kitchen. He'll find something."

Tandy shared a look with Kendra, whose eyebrow raised. *Definitely not like Momma.* She pictured Daddy cutting cheese slices and layering them on crackers and felt a twinge.

Her stool scraped across the floor when she pushed away from the table. "I'll be right back. I'll just go check and make sure he found something."

"Well, that's not necessary," Zelda said. "Like I said, he's a grown man. He can find dinner."

Tandy swallowed her desired reply. *Like you did? We brought you your dinner.* "All the same," she said instead and shot down the stairs before Zelda could protest again. She found Daddy in the kitchen, staring at a refrigerator whose shelves were depressingly bare. Daddy's smile held mischief though. "It looks like I should have placed my order tonight." He shut the refrigerator door.

"I'm so sorry, Daddy. I assumed she would fix something for you, or I'd have brought you a burger too."

Daddy shook his head before the words were out of her mouth. "I know, honey girl. Don't you worry for a second about me. I've got more food in this kitchen than some kids see in an entire year. I won't starve to death."

It's not starvation of the stomach I'm worried about. How does she feed your soul?

"Still, I feel awful that we're all chowing down on burgers up there and here you stand with not even a piece of turkey or ham to make a sandwich."

"Maybe I'll head on down to Clay's and get me a BLT. He knows how to make them right, and I've had a hankering for one ever since we got home."

"I'm sure he'll be glad to make it for you."

"Then that settles it." Daddy's work boots

411

clomped on the linoleum floor. "I'll leave you girls to the scrapbooking and go find me some male conversation."

Daddy's solitary figure looked lonelier than it had in months — probably because he shouldn't *be* a solitary figure anymore.

"I love you, Daddy," she called.

Daddy looked over his shoulder and said, "I love you too, honey girl."

Tandy stood until she heard the front door open and close, then the rumble of Daddy's truck motor, before going back through the living room and up the stairs to the scrapping studio. She didn't trust herself to be around Zelda right now, but if she left, all the sisters would notice and call her cell anyway.

Though I'll bet they're not happy with Zelda right now either. Especially Ms. Fix-a-Three-Course-Meal-Every-Night Joy.

Tension coiled in the room like a thick electrical cord frayed on its end. One spark and the entire room would go up in flames. Each sister sat with head down, eyes focused on the layouts in front of them. No one appeared to have touched their burger.

Zelda chattered away, either oblivious or uncaring.

I'm not sure anymore which. What is with her?

Tandy sauntered back around to the table, doing a pretty good impression of someone who wasn't angry, and once again picked up her photos. Zelda prattled on about the beautiful Florida beaches and gorgeous Florida sunsets and fabulous Florida night life and stunning Florida weather until Tandy felt certain that the State of Florida should be paying this one promotional dollars.

She glanced at the clock on the wall. Only five minutes since she'd sat down. Five minutes wasn't long enough to claim a headache and go home.

She tried to focus instead on the layout at her fingertips. With the wedding scrapbook finally done, she had begun her honeymoon scrapbook. Journaling had proven a bit harder because so much of the magical time they had shared wouldn't be appropriate to write in a scrapbook for familial consumption. Instead, she'd journaled those thoughts and tucked the journal away in the top corner of their bedroom closet. Tandy figured if she and Clay ever got in a huge argument, she could read about those first days of their marriage, of the fun they had, and remember better times.

A sudden silence filled the room and Tandy looked up. Zelda stood over at the wall of paper racks, running a stubby finger down the columns of color. *Guess she couldn't consider paper choices and prattle at the same time.* She should stop these unflattering thoughts, but Zelda's actions made it too easy. And too justified. Tandy pictured Daddy sitting all alone at a table down at Clay's and stood up.

"Look, y'all, I think I'm having an uninspired night. I can't think through this layout for the life of me. I think I better just call it a night and try again later."

"Me too." Joy pushed her paper cutter away. "I've been staring at the same pictures for ten minutes, and no inspiration is coming."

Kendra crossed her arms and rested on the table. "Then it's catching because I've got the same problem."

Meg sighed, and Tandy knew the sound was more theatrical than anything else. "I'm sorry, Zelda. I think we better try again another night."

Zelda brought the papers she'd chosen to the table and set them down. "That's all right, girls. I'll just go on downstairs and watch that Lifetime movie that we TiVoed while we were gone. Y'all want to come over after church Sunday?"

"We'll see." Tandy couldn't get to the

stairs fast enough. "Thanks for having us over." *To our own house. Where you've invaded.*

"Anytime, hon, anytime."

It took all of four seconds for the sisters to get outside and come to a halt between Tandy's car and Meg's van.

"Tandy, what did Daddy say?" Meg opened her passenger door and dropped her purse inside.

"He's down at Clay's getting a BLT. He checked the fridge first. There's nothing in it."

"How did she survive before they got married?" Joy had one small hand on an expanding hip. "Pizza?"

Meg ran a hand through her hair, tucking it behind her ears. "I don't know, but it must not have been by preparing her own meals."

Kendra leaned against the van. "So what are we going to do about it?"

"Is there anything we *can* do? Would Daddy want us to, even if there was? He had time to talk to me about it in the kitchen and he chose not to."

"What exactly could he say?" Kendra tossed her hair over her shoulder. " 'Oops, I married a woman who can't even put peanut butter and jelly between two slices of bread?' "

"He could ask one of us to teach her. You, Joy."

"Me?" Joy laid a delicate hand on her chest. "I have no intention of standing in that house teaching Zelda how to cook on Momma's stove. She'd just as likely break the thing as learn how to use it."

"But you'd be helping Daddy out," Meg cajoled. "You could cover the basics. Teach her a few soups, spaghetti, maybe a casserole or two."

"Because the stress of dealing with that woman is exactly what I need in my life right now."

Tandy instantly understood the dilemma. "You could wait until your second trimester."

"I'm *in* my second trimester. Hit it a week and a half ago, but haven't had a chance to tell y'all yet."

"What?!" all the sisters exclaimed at once.

"I had intended to tell you tonight, but that woman in there ruined my moment."

"Another reason to not like her," Tandy sniffed.

"Don't let her spoil the moment." Kendra threw an arm around Joy's slender shoulders. "This is big news and we need to celebrate!"

"Ooh! What about a fondue party? I've got a fondue set somebody gave Clay and me for a wedding present and I have yet to use the thing. Let's go dip stuff in chocolate!"

THIRTY-NINE

"Somebody remind me why they call pregnancy a blessed time." Tandy rested a hand on her belly while an October wind blew outside. "I'm only at seven months. This thing is just going to get bigger."

Joy rolled her eyes. "At least you've got a few inches of height to spread it all out. Being short isn't helpful when you're adding a basketball to your midsection. I look like I swallowed a cantaloupe."

The sisters sat in side-by-side seats at the A terminal of the Nashville airport. Boarding for their plane to St. Thomas had been set for thirty minutes from now. Tandy shifted in her seat. "They didn't make these chairs to accommodate pregnant women."

"That they didn't."

"Maybe we should have gone with Meg and Kendra to get manicures over in the other terminal."

"And walk all that way? Right before sitting on a plane for several hours and then walking all over an island? No, thank you." Joy sat back and crossed her arms, resting them on her round belly. "I'll sit right here and watch the world go by, thank you very much."

As her belly grew, so did Joy's ability to speak her mind. *Woe to the one who comes against you, baby sister.* She dared not use the "baby sister" phrase out loud. Between her haywire hormones and Joy's, no telling what kind of argument that could bring on. And they didn't need a fight right before Kendra's wedding. Tandy closed the *Fit Pregnancy* she'd been reading and let that sink in again. In three days Kendra would be Mrs. Darin Spenser. Wild-and-free Kendra, tethering herself to a man for the rest of her life. Wonders never cease.

She hoped Darin knew just what he was getting into. Probably not. Who could really know anyone anymore? Not until you've spent a lifetime together, and maybe not even then.

"Ouch!" She pushed in on a section of her belly. "Stop kicking me in there! And I mean it, obey your mother or you're grounded as soon as you show your face." The kicks subsided and she relaxed again.

"Okay, I'm impressed."

"Don't be. It rarely works, and I doubt it did this time. My command probably just happened to coincide with when he was tired of kicking anyway."

"Have you guys settled on the name yet?"

"Nope. We've narrowed it down to a short list, but we go back and forth between them all."

"What are the finalists?"

"Jack — for Daddy, of course. Clay, for obvious reasons. Oliver, which Clay says will label him a geek for life. Seth, just because we both like the name. And Charles, because it's an old name you don't hear every day."

"I think I'd go with Seth."

"Well, see, that's what we thought. We both like the name, but what if he has a lisp of some sort? He'd be 'Theth' and get made fun of by the other kids."

"All kids are going to make fun of the other kids no matter what you name them."

"That's true, but shouldn't I do whatever I can to prevent it, if possible?"

"I suppose."

"Have you and Scott thought through names?"

"We're leaning toward Madeline. I've always loved that name. Or Marian, after Momma."

"Must be nice to have it narrowed down to two."

Joy nodded. "It is."

"Hey, preggos!" Kendra had her arm linked through Meg's as they bopped down the concourse. "You ready for an island adventure?"

"I'm ready for a nice, long nap."

"You pregnant ladies, always needing naps." Meg plopped down into the seat beside Joy. "You'd think you were growing a human or something."

"Ha ha. Very funny." Tandy tilted her head back and let her hair fall down. The weight of it gave her a headache, but Joy hadn't felt like giving hair cuts the last couple of weeks. "You'd think you would show a little sympathy, having done this a few times yourself."

"This is the voice of a smug, satisfied woman happy in the knowledge that I never have to go through childbirth again and have three wonderful children."

"Speaking of which, where are they?"

"Clay and Jamison have them running up and down the concourse, trying to burn energy and wear them out before we get on the plane."

"Brilliant man I married." Tandy closed her eyes. "He'll make a good daddy someday."

"Yeah, I'd say in about two months."

"Where's Scott?" Joy looked around. "Oh." Scott sat in the corner of the terminal, his laptop plugged in and his head down, focused on the screen. "That man never stops working."

"Cut him some slack," Meg advised. "He knows in about two and a half months, he's not going to be able to work because that little girl will keep him up all night. Let him get ahead for now."

"I suppose you're right."

"Having endured three kiddos myself, trust me, sis. I'm right."

"How long until we board?"

Kendra checked her watch. "Twenty minutes. Anybody need a last-minute bathroom break?"

"Always." Tandy pushed up from her seat. "Let's go."

"Wait for me." Joy followed along behind.

Kendra clapped. "Look, it's the preggo parade!"

"Oh, shut *up.*" Tandy put a hand at the small of her back, which felt as if someone had sat an anvil on it. "Just you wait. First comes love, then comes marriage . . ."

FORTY

Meg hopped out of the hotel shuttle and led the group to the edge of Megan's Bay. "Wow, would you look at that ocean? I thought the postcard pictures were only from someone with a great imagination and a talent with PhotoShop, but that'll take your breath."

"It *does* look like a postcard." Tandy set her beach basket down in the powdery sand.

Kendra took in the beauty all around them, catching her breath on its perfection. Above the crystal-blue waters, hills covered in green rose on either side. The water's translucent quality was such that little fish could be seen as far as six feet beneath the surface. Yellow, blue, red, orange, bearing black stripes and white stripes, large fins and small, they darted about in small schools.

Kendra smiled. A fairy-tale place for a fairy-tale wedding.

"I feel like I just walked into a fairy tale," Joy breathed, echoing Kendra's thoughts. "Look at this place, Scott."

Early morning sun lit the water, sprinkling it with dancing points of light that played upon the waves created by a gentle breeze. Scott sat down the gear he'd carried and unfolded a chaise lounge. "No wonder it's one of the top five beaches in the world."

"Anybody want to snorkel?" Clay held up rubber snorkel hoses and face masks.

"I'm in." Darin snagged a face mask.

"Me too." Scott caught the mask Clay tossed his way.

"Jack?"

"No, no, you boys go on ahead. I'll sit here and keep the girls safe from beach bums."

Kendra slathered sunblock along her arms. "Make sure you put on lots of sunscreen. I can't have my bridesmaids looking like lobsters tomorrow."

"Yes, your majesty." Tandy pulled a bottle of SPF 30 from her beach bag.

"Daddy, I hope Zelda's feeling better when we get back to the hotel."

"She'll be fine, Meggy. Just a little tired, I'm sure."

Yeah, tired of us. And the feeling's mutual. Kendra kept her thoughts inside. "I hate that she's missing out on this beautiful beach. Her being such a beach lover and all."

"She knows where we are and can catch the hotel shuttle if she wakes up and feels like getting out."

"How's married life?" Kendra couldn't help but ask. "Is it different from the first time?" *As if we don't all know.*

"It is, but different isn't necessarily bad." Daddy gazed across the water. "It's just . . . different."

"So long as different makes you happy, then different is fine. But if you decide you don't like different —"

"I'll decide to be happy with different. Marriage is no less sacred when it's your second, Tandy. I made vows to Zelda, and she made vows to me. Don't any of you daughters be thinking either of us is about to break a vow just because this start is a little rockier than we'd planned."

"We wouldn't want you to break your vows, Daddy." Joy laid a hand on his arm. "We simply want to be sure you're happy."

"I suspect I'm like a lot of married folks, Joy. Some days I'm happy, others I wonder what in the world I've gotten myself into."

"Did you ever wonder that with Momma?" *You've got to learn to shut your mouth, Kendra.*

"Sure I did. I'm certain your momma had her doubts about me too. Like I said, most married couples, if they stay married long enough, are going to wonder if it would be easier to be single. And it might be for a while. But if you've made a vow to somebody, then an honorable person sticks to that vow."

"It's hard though, Daddy." Tandy piped up. "We want you to be loved and taken care of, and we don't see her doing that."

"Y'all don't see everything that goes on between Zelda and me. It's been a little rough, adjusting to each other's habits, living in the same house. We're old and set in our ways. That's to be expected. But I can learn to cook my own bacon, and Zelda can figure out the washing machine. So we'll be fine in the long run. It'd help a lot if she didn't have to worry about you girls so much."

"She doesn't have to worry about me at all." Kendra shook her head. "I'm a grown woman who ain't in need of a step-momma to make my decisions."

"That isn't what I meant, and you watch the attitude, missy. She's worried you girls don't like her or accept her, and she spends a lot of time fretting over it. If you could give her the benefit of the doubt, help her learn some new things, then this would be a little easier on everyone involved."

Joy sighed. "I suppose I can help her learn a few dishes in the kitchen."

"That's my girl. Thank you. That'd be a good start."

Tandy bit her lip. "Did she skip the beach today because of us?"

"I think so, but she didn't say that out loud. She wants this trip to be about Kendra and Darin's wedding, not her relationship with the four of you. She thought her being here might add tension to the day and y'all wouldn't have as much fun. Again, she didn't say it in those words exactly, but that's what I think kept her back at the hotel."

"We should call and see if she wants to come."

"I think that'd be a good idea, Tandy."

Tandy dialed Zelda's number on her cell, and Kendra listened to her invite Zelda to join them. The thing was, this trip *should* be about her and Darin, not Zelda. And yet here they sat, discussing Zelda and her absence. As though, by her absence, Zelda had made the day about her.

Kendra closed her eyes and let the sea breeze wash over her face. No more Zelda thoughts. In less than twenty-four hours, she'd be walking down the aisle to become Mrs. Darin Spenser. A grin spread across her face. Now *there* was something worth thinking about. She ran through the checklist in her mind. Flowers were confirmed — the bougainvillea and wildflower bouquets were explosions of purple and red color. The organist had confirmed. Reverend was ready and waiting. Limo service hired. Airplane from St. Thomas over to Virgin Gorda booked. Everything she could think of had been taken care of and confirmed. Only an early morning wake-up and trip to the church stood between her and marital bliss.

Kendra breathed deeply of the salt air. Coming to the islands had been the perfect decision for her and Darin. His parents hadn't wanted to come over to Megan's Bay either this morning, but they'd be at the service. She couldn't decide if they disapproved of the marriage or simply weren't beach people. Not that it mattered. Nothing would stop this wedding, short of Tandy or Joy going into labor. And since that shouldn't happen for two months, all should be fine.

Kendra's heart galloped in her chest and she felt certain everyone could see it above the neckline of her strapless gown. "Do I look okay?" she hissed, causing Tandy to turn around from her place at the sanctuary doors.

"You look like an island princess. Ready to get married?"

Kendra nodded, careful not to upset the wreath of flowers in her hair holding down her veil.

Organ music spilled out of the open church windows, causing those in the street to stop and enjoy the sound. A slight breeze blew up the church stairs, giving Kendra relief from the rising heat of the day. The men in their linen suits were probably sweating buckets by now. She knew she was reconsidering her wedding dress. A nice slip dress would have been a lot cooler in the island heat. But the pictures would be amazing, so she could ignore the slight rivulet of sweat rolling down her back beneath the corset.

"There's my cue!" Tandy whispered. "See you in there!"

Kendra grinned and laced her arm through Daddy's, standing just to the side so that Darin couldn't see her when Tandy opened the door and entered the sanctuary. This was finally it! In just a few minutes, Kendra Sinclair would become Kendra Sinclair Spenser.

"You ready?" Daddy's eyes twinkled.

"Like ice cubes for the tea glass."

"Because we could go right back down these steps and over to the beach if you'd prefer."

"Not on your life."

"Just checking."

The organ music changed again, this time to Jeremiah Clarke's "Trumpet Voluntary." Kendra tugged on Daddy's arm. "They're playing my song."

Daddy opened the door wide and in she walked, putting her eyes on Darin and nowhere else for the entire procession. His face, wide open with love and trust, beamed back at her.

She barely heard the vows, the prayers, even the songs they'd chosen, so intent was she on watching his sweet face.

It was all over before she knew it, and she listened as the reverend introduced Mr. and Mrs. Darin Spenser to the crowd.

Darin squeezed her hand. "That's us!" he whispered.

"Amazing, isn't it?" Kendra whispered back, and he swept her down the aisle and out the door to their waiting limo amid claps and cheers.

FORTY-ONE

The wind makes every red velvet bow on our antique streetlights dance like elves on parade. I love Christmastime. I love every single thing about it. Wreaths of holly and evergreen. Music wishing good tidings and peace. Giant shopping bags swinging from everyone's arms. Bright holly berries peeking out from snow-covered branches. Majestic trees whose boughs bend under the weight of ornaments and lights.

And best of all, the smell of gingerbread, fruitcake, and wassail in my kitchen.

Next year I'll begin to teach Maddie all of our traditions. My belly is the size of a watermelon now. I have two and a half more weeks to go, though I cannot imagine how my skin could stretch to accommodate this child any longer. I wonder sometimes if my birth mother patted her belly as I find myself often doing. Did she wonder if I would have her eyes? Her laugh?

Since seeing her homeland, I think of her more often. I have more sympathy for her. I am blessed that, in this country, I could choose to give birth alone, were that my lot, and endure that hardship without fear of retribution from my government. She did not have that right. I worry for her. I hope she knows, wherever she is this day, that her little girl is safe, happy, and loved.

I hope she knows that.

Tandy is due tomorrow. I plan to be there every step of the way, taking notes on the entire process so that I can prepare for my own delivery next month. Tandy's belly is larger than mine, though not by much. I've decided she's a prettier pregnant woman because she has a little more height to balance out the watermelon. I just look like I swallowed something — like one of those cartoon characters I watched as a child.

The wind is so cold on this night of the Christmas parade. People line the sidewalks, decked out in their holiday finery. There's Sara in a new red coat with big brass buttons. And Ms. Corinne with a deep purple coat of her own, trimmed with red and green. She looks beautiful, that snow-white hair shining in the streetlights.

My clan waits a block away, down by Clay's. We decided to not stray far from the hot cocoa this year. The best place to watch the parade, of course, is down by Wendy's. There's plenty of parking, and it is early enough in the procession that each float still has lots of candy to throw out.

But Wendy's is a good quarter mile from Clay's, and Wendy's doesn't serve hot chocolate.

It most definitely does not serve hot chocolate made with Ghirardelli chocolate ordered directly from the Ghirardelli store in Ghirardelli Square in San Francisco. Thus our position at the corner of Oxford and Lindell.

My family makes a lovely holiday picture in their red, black, green, and white coats, mittens, scarves, and gloves. Only Zelda stands out — she's chosen to wear a light-blue coat. Why light blue I have no idea. Who associates light blue with Christmas-time? Perhaps she found it on a clearance rack.

No matter. I will not allow Zelda to mar a perfect evening, which is what I'm set on having. This is the final parade before Scott and I begin sharing our lives with a little one. Next year Maddie will be up on Scott's shoulders, and I'll run into the street as the candy is tossed so that I can fill her bag with sweets and treats.

We won't let her eat much of them, of course, but she can share it with her cousins.

Ouch. There comes that twinge again. Meg assures me it's false labor. She should know. She had false labor with every single one of hers. They don't come with any regularity, really, but they certainly are uncomfortable. They've changed my mind about the epidural. I'll be asking for it the second they wheel me into the hospital. If false labor hurts this badly, I want no part of the pain of the real deal. I'm a strong woman, but I also like to think I'm a sensible one.

I hear the police sirens now. They must be down around Wendy's. I pick up my pace, wanting to be with the family when the cars round the turn from University to Lindell.

Heavens, there it comes again.

I guess the first pain wasn't really finished yet since no two have come that quickly yet. Meg tells me when the false pains come to get off my feet and they'll go away. But how can I get off my feet in the middle of a Christmas parade?

I suppose I'll just have to grit my teeth and bear it, as Scarlett O'Hara would advise us Southern women. Of course, when it came time for Scarlett to give birth, I didn't see her keeping her cool.

Maybe Tandy will go into labor tonight.

We've had a lot of excitement today, and the magazines and books I've been reading tell me a lot of mothers go into labor after a strenuous day of activity. Today alone we walked the mall up in Cool Springs, gathering last minute Christmas gifts, finished putting Christmas ornaments on Tandy's Christmas tree (the woman waits until the last minute for so many things), put together her crib (which was *finally* delivered this morning), and now are down here at a Christmas parade. I'd say that's a day full of activity if ever there was one.

"There you are." Scott reaches out an arm and snuggles me to his side. Well, the part of me that still fits. "I was beginning to think we'd see the parade without you."

"Oh, don't worry about that. I got the bow fixed and, look, the police cars haven't even made the turn yet."

"You know, someone *does* have the job of making sure the bows are correct on city streetlights. I'm sure Tanner has taken care of that." Meg shakes her head.

"Then Tanner should be informed that his chosen person should be reprimanded. That bow was so crooked, it was almost upside down." I cannot stand it when cities don't take pride in their decorations. Tanner did an exceedingly good job this year of sprucing up our little Stars Hill and creating a most festive air. But how could one feel jolly in the face of a bow askew?

"That's it. I'm making you take the OCD test when this is over." Tandy leans on Clay, smiling.

Another pain comes and I cannot help but wince.

Tandy is at my side in an instant — well, as short of an instant as she can haul her watermelon-laden self over to me. "Hey, are you okay?"

"I'm fine. I'm fine. It's just more of this false labor."

Scott pats my back. "Maybe you should sit down to watch the parade. Didn't Meg say they stop if you get off your feet?"

"If I sit down, I won't be able to see anything." I indicate the people lining the sidewalk in front of us. "Unless you have a plan for making all of these people sit down as well."

"You've seen this parade nearly thirty times." Tandy tucks a curl up in her lime green toboggan cap. "How about you sit down for this one?"

"I'm fine, really. I don't see you sitting down, and you're farther along than me."

"Yeah, well, I've just got a better-behaved kid. Mine's not giving me fits."

436

"Hey, my child is perfectly behaved." Another pain comes and I bite my lip. "She's just making a couple of test runs before the real show, that's all. She likes to prepare. She's like her mother."

"Mm-hmm." Tandy pats my shoulder. "Clay, could you go get Joy a chair, please?"

"You bet!" Clay trots back into the diner, reappearing a moment later with a chair. "Here ya go, preggo."

"I will be so happy when I give birth to this child and can stop being referred to as preggo." I sit down, trying not to show how grateful I am to be off my feet. How Mary rode on the back of a donkey at this stage of her pregnancy is beyond me.

"Mom! Look! It's the firemen!" James jumps up and down, his Santa hat bouncing. In a few years Maddie will jump like that. I'll have her in a red velvet dress with giant black, shiny buttons and a white fur sash. She'll be adorable.

"You sure you're okay, hon?" Scott's forehead is creased and I reach to smooth it.

"I'm fine. This is just false labor. Ask Meg."

Meg is busily running into the street, one hand holding James, the other Savannah. The kids scoop up candy as she keeps an eye out for the next float.

"Meg?" Scott gets her attention when they've returned from their sugar-grabbing expedition. "You're sure this isn't the real thing?"

Meg pushes hair out of her face, which has grown pink with exertion. "Are you having contractions again?" She weaves her way through family members and kneels at my side.

"Yes."

"Have you been timing them?"

"Not really. They come every few minutes and I had two in a row while I was walking back over here. That's not regular, so it's not real labor, right?"

"Mostly right. Real labor can have irregular contractions thrown in."

"What?" A tiny bit of alarm floats through my brain, but I stamp it out. "What are you talking about?"

"I mean, when I had Savannah, I had regular contractions. But every now and then, I'd have an extra one or I'd skip one. It was like that right up until I had her."

"You didn't tell me that before."

Meg shrugs, and I consider decking my sister but decide pregnancy hormones will only excuse so much. "Your other contractions were all so irregular, it didn't apply.

But you said these are coming every few minutes. That sounds pretty regular to me. Do they feel different than the other ones?"

"Heavens, I don't know." I throw my hands up. I hate having to do something I can't prepare for any more than reading other women's experiences, no two of which are exactly alike. "They hurt. They always hurt."

"But do they hurt in the same way?"

"I can't remember! It's been a week since I had those other ones. I was pretty happy I'd forgotten what they felt like. *Ouch!*" Another *whatever* starts building, and this one isn't going away as quickly as the others. I grab the arm of the chair, hanging on and waiting for it to end.

"Sister, I think you're having a baby."

"No, I'm not. I have two and a half more weeks. Tandy's going first."

Meg's chuckle only raises my hackles more. "I don't think Maddie got the memo, sis."

I look at her, not quite believing what I hear. I'm having a baby? *Now?* But this isn't right! Maddie needs to grow two and a half more weeks! She isn't fully developed. I'm not sure of everything that can go wrong at this point, but I'm certain there are plenty of items that need to be checked off the developmental to-do list before Maddie makes her grand entrance into the world.

"Hey." Meg lays a gloved hand on my arm. "Stop freaking out. You're two weeks from your due date. You're fine. Maddie's fine."

"But —"

I pause as a warm, wet feeling enters my consciousness. Either I just peed on myself or —

"I think my water just broke!"

The entire family turns as one, eyes wide and mouths open.

"And that seals the deal." Meg puts one hand under my arm. "Scott, get her other arm. She's got to get up out of this chair and into the car. Where's your car?"

"We parked over by the park."

I groan. The park is an entire block away.

"Take Tandy's." I see Clay put his keys into Scott's pocket. "It's right there." I look up and see Tandy's little Beemer sitting underneath one of the streetlights. I have no idea how I will push up out of that thing once we get to the hospital, but I also know it's better than walking a block to our vehicle.

"Thanks." Scott puts an arm around my back and supports me while the entire Sinclair clan trails along. Behind us, parade floats bedecked with thousands of yards of tissue paper and tinsel continue rolling past. The Westview marching band has just turned the corner from University onto Lindell, and I hear them break into song as Scott opens the car door.

Well, this certainly wasn't the procedure I had planned. But then again, when does life ever follow the plan we make?

As another pain hits and I hear my family members calling out their assurances and promises to "Be right there!" I close my eyes. No, this isn't what I had planned. But I'll take this chaos over a planned quietness any day.

EPILOGUE

"I can't believe she's here." Scott's whisper tickles my neck as we stare at the beautiful pink bundle before us. "She's so tiny."

"Six pounds is not tiny. Trust me, I've birthed it."

His chuckle causes Maddie to open her eyes. "Oh, look! Hi, little one!"

She blinks, then goes back to sleep.

"I love you, Joy."

The tears that blur my vision remind me of God's promise to bring joy for mourning. "I love you too Scott."

He cups her little head in his tanned hand. "I'll be right back, sweet girl. Pretty soon Daddy will teach you all about coffee and its amazing powers."

I swat his hand away and laugh. "You'll do no such thing. No child needs caffeine to grow healthy."

Scott backs toward the door, that crooked grin of his in place. "I didn't say she'd drink it, just learn about it."

"Oh, you." I roll my eyes as he pushes through the door.

"Be right back."

A few seconds later Tandy's belly appears in the door just before I see her smiling face.

"You were supposed to be first," I whisper, mindful of the sleeping angel in my arms. I ache all over, but I don't mind. I would do every bit of it again a thousand times ten thousand if it resulted in someone laying in my arms this pink little bundle on which I now gaze.

Tandy smiles and runs a finger down Maddie's blanketed body. "Yeah. My kid must have gotten my procrastination gene. I'm praying he makes an appearance before Christmas."

"I didn't get to take notes and be prepared."

"Does it matter?"

I look again at Maddie's perfect little nose that I'm fairly certain she got from Scott. And I see her thick, black lashes resting on skin the shade of my own. And I hear her give a little baby sigh. "No, it doesn't."

"Sometimes planning isn't the best idea."

I smile, realizing I've taken that lesson deep into my soul. I think Maddie will benefit from me taking life as it comes, not preparing for every single circumstance.

As if we could ever prepare for all circumstances.

Obviously my birth mother didn't prepare. And that turned out all right.

In fact, as my newborn daughter's eyes open and she looks up at me, I'd say it turned out, quite simply, perfect.

ABOUT THE AUTHOR

Rebeca Seitz loves to sit under the oak trees in the front yard of her southern Kentucky home while writing on a laptop. If you don't see her there, check the barn in the back pasture where she's probably looking to find another batch of kittens. Her husband and two children will also be nearby.

The employees of Thorndike Press hope you have enjoyed this Large Print book. All our Thorndike, Wheeler, and Kennebec Large Print titles are designed for easy reading, and all our books are made to last. Other Thorndike Press Large Print books are available at your library, through selected bookstores, or directly from us.

For information about titles, please call:
  (800) 223-1244

or visit our Web site at:
  http://gale.cengage.com/thorndike

To share your comments, please write:
  Publisher
  Thorndike Press
  295 Kennedy Memorial Drive
  Waterville, ME 04901